Who's Mack Oliver

John Thanks
for your support.

Jota 2007

This is a work of fiction. Names, characters, places, and incidents either are the product of the author's imagination or are used fictitiously, and any resemblance to actual persons, living or dead, business establishments, events, or locales is entirely coincidental.

ISBN: 1-4196-5117-X
ISBN-13: 978-1419651175
Library of Congress Control Number: 2006910271

Visit www.booksurge.com to order additional copies.

Who's Mack Oliver

Jonathan W. Dunning

2006

Who's Mack Oliver

TABLE OF CONTENTS

Who's Mack Oliver

"At the heart of this deftly-written novel is the question of its title, Who's Mack Oliver?, a question that is answered in several ways, lending the mystery a dimension beyond the obvious *whodunit.* Indeed this is a novel as much about perception as it is about mystery – perceptions of race, of the homeless, of the mentally disabled – and about the long and painful process of correcting those perceptions – ours as much as the characters' – in order to arrive at the truth. ...Any debut murder mystery is up against very exacting standards. ...Jonathan Dunning has succeeded, in very capable prose, in standing up with the best writers of this genre, including Agatha Christie and Ngaio Marsh."

- *New York Times* best selling author Ellen Tanner Marsh

"Precious few novels have captured the gut-wrenching complexities of life on the streets of our urban cities. Who's Mack Oliver? gives insight, understanding, and hope for anyone willing to listen to the remarkably clear and cogent voice so expertly crafted by Jonathan Dunning. Read this book because you care about your neighbor."

– Max Michael, MD, Dean, University of Alabama at Birmingham School of Public Health

"Who's Mack Oliver? is a compelling and provocative look at class, addiction, mental illness and homelessness. Jonathan Dunning skillfully dissects and guides us through a culture so ingrained that even its victims believe in its values. It is a brilliant education in cultural diversity that is masterfully woven into a psychological thriller that quickly hooks the reader through superb character development. Dunning's characters are richly complex, realistically heroic and flawed. Both enlightening and entertaining, I couldn't put it down. A must read for everyone."

– Dr. Sharon Waltz, Licensed Clinical Psychologist/Adjunct Professor

For the thousands of Mack Oliver's
who live in the shadows with silent dignity.

CHAPTER ONE

Making Amends

"Dr. Sam, what we talk about, is it just between me and you?"

Dr. Sam leaned back in her desk chair. "Yes, it is, unless you tell me you're going to hurt yourself or someone else. Are you going to hurt yourself or someone else, Cassius?"

"Not today," replied Cassius sarcastically.

"Then what you tell me is confidential; it's just between us. I can't disclose that you are here or that you have ever been here unless you say it's okay."

"To no one?"

"No one."

"I feel safe here. I've never felt safe anywhere," he replied with a look of defeat.

"Good. You've been concerned about this before, if anyone will know what we talk about or will know you are here. Are you ready to talk about what is bothering you, Cassius?"

Cassius hesitated, his dark eyes avoiding Dr. Sam's, searching about her office. His eyes eventually found the floor in front of him. He shuffled his right heel around on the floor where his eyes had focused, moving the carpet fibers, first, with the grain, then against. His heart pounded. Nervousness showed in his eyes, a feeling he was unfamiliar with. He swallowed so hard he was afraid Dr. Sam could hear it. She could. Then he answered slowly, "What if these things are very bad?"

Dr. Sam's demeanor was reassuring and her voice supportive. "That's why we're here, to talk about those things. I'm sure it's nothing I've never heard before."

But Cassius was sure she had never heard a problem like his before. Her disarming and comfortable manner with Cassius were coaxing him toward taking a first step.

"Let's talk about it," she said.

Cassius again checked the room, briefly looking into Dr. Sam's eyes, the trusting eyes he had come to know during the past thirty days. Dr. Sam waited patiently. She knew Cassius wanted to release his secret.

After a brief moment, Cassius replied, "I am working the Steps, and I am having trouble with Number Five. I've always had trouble with Number Five. This is my fourth time in treatment, you know. It says…do you know what it says, Dr. Sam?"

"Yes," she responded, as Cassius pulled out his heavily worn, stained Narcotics Anonymous book with folded pages and began to read Step Five aloud.

"'Admit to God, to ourselves and another human being the exact nature of our wrongs.' Well, God knows and I know and I've asked Him for forgiveness, if He's listening or even knows I'm here. Do you think that is enough?"

"Maybe, Cassius. What do you think?"

"I've hurt people, and it's all I can think about. I've never felt like this before."

"Then I think you have answered your question. It doesn't matter how bad it is, you can face it here."

Cassius exhaled, but only partially released his defenses. "My brother was hurt. He died, ten years ago."

"How?"

Speaking rapidly and turning his head away, Cassius blurted out a part of his secret. "I am not sure; he bumped his head, fell, and died. I was drunk, high. It's blurry. It keeps me up at night. I see his face every night. I hear his voice. I dream about him. It tore my family apart."

Pausing abruptly as if his mind had shut down, he changed the subject. "My mother will be here Sunday, Family Night. Will you be here that night, Dr. Sam?"

Cassius disclosed more in that moment than he had in four weeks of his anticipated two-month stay. The powerfully built, solemn Cassius exposed glimpses of the torment and agony that had landed him in and out of treatment centers and halfway houses for the past decade.

"Yes, Cassius, I will. I look forward to meeting your mother. Any other family coming?"

"No, she's all that's left."

Thinking this was a good stopping point, and that Cassius had given an exhaustive effort, Dr. Sam looked at the digital desk clock. It read 6:00 p.m. "Our time is up, Cassius. We're scheduled again for next week. Think about what we have discussed today and we will continue at our next session."

January 25. Cassius Carey, a thirty-five-year-old, Black male, unmarried. Severely addicted to crack cocaine and alcohol with Antisocial Personality Disorder and signs of Posttraumatic Stress Disorder. Prone to embellishment in an effort at self-importance. Self-admitted to the inpatient treatment center December 24, thirty days ago. He is indigent, homeless, has a high school equivalent education, and is a skilled carpenter. After much resistance over the past few weeks during addiction and mental health treatment, Cassius is approaching a breakthrough. The patient described urges to disclose core issues. We will continue the current treatment regimen. The patient is scheduled for a family visit Sunday and an individual session seven days from today.

Dr. Samantha Williams concluded her brief therapy note about the one-hour session with Cassius Carey. She grabbed her gym bag, cut off the lights in her small but comfortable office, locked the door, and told her assistant, Cicely, she was headed to the downtown Atlanta YMCA for a game of racquetball, a four-day-a-week routine she has had for the past two years. This was not an unusual day for the thirty-three-year-old clinical psychologist, who, as a clinician at the Atlanta Mental Health Center, had seen a lot.

CHAPTER TWO

The American Dream

The country club stood sublimely atop the windward crest of Birmingham's Red Mountain, flaunting a resolute perdurability. The bountiful foliage surrounding the brick and stone mansion parted only by a perfectly smooth, narrow asphalt drive winding up the peak that ended at a two-story limestone veranda, nestled among a parterre and a thick bed of deep violet pansies that declared *Merry Christmas.* The dogwoods and oaks that dotted the estate were besprinkled with thousands of white lights, the glitter reminiscent of diamonds. As the hundreds of members and distinguished guests arrived for the evening's celebration, dozens of valets clad in crimson coats, white shirts, black bowties and trousers – all African-American - promptly greeted and escorted them from their fine automobiles with perfect decorum. Every guest was addressed as "mister" or "ma'am," regardless of age, at all times. It was expected to be the best-attended Christmas Gala in ten years.

Millicent Wallace, this year's chairwoman of the event, had missed no detail. As was customary, the wife of the country club's board chairman planned the festivity. For this year's chairman, Draper Wallace, the occasion was particularly sweet. The newly renovated ballroom was complete and more splendid than any had imagined. The construction had been completed by the Wallace Corporation. Many of the members had opined that the project wouldn't be finished by Christmas. Some felt it wouldn't be finished by Easter. They had remarked that the construction was too ambitious, that the cost had been grossly underestimated – but it had been finished on time and within budget, and now the ballroom was parexcellence among the best.

The eastern ballroom possessed an unrivaled grandeur. The grand entrance of the room, with double brass doors fifteen feet tall and ten feet wide together, highly polished and resembling gold with beveled glass panes, opened to a cavernous hall with a cathedral ceiling three stories high. Eleven crystal chandeliers sparkled with such a brilliant radiance that they appeared to be spotlighted. Five adorned each side of the room, each one between Roman columns, set one hundred feet apart from each other and the walls, that ascended to the height of the ceiling and created an impressive image of power. One chandelier equal in size to three of the others hung above the middle of the room. Four Douglas firs, taller than anyone had seen indoors and decorated with white lights and gold ornaments, anchored each corner of the hall. The marble floor reflected their glow.

The Gala commenced with a toast from a black tuxedo-attired Wallace, Millicent standing beside him in a black gown and adorned with rubies and diamonds. Sapphires, rubies and diamonds – the unspoken but preferred, time-honored motif among the committeewomen and those privy to the tradition. The Mountain Brook modiste had paid particular attention to what all the club's women would wear to the Gala so as to not create an embarrassing situation of any women showing up in similar jewelry or gowns. The members were in silent awe of the size and brilliance of the jewels worn by this year's chairwoman.

Wallace's toast was discreet and tasteful. There was no need to point out the obvious. He was one of the wealthiest men in Alabama and, as CEO of the Wallace Corporation, he had accomplished what no one else could: the most successful capital campaign in the history of the club. The completion of the facility would have the richest clamoring for membership for years to come, and tonight a more opulent celebration than even the wealthiest had ever seen. He would be humorous and self-deprecating. His place of honor on the dais, reserved for the board of governors and head and shoulders above the others in attendance, had been well earned.

Cases of champagne poured freely during the cocktail hour as the members sampled exquisite hors d'oeuvres, caviar and Gulf Bay shrimp the size of plantains. For dinner, a choice of lobster, hand-carved prime rib, or wild pheasant from South Alabama served in wine sauce. Pre-selected weeks earlier by the members attending, the entrées were served to them with flawless precision by waiters – all African-American - who never spoke to each other, but used a complex system of hand gestures, nods and winks so as to not disturb the attendees with their voices. They, however, had mastered the art of always being near, but not being seen, never letting a glass be empty, picking up a dropped utensil or napkin without it being requested, and in a way that no one noticed, anticipating every need. The stemware, china, and silverware all polished to a high gloss set atop white linen tablecloths, all under the attentive watch of the club's experienced maitre d' of the past forty years, Mr. Jefferson Drake. He, too, was dressed in a black, perfectly tailored tuxedo; however, he appeared slightly thinner than usual due to the advanced stage of prostate cancer from which he was suffering. His condition was unknown to his employers and, although his family knew of his condition, they – as well as everyone else - were unaware of his acute physical weakness. He had assisted Millicent Wallace in ensuring that this year's Gala would be the best. He feared it would be his last.

Jefferson wore two military medals on the left lapel of his tuxedo: a Silver Star and a Purple Heart that he had earned for bravery and wounds received in combat during World War II as an Army tanker. Although wearing the medals was highly unusual, he thought it necessary to counteract the myth that all black soldiers were servants during the War, lacked patriotism, and had not sacrificed. His medals and perfect execution of his vocation had earned him the rare title of "mister" among the board of governors and the club's hundreds of members. This salutation was a required propriety by all servants at the club when addressing members, and only first names were used by members when addressing the servants. The etiquette was broken only for Mr. Drake.

Jefferson was also exceedingly proud this day. His son, Dr. Lincoln Drake, a psychologist, was accepting a $100,000 donation from the Club tonight for needed renovations to the Catherine Fairchild Center, a non-profit organization devoted to the rehabilitation of the homeless. Jefferson's wife, Genevieve, was also present, accompanying her son. Her attendance was an added treat for Lily McPeake. The dining tables in the hall were large enough for sixteen guests at each one. Genevieve and Lincoln Drake (non-club members) were seated with Lily McPeake, whose husband, Jedidiah McPeake, was a founding member of the club. Also seated at the table were Lily's sons, Wilburn McPeake (member), president of the Bank of the South founded by her husband, and Judge J. B. McPeake (member), and their wives, Bernie and Haley (members); Alabama Supreme Court Chief Justice Harold Hawk and his wife, Francis (members), their son Seth and his wife, Justine (members); the Mayor of Birmingham, Peyton Castelle, and his wife, Joyce (non-members); Jefferson County District Attorney William Penick III and his wife, Ann (members) - both their fathers being past members of the board of governors; and widow Ruth Levin (member). Seated at other tables were three of the Wallace children (members); their eldest son, Draper Jr., their other son, Michael, and their eldest daughter, Vicki. Their youngest child, Jodi, was not in attendance. Governor Herbert Charles (member) was there, as were congressmen past and present. A total of one thousand potentates regaled in the night's ambiance.

Ben, the club's longtime, self-taught pianist on his baby grand, along with George on double bass and Raymond on soprano saxophone, entertained throughout the night. As the ice sculptures and hundreds of candles started to show the late hour of the evening, Jefferson Drake retired to his favorite place in the club, the Men's Grille, set off from the men's personal chambers. The room was lined with dark oak lockers, with the members' names engraved on them in gold. The names of some notable members, although deceased, were still affixed to their lockers. The dark-paneled walls were lined with oil portraits of past chairmen and notable members of the boards of governors, most gone now. Jefferson had known most of them. It felt to him as if they had never left and, at any moment, might walk in and surprise him, say hello, make a personal request, or just sit beside him and discuss their golf game. The evening had taken its toll on the seventy-five-year-old. He'd dozed off in an aged oxblood lounge chair, his drink unfinished but still held loosely in his hand, the napkin around the glass soaked with condensation, and the water trickling down his fingers. The ballroom, too, showed the signs of an enjoyed celebration. Only Draper and Millicent remained, and two or three other couples who did not want the party to end. Ben played "Stars Fell on Alabama," the most requested song of the evening, one last time. The Wallaces waltzed to their favorite song and gazed into each other's eyes, assured that this was a night neither they nor the members would ever forget.

CHAPTER THREE

Christmas Eve

Saturday, December 24, Christmas Eve, 4:00 a.m. Millicent Wallace was restless after arriving home at 1:00 a.m., expecting her youngest daughter to be in bed. Jodi Wallace, eighteen years old, was supposed to have returned home by midnight, her curfew. Jodi had gone shopping earlier that evening, electing not to attend the Christmas Gala with her family. Her mother recalled the extra-long embrace Jodi had given her before she left the house. Mrs. Wallace had always worried about her youngest daughter going to Birmingham's Southside to shop. The teenager had come home for the Christmas holidays from her freshman year at the University of Alabama in Tuscaloosa, an hour away in traffic southwest of Birmingham. Jodi's request for her mother not to worry had never been a request her mother could grant. She always worried about the trusting, dainty girl, much more than she ever had about her two older sons and her other daughter, seven years older than Jodi.

Jodi had come unexpectedly and had breathed new life into Millicent Wallace's marriage, now in its fortieth year. She had brought a summery warmth and a youthful exuberance to the old Mountain Brook, Alabama estate where they resided. Her absence the past few months while she was away at college had already created a sadness and a void that her mother and father were having trouble adjusting to. Mrs. Wallace had awakened her husband several times throughout the night because Jodi had not come home. Although Draper had told his wife not to worry, he had not slept soundly. By four o'clock, Millicent's unease – with her daughter not being home, not calling, and not answering her cell phone – had reached the point of panic. Draper Wallace, who did not want to imagine anything errant with his daughter, relented and called Birmingham Police Chief Bo Canon, a friend of Draper's and Millicent's for the past two decades.

Chief Canon had received many early morning phone calls over his thirty-year police career, but never had he received an early morning call like this from Draper Wallace. From the moment the chief picked up the phone, even before Draper gave his name, the firm and commanding voice of Draper Wallace brought him to his feet.

"Chief, sorry to disturb you so early. This is Draper Wallace. My daughter is missing. Jodi, my youngest. We've called all her friends and no one has seen her since last night. She's not answering her mobile phone."

Over all the years the chief had known Draper, he had never known him to be shaken or given to irrational concern. He also had watched, as had all of Birmingham, the Wallace's youngest daughter grow up. The parent's concern was immediately absorbed by the chief.

"Where was she last seen, and what's her tag number?" asked Canon.

"She was last seen by her friends on the Southside. She was driving a red Mercedes convertible, tag number UA JODI."

"Mr. Wallace, I am sure I don't have to tell you and Mrs. Wallace that every resource will be put on this. As soon as I know something, I'll be in touch. If she returns, please be sure and let me know."

Chief Canon promptly instructed all shift captains to put out a be-on-the-look-out for Jodi Wallace and her red Mercedes.

CHAPTER FOUR

The Unimaginable

By 6:00 a.m., minutes before daybreak, two Birmingham police officers found the car matching the description and tag number. Jodi Wallace's car was parked in a semi-secluded lot of an outpatient medical office behind a strip of stores on 11th Avenue South, on the Southside of Birmingham. The storefront blocked the view of the rear parking. The area was not well lit, nor was it conspicuous to pedestrians or passing cars on 19th Street and 20th Street, which ran north and south with the secluded lot between them. The local YMCA, the Union Labor Center, Five Points Hardware, and a nightclub for novice bands blocked the view of the lot from 10th Avenue South. The lot that was surely packed with cars the night before was now void of any except the Mercedes coupe, which sat there eerily. The car was cold to the touch, telling the officers it had been parked there awhile. The thirty-degree weather had the windows of the crimson Mercedes thickly frosted over. The officers used their flashlights to peek inside. A check of the doors revealed they were unlocked. As one door popped open, the tan interior was illuminated brightly against the dawn of the frigid Christmas Eve morning, but did not reveal any immediate clues. One officer inspected the ground around the front and sides of the car, then the rear. He approached the trunk, and one squeeze of the trunk latch with his gloved hand revealed a crime that stunned both officers.

Speechless, the young officers stared in shock at the discovery of the body of their missing person. Moments went by. A quick assumption by the officers that the victim had been there for hours was made due to the rigor mortis and blue hue of the young girl's face, hands and body. Her once well-kept, deep blonde hair was now tangled. Her dark tights and panties were ripped and pulled down around her ankles. Her blue jean skirt was inverted and pulled up around her midsection. A large bruise that seemed to wrap around her neck was visible to the officers. Her eyes were open. Her body was squeezed in among shopping bags and gift-wrapped packages, some torn open, and her emptied purse and her keys. The missing person search had now shockingly turned into a homicide investigation. The men quickly and automatically went through their routine. The officers' call to their sergeant would start the chain that reached Chief Canon. The call reached him as he was leaving his house, headed for the police headquarters downtown.

Bo Canon had not prepared himself for the worst case scenario. The chief sat on the edge of his bed in dismay and grief after hearing the shocking news. He knew the Wallaces and this innocent young child. He considered them friends. A two-time heart attack survivor, he popped a nitroglycerin tablet from the bottle he always carried in his top left pocket to alleviate the heaviness and tightness he felt in his chest. He had hoped that this year's murder rate would go down. The rate had gone up and it looked like the last murder of the year, if it was the last, was surely it's most shocking and gruesome.

The chief, now in his thirtieth year on the force, had for the past five years been hoping that each of those years would be his last. He wanted to go out on a high note. The trend was going in the opposite direction with more crime each year. This was the worst crime of his career: an innocent child of a friend. The high note had slipped away. His boss would want to hear this news before anyone else and deserved not to be blindsided. Bo Canon placed a call to the mayor, Peyton Castelle.

"Peyton, this is Bo. I know it's early, sir, but we have another murder on the Southside."

Mayor Castelle, sitting down to breakfast with his wife, got up and walked to a quiet room and closed the door.

"What do you mean another? Didn't know we had the first one."

"This murder looks similar to the Tiffany Miller murder on the Southside nine months ago. This would be the second one, sir."

"Who the hell is Tiffany Miller?"

"She was strangled, raped, and murdered, Peyton – a black woman on the Southside – nine months ago."

"What aren't you telling me, Bo? Why are you calling me at six-thirty in the morning on Christmas Eve to report a murder?"

"Peyton, the victim is the daughter of Draper Wallace."

"*The* Draper Wallace? As in built every damn building in the city, Draper Wallace?" responded the shocked mayor.

"Yes, him. I wanted you to know because I'm sure the media is on the way to the scene."

"How was she killed?"

"She was strangled and raped in the same fashion as Tiffany Miller."

"Who did it?"

"We don't know, but that side of town is infested with drug addicts and homeless people."

"But kill someone like her? Come on! Where are we on the case?"

"The Tiffany Miller case went nowhere. This one was just discovered ten minutes ago. We are no where yet."

"You mean we have two murders. A serial killer?"

"Well, let's don't get ahead of ourselves."

"Bo, are you sure it's her?"

"Yes," the chief replied. "It fits her description: blonde hair, blue eyes. It's her face, her little Mercedes, and her ID."

"Damn, damn, damn!" responded the mayor, loud enough for his wife, Joyce, to hear in the next room.

"Draper called me this morning and reported the child missing himself. I'm going to have to inform him and Mrs. Wallace."

"I will give you a while and then place a call to the family myself," said Peyton anxiously. "Jesus Christ, man! Draper Wallace's daughter." Even louder, he repeated, "Damn, damn!"

Joyce had come to the door, concerned. "Peyton?"

"Mayor, anything else you'd like me to do?"

"No, Bo, just solve this damn case. Get someone quick. This is bad."

"Yeah, yeah," responded Bo. "It's a messy crime scene. Hopefully there's a lot of evidence there. I'll call you shortly with what we have."

"Do that," the mayor replied. "Joyce, I'll be right there. I'm washing my face."

Bo Canon knew his next call wouldn't be an easy one. His trembling hand mis-dialed the number three times. After taking a few deep breaths to calm himself and looking at his trembling hands, he poured a bourbon. Taking several large swallows, he tried dialing again. Basil, the Wallace's butler – a member of the Wallace's family since before Draper was born – answered the phone with a deep and articulate, "Wallace residence."

"It's Bo Canon. I need to speak to Mr. Wallace. Is he available?"

"Just a moment, Chief."

Draper hurriedly answered the phone, relieved that Bo was calling so soon.

"Bo, I was just leaving. Where was she?"

Solemnly, Bo stated, "Draper, you need to come downtown."

"What do you mean come downtown? Where's my daughter right now, Bo? What's going on with her?"

Canon was silent for a moment, and then remorsefully said, "We found her body, Draper. I'm so sorry."

More silence. Wallace shrank in disbelief, immobilized, no words immediately coming out. Then a whisper, "No. Christ... God...her mother said last night that this felt bad. I was sure it was nothing. Oh my God. Where is she right now, Bo? I'm coming there."

Draper left the estate without telling Millicent the news. He, too, had not considered this outcome.

Bo Canon was at the scene when Draper Wallace arrived. Although the officers and investigators were professional and busy collecting evidence, Draper's arrival caused each of them to stop and observe the grief-stricken father as he absorbed the magnitude of an unimaginable tragedy. They all understood the implication it bore.

At this time of the morning on Christmas Eve, Five Points South was devoid of traffic. The alley where Jodi's car was discovered was the only one there, besides the police cars and an ambulance. Their emergency lights lit up the whole block as the night gave way to a gray, dreary morning that bore no resemblance to Christmas Eve, except for the pleasant, early morning aroma floating through the air from the local Southside bakeries.

Every officer on the scene had a cup of coffee and the smokers, and recent non-smokers, all had a cigarette. There was no pedestrian traffic. A very thin, lactating stray dog was scrounging for food. An alley cat scurried past, and a homeless man hurriedly pushed a grocery cart by. It was an ugly, cold day.

Broken, Draper Wallace looked hesitantly inside the trunk of his daughter's car - her sixteenth birthday present they had selected together. No one had the courage to tell him he shouldn't look. The officers knew that if he saw her, he'd never be able to erase her last image from his mind.

After many moments of silence and internal questions, he gulped and asked, "Who would do this? Put my child in here like she was trash? Why? How could someone do this? She was an angel. What have we come to? I don't want a word of this out until I've talked to her mother." Draper was inconsolable. "Who could kill my precious baby? Why?"

Pulling himself together, he stared at Bo Canon. "Who are you putting on this?"

"Jackson Connolly and Vincent Franks," replied Canon. "They'll find out what happened to Jodi, sir."

"Connolly...good choice, good choice," replied Draper.

All the crime scene investigators were frozen as Draper Wallace observed the tragic scene, trying not to let him see them stare at him with remorse. His presence reminded everyone that Jodi was a somebody; that this was a real person, a person who was loved. His anguish silenced the officers as they tried ever so carefully to resume their work. What Wallace had anticipated would be a regular day had so quickly and unpredictably turned into the worst day of his life. The moment seemed unreal. Impossible. Unimaginable. How could he give this news to his wife? Draper stood in what seemed to be the middle of the crime scene, his arms folded and his head resting in his right hand. Everyone worked around him. His reputation and presence communicated what he was not saying with words. This was the first time many of the policemen had ever seen Draper Wallace in person. They had read about him and seen him on television, but there he was – even more intimidating in real life.

The Wallace Corporation was known nationally. Wallace was an icon in Birmingham, Alabama. His multibillion-dollar business in construction and construction finance was one of the few businesses of its size that was still privately owned. Wallace was credited with changing the landscape of Birmingham. His ideas and will had made Birmingham look like a modern city. Wallace's reputation nationally had also helped to change the image of Birmingham among businessmen and investors. He had reached the pinnacle of success, and had become influential in affecting state and presidential politics and national policy. He was just as involved with local politics down to who was on the city council, and who would be mayor, police chief, and judge. He was one of the few people who could also get long-time bureaucratic city officials fired, something even the mayor couldn't do. Wallace did not want his building permits bogged down in bureaucratic red tape, something Birmingham City Hall was notorious for. And he did not want politics – local or national – to interfere with his business; chiefly, the migration of his cheap Mexican construction labor or meddling with his unions. His involvement in politics was for one purpose: profit.

Many years earlier, Draper and his three brothers had inherited the construction company from their father. The ownership of the company was split into fourths when he died. Draper, the second child, was always the better businessman. Taking full advantage of his superior business skills, he loaned his brothers money for them to pursue business ventures – which were seldom well thought out. They used their 25 percent of the construction company as collateral. One by one, they got in financial trouble and Wallace called the loans; first his youngest brother, then his other younger brother, and finally his older brother. Draper's two younger brothers still worked for him. His older brother hadn't spoken to him in twenty years. Wallace had never seen anything wrong with what he had done. He remarked to his older brother, "What bank or businessman would do anything different?" The loans to his brothers were what got Wallace into the construction loan business, where he proceeded to make a fortune.

Wallace was so astute at getting a construction job financed and completed that other competing firms would ask if the Wallace Corporation was going to bid on a job before they got involved at all. If it was, they wouldn't even consider it. However, those that did in the beginning soon learned that Wallace would stop at nothing to win. If he was outbid, his competitors often experienced misfortune. Sometimes building permit applications got lost at City Hall or Immigration might visit their worksite. A building inspector might not approve their work, or delay them so long that they were driven into bankruptcy. Or, they might just have an unexpected union strike. No one ever accused Wallace publicly, but his luck was uncanny. His construction jobs, though, were known for two things: they finished on time, and the job cost what he had said it would cost, something unheard of with other companies.

The Wallace Corporation was in a class all its own. Alabamians idolized Draper. He had made it and was the quintessential American businessman. In Mountain Brook where he had lived all his life, and where his parents had lived, and also in Birmingham, he was a pillar. He was born into the right circumstances. The good-looking, ambitious Draper had married his high school sweetheart, the beautiful Millicent Greenwood, whose family was richer than Draper's when they married. He had four beautiful children. He had built an empire and was respected by all. Now at fifty-nine, Wallace was Alabama royalty. He knew it, accepted it, and acted like it.

Wallace's mother had lived into her late eighties, his father into his late sixties. No one close to Draper had ever died of anything except old age. There had never been a tragic accident that took anyone he loved, and certainly not a murder. And a murder of someone young and innocent like Jodi was unthinkable. No one had ever taken anything away from Wallace. Until now – the youngest of his children, a little girl, one with such promise. He had always felt that he and Millie had finally gotten it just right with Jodi. She was born at a time when both of them had had more time to spend raising her. They had learned from the mistakes they had made with the older children. She was beautiful, with aqua blue eyes and with thick locks of golden hair. Her brilliant smile and spirit were unequaled. She was well adjusted and exceptionally loving. Her personality had made her a favorite at school and among her friends. Wallace could not comprehend that she could have died so violently. That he would outlive her. That she wouldn't graduate college, get married, or have children of her own. That her first sexual experience would be a gruesome rape at the hands of a murderer. The vulgarity of what had happened to his child had made him sick and enraged. How could he go on? How could he move from this spot where he was standing and leave her here? He had always protected her.

He should have made her come to the country club last night with him and Millie. He blamed himself. He had let his daughter leave his protective care. She should have been at the club – where she belonged, with her kind of people – not on the Southside with vagrants and that crowd. His acquiescence to the liberal leanings of the present times and to his daughter's youthful pleading to let her skip this year's annual celebration had been a mistake. He had given in. He'd always given in to her. Millie had wanted her at the annual Christmas party, but Draper had talked her into letting Jodi skip it. He understood that nearly all the people at the Christmas Gala had to be members of the club, even the dates that accompanied any girl or boy had to be members. Only certain invited luminaries were not members. Jodi had made many friends that couldn't attend, and her boyfriend, Davis, was a member but had not arrived home yet. Jodi had helped her mother plan the ball, but she'd grown up. She didn't want to go to what she called "the old boring Moth Ball." Draper had laughed, confident that one day soon she'd change, perhaps when she married and had her own family, and realized the benefits of being one of the chosen few belonging to the club. He remembered that Millie had been just like Jodi at that age, and now Millie was one of the club's staunchest supporters. God, how was he going to tell her?

Before his daughter was taken away in the ambulance, Wallace kissed and embraced her. He looked at Bo Canon and the investigators there. Who he was, who the victim was, and the importance of solving this crime was unmistakably conveyed. The solemn father left the scene to give Millie Wallace the worst news of her life.

CHAPTER FIVE

The Hunt

Detectives Connolly and Franks arrived at the crime scene having been briefed on the way.

"What do we have here?" asked Connolly.

"A white female, eighteen, appears to have been sexually assaulted, her clothes torn, strangled, bruises on her neck," one of the crime scene investigators responded. "She was robbed; the contents of her purse strewn about, but no money in it. She was clutching a bangle made of tin in her left hand. The car doesn't seem to be damaged, though."

"Do we know if the crime was committed here or was the car brought here?" asked Connolly.

"The car has been here for hours. She was probably shopping in the area, but we aren't sure yet."

"The stores will be opening soon. Franks and I will ask around, check with the local merchants, see if any of them saw anything."

Talking to the scene investigators, Connolly stated with emphasis, "Do better than the usual. This is the most important case you'll ever work on. Do it fast, but do it right. The first forty-eight hours are critical. You call only me. Everybody clear?"

Connolly masked his grief effectively. He had known Jodi all of her life. She called him Uncle Jack.

The shops had opened early on Christmas Eve for late holiday shoppers. The two detectives had spent the last few hours talking to several merchants, none of whom knew anything. At ten a.m., they entered Alan Alman's shop, The Urban Clothier Southside Boutique.

"I'm Detective Connolly, this is Detective Franks. We are investigating a murder that occurred last night. The victim is a young woman named Jodi Wallace. She's blonde, blue eyes, five-foot three-inches tall."

Mr. Alman appeared faint as he heard the news.

"Mr. Alman, are you okay?" Detective Franks asked.

He stammered, "When did this happen? I know Jodi. She's a regular here, in almost every weekend before she went off to college. She was here just last night."

"What time did she leave, sir?"

"A little before ten p.m. We closed later than usual last night for late Christmas shoppers. The door was locked because it was so close to closing time, so I had to unlock it to let her out. I bet it's one of those homeless people – fighting, doing drugs, defecating on the sidewalks."

"Were there any around last night?"

"Yeah, I ran one of them off that's here all the time. He was asking customers for money when they came in and left. He asked Jodi for money. She told him she didn't have any change. I told him to leave. She was always real nice about it though, never scared."

"Did you see who she left with?"

"No."

"Did you notice if she got in her car or drove off?"

"No, no, I didn't see anything. I had customers still inside. I just saw him talking to her, asking for money. I told him to get the hell away from my store."

"Did you see him leave?"

"Well, he went around the corner."

"Did you see him anymore that night?"

"No. No. I didn't."

"Mr. Alman, would you be able to pick this guy out of a lineup?"

"I sure could."

"By chance do you know this person's name?"

"No, I don't know."

"We need a description of him," added Franks.

"Well, he has a long, straggly beard. And he has a bike; looks like he has everything he owns on his bike. And he wears a lot of jewelry."

"Lots of jewelry?" Connolly asked.

"Yeah, lots of bangles on his arms. He's black, dark-skinned, red eyes, long tangled hair... like he hasn't had a bath in years. Real scary looking. He looks like a killer."

"Mr. Alman, how tall was this man?"

"He was black, mean looking."

"His size, sir. How tall?"

"Average, I guess."

"How old?"

"Forties, maybe. They operate the damn street like a toll booth. Patrons can't get through without giving them money. Those that don't get dirty looks. Those that do, it's like throwing pieces of bread to pigeons. They come out of the woodwork, following you around, harassing you. Folks can't eat dinner outside around here anymore. The restaurant owners constantly have to run them off. They come right up to the tables, drooling, cracked out, and smelling like shit and cheap wine. None of them work. Most of them just sit out here talking to themselves and acting out war scenes. They are very dangerous. I knew it was only a matter of time before they started killing people. You know, because of those liberals you can't do a damn thing about them. They think the homeless people own the streets, that the streets are the homes for the homeless people and not all of our property. These are not their homes; these are damn public sidewalks and parks. Then they've got those grocery store shopping carts all over the damn place. Can't you arrest them for stealing those? They come down here selling drugs, prostituting, using drugs right out in the open, and think they have the right to harass good people. There are only a few good folks left down here. I'll be happy to pick that son-of-a-bitch out of a lineup."

Alman wanted to continue his rant, but Connolly cut him off, "Well, here's my card. If you think of anything else, or if he shows up, give me a call."

"I'll be happy to. She's Draper Wallace's daughter, isn't she? It's a shame it took them killing somebody like her. Maybe something will get done about this now."

***

Dozens of phone calls flooded City Hall filling the answering machine and the weekend *Express Yourself* hotline as the press descended upon the biggest story in recent memory. Calls came from the press, concerned citizens, and politicians whose careers Draper Wallace could end with a phone call.

Peyton Castelle had been a political hack all his life. He had been a state representative, worked for the governor, and was now mayor. In the past, Peyton had never been one to shun any publicity or cameras, but this was a press conference he would rather have done anything else but give. But as an astute politician, he had quickly assessed that his career was inexplicably tied to the life of this murder.

Chief Canon was a three-decade veteran of the force and had been the police chief for the past fifteen years. He was a traditional southerner. He had served on the force in Birmingham through segregation and protests, and he was hardened by his many years as a police officer. But he was considered by all who knew him to be fair and intelligent, which was not what one would assume from the "good ol' boy" image he tried hard to cultivate – a necessity for success in the South.

The mayor and chief were not looking forward to the noon Christmas Eve conference with the Birmingham press corps, who had long ago learned to be distrustful and suspicious of local politicians and the police department. The press couldn't wait for the two men to get to the microphones before starting their questions. The first question hit while they were still five feet away.

"We hear there has been a murder. Are there any suspects?"

"No," answered the chief.

"We understand that Draper and Millicent Wallace, pillars of our community, lost their daughter."

"That's the unfortunate truth. We are investigating, but have no leads yet. We will keep you apprised. Remember, these parents have lost their daughter, a precious member of their family. As is feasible, we will keep you apprised of the case," replied Canon.

"We want to assure the citizens of Birmingham, however, that we are committed to solving this case and keeping everyone safe. There is no reason to be scared," added the mayor.

A seasoned Birmingham news reporter, Jacob Levin, asked, "What about the young girl strangled and killed just nine months ago, chief? Where are you on that investigation?"

The mayor responded hastily, "We can't take anymore questions at this time."

"Mr. Mayor, sir," Levin continued, "the citizens have long asked for protection on the Southside. Where is it? This police department is fraught with civil suits and wrongful death cases brought against it, yet the citizens of Birmingham are being killed in the streets right under your nose. How in the world could the richest kid in Birmingham get killed downtown right under your nose?" Levin threw his questions like spears. "A mayor with five city officials and two council people under investigation for corruption – are you people too preoccupied to do your jobs?"

Another reporter asked, "Why doesn't this city have any ordinances against panhandling? And why aren't you enforcing laws against drunkenness and this street harassment?"

"There is a homeless man that is under investigation, is that true?" Another reporter added.

An irritated Chief Canon responded, "Sorry, we can't take anymore questions at this time. We will keep you informed of our investigation. Thank you."

The mayor and chief hurried from the microphones to take refuge in City Hall, as if retreating to a garrison.

✲ ✲ ✲

As the night claimed this uncharacteristically cold, dreary Christmas Eve, all of Birmingham learned of the Jodi Wallace murder. All other matters had become insignificant in light of the story. Late shoppers were watching television updates at the malls, forgetting the lack of time left to finish their Christmas shopping. The restaurants lacked the customary chatter, as patrons whispered of the brutal crime and craned their necks to see the televisions. People who did not need to leave their homes stayed in and made sure the doors were locked. The Birmingham police acted as if they were under assault. The mounted police were working the Southside and there were extra bike police patrols. Patrol cars sped in every direction. Suspicious characters were being questioned and minor offenses normally overlooked were getting citizens arrested. The investigation into the murder had started immediately and determinedly. Detectives Connolly and Franks were en route to the Wallace estate to meet with Draper and Millicent Wallace, before memories of small events leading up to the murder faded or became exaggerated.

At 7:00 p.m., Detectives Connolly and Franks arrived at the Wallace home in Mountain Brook. The occasion for their visit made it exceptionally sad, with the backdrop of beautiful Christmas decorations. The atmosphere inside the Wallace mansion was somber, and an uncomfortable silence expressed every draft in the old house as they entered. Connolly knew the estate well. He had worked for Wallace for twenty years on special projects. It was also not Franks' first visit to the estate. The eldest Wallace son had had many brushes with the law in the past – fighting, drunken car wrecks – but nothing that would have gotten a Wallace arrested. There had infrequently been some sort of domestic disturbance in the neighborhood over the years, including a wife who mysteriously fell down a flight of stairs, officially ruled an accident due to slick hardwoods. There had also been a rape investigation that turned out to be just a misunderstanding. There were no violent crime statistics for Mountain Brook, the safest suburb in Birmingham. It had only been twelve hours since Jodi's body was found, yet Connolly and Franks already knew this case was very different. Every resource available would be used to solve it in record time. Connolly led the way to the front door.

"Good evening, Lieutenant Connolly," greeted Basil.

"This is Detective Franks. We're here to see Mr. and Mrs. Wallace."

"Yes, please come in and have a seat. Mrs. Wallace is expecting you."

The two preferred to stand in the foyer as Basil informed Mrs. Wallace.

"Good evening, Mrs. Wallace."

"Hello, Jack," she responded, a tremor in her voice.

Mrs. Wallace was shaken, Connolly observed, but seemed to be trying hard to hold it together. Connolly thought she showed exceptional poise and looked quite dignified, but the moment seemed to have aged her considerably. Her eyes were dark and swollen. Her blonde hair seemed grayer and less together. Connolly had never hugged Millie before and felt awkward. They did not embrace, but she placed a hand on his shoulder, offering him reassurance.

"I'm so sorry, Mrs. Wallace. This is Detective Franks from the Homicide Division, ma'am."

"I'm very sorry for your loss. Thank you for agreeing to see us tonight," added Franks.

"Please come in. Draper is in the family room, and we have some guests here, family and friends. Can Rose get you gentleman some coffee or something?" Rose was the Wallace's house lady.

"No, thank you, ma'am."

"Basil, will you please show the gentlemen to the study and get the Winters and Drover girls."

Basil nodded.

The detectives were escorted through the expansive foyer of

the old mansion and into the dark mahogany study. They waited a few moments and observed the massive room, which was as large as a small public library and contained several thousand books.

Connolly was not looking forward to meeting with Wallace under the circumstances. He had met Wallace when he was twenty-eight years old and a rookie on the police force before he understood power and corruption. During the twenty years that had passed, Connolly surprisingly had managed to hold on to much of his idealism. He'd stayed on the Birmingham police force, although most of his colleagues had left Birmingham for surrounding cities. They received higher pay and less dangerous duty. But Connolly didn't want to work the school crossings Monday through Friday or a church parking lot on Sundays. He wanted to be a cop, work vice, and investigate murders. But he, like his colleagues who had left Birmingham, was drawn by the allure of extra cash, so he worked for Wallace as well. The projects that Wallace put Connolly on were often more exciting than vice. He respected and admired Wallace the way one respected a boss that had become a mentor and somewhat of an arms-length friend. Wallace also respected Connolly, but they were from different worlds.

As he waited, Connolly reflected on Birmingham. Alabama's largest metropolitan area had more than legitimately earned its reputation of being a city of racial prejudice and cronyism, he thought, and of politicians who made their living on exploiting racial division. Even in the present day, after Birmingham's bitter struggle toward racial integration, it was still a city divided along racial lines. It was also the quintessential city of the haves and have-nots – with the ultimate haves no more aptly represented than by the residents of Mountain Brook, at one time the richest suburb in the nation. Draper Wallace was one of its most notable citizens.

He knew that being from an old Mountain Brook family, Draper had inherited millions of dollars and could have done nothing, as is so often the case. But Wallace turned his millions into billions. By all accounts, if you didn't consider his extreme wealth, Connolly had always thought that Wallace came across down to earth – as down to earth as he could, as one of the richest men in the state and having had such a privileged existence. Connolly's twenty years of working with Wallace had given him a jaded opinion of Wallace's world. He, like most, desired to have what Wallace had, but Connolly knew that even if he won the lottery, he could never fit into Wallace's world.

People in Mountain Brook were set apart from Alabama socially, but enjoyed the position that came with being so rich and wealthy in a poor state. It was where the Old South thrived and where the obvious separation of people by economic class was still in vogue. Each time Connolly had seen Wallace stroll the grounds of his estate, he had felt it was reminiscent of a master lording over his plantation 150 years ago, with all the characters gratefully obliging their traditional roles.

Connolly observed that it was a city frozen in time, the old mansions complete with carriage houses behind them and overgrown trees that were just as old. The mountain perch and deep foliage made Mountain Brook ten degrees cooler than the rest of Birmingham, saving its residents from the scorching heat of Alabama summers. The temperature differential caused a gentle whisper of wind that created a hypnotic allure for the residents and non-residents as they passed by, dreaming of a life in the privileged community. The mountain also shielded Mountain Brook from the dirt, dust and black coal soot that covered the rest of Birmingham, the only city in Alabama built on steel and industry rather than agriculture. The appearance of Birmingham was gray and dusty, with smoke stacks, railroads, and aluminum buildings dotting the landscape. The money from that steel built Mountain Brook. The Wallace mansion was old world; no marble, no gold, nothing shiny, the ground slightly damp, cool and musty.

The enclave city of Mountain Brook had an aura of unwelcomeness to outsiders, and a certain illegitimacy was bestowed on new people who moved in. There might as well have been signs throughout the community that read New Money Need Not Apply, Connolly had always told his wife. It was a place where the servants still wore uniforms and one of the rare places in America where black house servants, cooks, and nannies were still preferred, most of whom were veterans of their jobs for many years. The mastery of their domestic skills was obviously inferred by their advanced years, but this also gave the impression of an era that would soon end – an era that they, as well as their employers, were desperately clinging to.

But Connolly knew from his years on the force that the thought of one of theirs raped and killed near their back door was outrageous. The encroachment of that kind of problem and issue on Mountain Brook was extremely distasteful. The unspoken outrage and sense of urgency, although not openly expressed, was palpable.

Lyndon Johnson's civil rights bills and voting rights acts had already been the catalyst to turn Alabama conservative, a euphemism for bigot in the South, and integration and urban sprawl had greatly accelerated the process. It seemed that the death of Jodi Wallace was the symbolic crescendo that would forever remind Birmingham and the elite class of Mountain Brookians that there were holes in the levy that needed plugging.

Connolly knew in his soul that Birmingham would never be the same.

Connolly was brought back to the mansion as Mrs. Wallace announced, "Officers, this is Allison Drover and Stephanie Winters. They were with Jodi last night. Jodi told me she was going to do some Christmas shopping and meet the girls later. I just never imagined." Tears rolled down Millie's cheeks, but she wiped them away quickly. She remained in the study as the officers questioned the girls, showing a strength that was guiding others through the tragedy.

Franks was amazed at how much Allison and Stephanie resembled Jodi. They could have passed as siblings. Their looks appeared almost as a prototype, a product of selective breeding. They were exceptionally beautiful, with thick hair, big eyes, and perfectly straight, white teeth. They were well-spoken, polite and poised. Franks recalled how easy it had been, during the years he was in the Navy and traveled abroad, to pick out Americans wherever he saw them, whether in a café, on a bus or shopping. The Americans stood out. These girls would also stand out wherever they were. His investigative skills told him how much the girls must have stood out last night, too.

"Miss Drover, would you mind telling us what you girls did last night?"

She responded emotionally, her hands visibly trembling. "No sir, I wouldn't mind. We met Jodi at Starbucks around ten and ordered our usual, toffee nut latte. We talked about the Christmas pageant, our first semester at school, looked at Zaps from the Tri Delt Formal, stuff like that. We all had a midnight curfew and it was getting close to eleven. I remember she was so excited that Davis was coming home."

"Davis?"

"That's her boyfriend."

"Anything else you can remember?"

Both girls began to cry, "No, nothing I can ...," Allison managed.

"Wait, Ali, I remember something else," Stephanie interrupted. "She asked me for change. All I had was a five, so I gave her that. She said she needed it to give to the homeless guy outside. Remember, Ali?"

Allison wiped her eyes. "That's right. We all walked out and she gave the money to the homeless man as we were leaving. He was standing on the corner with his bike. Steph and I rode together, and Jodi parked in the opposite direction. We said goodnight and she started walking toward her car. The homeless guy trailed behind her on his bike. Then we turned the corner and she was out of sight. We didn't think anything about it. The bums are always down there. They're usually harmless if you give them money."

Franks asked, "Do you girls remember what this man looked like?"

"Yeah, like a smelly homeless guy, and he had bangles all over his arms. He was black, nasty, had a bunch of stuff on his bike. We should have known. God, we should have known," Allison remorsed.

"His age?"

"God! Old." Stephanie replied.

"How old would you think?"

"Umm, fifties, sixties maybe," Stephanie added.

"Was his hair gray?"

"No, he had black, straggly hair and a beard, a long beard. Gross, very scary looking," Stephanie continued.

"Anything else?"

"No, sir," replied Allison.

"No, that's all I can remember, too," said Stephanie.

"Could you pick him out of a lineup?" asked Franks.

"Absolutely," Stephanie replied.

"Yes," Allison added.

"Thank you, girls." The girls, eighteen and nineteen, both badly shaken and lifetime friends of Jodi, returned to the other guests.

As they did so, Connolly and Franks focused their attention on Mrs. Wallace.

"Mrs. Wallace, can you tell us about your conversations with Jodi last evening?"

"Well, she said she was going shopping and then to meet the girls at Starbucks. She said she would be home by midnight. That's her curfew. Draper said she was getting too old for a curfew, but I still insisted. She was just eighteen, you know, a freshman at Alabama. She wanted to be a journalist."

"Was she having any problems at home or school that you were aware of?"

"No, none."

"Any enemies? Anyone mad at her?"

Millie was incensed. "My daughter was loved by everyone. She didn't have any enemies. Everybody loved her. She was in the sorority, the church choir. She was an honor student, with perfect grades."

"How about her boyfriend, Davis? Any problems there?"

"No, he's a perfect gentleman. They've been together since tenth grade. He graduated with her and earned a scholarship to Harvard. He's going to be a doctor. He's devastated. She was Christmas shopping for him."

"Is he here?"

"Yes, his plane arrived at six. He came straight here from the airport. He flew in from Massachusetts. I was always nervous about her shopping in the city because of the people you see down there. She told me all the time, 'I'll be careful, it's fine, you don't have to worry, Mom.'" Millie was sobbing again. "She was supposed to be with us last night. It was the annual Christmas party at the country club. She thought it was corny, and she wanted to be with her friends. I should have insisted."

"What time did you return home, Mrs. Wallace?"

"Draper and I returned to the house around one. Jodi had helped plan the party. I went up to tell her what a success it was, but her bed was empty."

The door of the study opened and Draper entered, without the swagger and confidence that Connolly had come to know.

"Give us just a moment alone, Millie. I want to have a few words with these officers." He put his arm around his wife and gave her a quick squeeze. After he had closed the doors behind her, he turned to the two detectives.

"Where are you on this investigation? I understand that there is a homeless man who's a suspect."

"It's too early to call anyone a suspect, but we are following up on all leads, sir," Franks replied. "Anything you know that you want to tell us, Mr. Wallace?"

"Only this - we are a normal family. Don't waste any time ruling us out, and Davis has an airtight alibi. He was a thousand miles away. Trust me, I've already checked that out."

Detectives Connolly and Franks both considered the multimillion-dollar Mountain Brook estate behind gates and the half-dozen servants and house attendants they had seen so far within their first thirty minutes in the house, and thought to themselves, *Normal?* There was nothing normal about the Wallaces.

"I'm sure I have made my enemies over the years, but my

little girl didn't have any. She was damn near perfect. The way I see it, this was some of those hoodlums on the Southside wanting a few extra dollars to buy some drugs or alcohol."

Connolly decided it was time to wrap up. "Well, Mr. Wallace, we are following up on all leads. If anything else comes to mind, here's my card." Detective Connolly made his best attempt at formality in front of Franks. Wallace knew exactly how to get in touch with Connolly, and had often. The two would talk later.

"Well, anything that you need, we're here, sir," added Connolly.

Wallace moved closer to the two men. "I'm gonna give you a couple of days because I trust you. I wanted you on this case because I trust you. But that's all I'll give you before I start my own investigation. Now y'all excuse us. Millie and I have things to tend to."

As they left, Connolly asked Franks to call the lab contact.

"Compare any forensic evidence on Jodi's body or in the car to the Miller girl who was murdered. See if anything matches the forensic evidence that was kept from her case."

"She was raped, right?" asked Franks.

"Yep, and strangled." The detectives locked eyes, sharing their silent hypothesis. Both twenty-year veterans of the Birmingham Police Department, they had investigated more homicides than any two detectives on the force. They knew that whatever cases any other detective had would be dropped, every beat cop would ask questions and run down homeless people, and all known black criminals with any record would be called in. If there was any DNA evidence on Jodi Wallace, every black man hauled in was going to be tested – with or without justifiable cause.

As Connolly and Franks left the gated estate, Connolly remembered, "The chief wanted us to brief him. We better call him." He made the call.

"Chief, it's Connolly."

"What have you got, Connolly?"

"It's only been half a day."

"I know how long it's been – it's been the longest day of my life. What do you have?"

The fact that it was Christmas Eve and a holiday weekend didn't matter. This was not Tiffany Miller.

"We talked to all the merchants in the Southside area where Jodi was shopping last night. One, the owner of the Urban Clothier, Alan Alman, said that she left his place around ten p.m. He had to run off a homeless man who was harassing her. The man asked her for money, but she didn't have any. Alman said these homeless people harass his patrons all the time. He gave us a description. He didn't know which direction the girl went in when she left the store, or if the man accompanied her or not. We also interviewed Mr. and Mrs. Wallace, and two girls, eighteen and nineteen, who grew up and attended Alabama with Jodi. They met her at Starbucks after Jodi left the clothing store a little after ten p.m. They stayed there for an hour. Jodi asked one of the girls, Stephanie Winters, for change because all she had was a credit card. Then when she left the coffee shop, they watched her give the money to a homeless black male standing on the corner. They described him as having a bike. He followed Jodi to her car. She was parked in the opposite direction from the girls. They waved goodbye, and that was the last time they saw her. Besides Draper saying he's going to take things into his own hands if we don't get him something soon, that's all we have. We got a description of the man: bearded, bracelets on his arms, bike loaded down with lots of items. We are going to give this description to our guys on the street."

"Well, damn it boys, that sounds like great progress. Find this man and we may be in business," Canon added with relief and excitement. "Keep this quiet. We don't want folks going off the deep end. We need a dignified investigation. If the mayor hears this, that man will be convicted before Christmas dinner."

"We're going to take a trip to the homeless shelter tomorrow and see if anyone there fits the description."

Connolly and Franks suspected that if a transient or homeless man had committed this crime, the man could have left immediately following the incident. Unless there was DNA evidence left at the scene and the perpetrator was in an offender databank, the person could have committed the crime, left Birmingham, and quickly blended in with the homeless population of another large, nearby city. The man could be in New Orleans, Memphis, or Atlanta. And at that point, the lead suspect sounded like every other homeless person in Birmingham, except for the bangles. The age given by both the girls and Alman was so disparate that it was invalid. Lose the bangles and the description would be a black male, average build and height, dark complexion, with a beard, between forty and sixty years old. He could be anyone. The two detectives feared they might have already lost their suspect – he could have gotten on a bus and left that night.

They didn't want to visit a shelter on Christmas Day, but this was Draper Wallace's daughter and no one wanted this suspect to slip through. Franks and Connolly knew that the meals on Christmas Day were pretty elaborate at the shelter, and the goodwill of the local citizens was at a peak. A police investigation on Christmas Day might not be what anyone wanted, but time was critical. The two men knew the local shelter operator, Jasper Thrash. If the people he was providing shelter to weren't society's throwaways, they also were aware he would be arrested and put in jail. The city gave a million dollars to him annually for a warehouse the city already owned and the 200 cots and pads that lined the walls. The food was donated by local restaurants and grocers. Many suspected the life-appointed rabble pack of city bureaucrats used the million dollars as a slush fund. Jasper was more than willing to oblige.

There were no expectations put on Jasper to operate the shelter, no accountability. There were no objectives to achieve for the homeless men who used the facility. The money made many people feel that they had done all that could be expected of them. The mayor and city council approved the expenditure every year, never asked any questions, not even the least intrusive. Many of them were suspected of using the fund as well. The annual auditors report was always clean, but most knew there were problems. The corruption was blatant, and it would get much worse.

Connolly and Franks left the Wallace estate at 8:00 p.m. on Christmas Eve. The veterans shared their thoughts as they left, feeling very fortunate that their families and loved ones were safe. They knew policemen were like soldiers: they took orders. What was important to them was what was important to their leaders: the mayor, the chief, and powerful citizens like Draper Wallace. Policemen get their priorities and the tone in which those priorities will be carried out from them. However, Connolly and Franks were disturbed about the complete lawlessness evident in these murders, although there had been no priority placed on solving the Tiffany Miller murder. It didn't matter how gruesome it was. Tiffany was a homeless, black, crack-addicted street hooker. Who cared? Her parents, even if outraged, were surely poor and powerless. She was gone and few noticed. These things happened to those kinds of people.

The lawmakers and the criminals understand explicitly that there was a line drawn in the sand, which if the criminal element doesn't cross, they can scrape out an existence. But that line cannot and must not be crossed, just as soldiers understand that in war they will kill each other, but that it is not acceptable to kill non-combatants or civilians. When the innocent were killed and those living outside of the communities where drugs and crime were rampant and allowed, then the community and the law take notice.

As the men approached their suburbs, they were thankful, grateful that their children were safe, but anxious that someone had crossed the line. They would be at the shelter at 5:00 p.m. Christmas Day, the time the homeless wanting Christmas dinner would arrive.

☆ ☆ ☆

Detectives Connolly and Franks had visited the shelter many times over the years. The residents were often good sources of information for street crimes. They had several informants who, if they knew anything, would be more than happy to cough it up for a few dollars. Franks was hoping to get lucky. Maybe someone had seen something, or knew the homeless man with the bangles. Maybe the bangled fellow would show up for Christmas dinner himself. Connolly, however, wasn't counting on it. The detectives preferred to encounter the homeless men on the streets, because the shelter was a particularly dark and sad place. The masses of homeless men all huddled together could also be intimidating, and Connolly and Franks were seasoned veterans not easily intimidated.

The scene was reminiscent of a prison and an asylum combined, without the protection of bars and guards. Connolly had seen prisons, however, that were more hygienic and had a sense of order and control. There was no order or control at the shelter, and it certainly wasn't hygienic. Many homeless men elected not to stay in shelters because the close quarters made it easier to catch colds and the flu. They knew that a bout of the flu on the streets could kill you. The cots lined the walls in a storm shelter fashion, and at least half of the men seemed to be suffering from a mental illness, talking to or even having heated arguments with themselves. There was rampant theft of each other's belongings and violent assaults. The staff, immune to it all, mundanely went about their tasks.

The detectives had encountered many people over the years that genuinely cared about these men, who had dedicated themselves to fighting the injustices that created the environment the two detectives witnessed at the shelter. Some had made great progress treating them. The detectives knew of such centers that were actually effective, and had taken many homeless people to them and had watched them change their lives. Unfortunately, this was rare. Most of the time, the homeless would continue this existence, in and out of treatment centers and in and out of jail - doing better and then relapsing back into their old behaviors. They were ill-equipped to manage their lives due to mental illness, addiction, poor education, and no job skills or coping skills. Many would never leave the streets. The men also knew that they were society's throwaways. They were the forgotten. There was little sympathy for young, middle-aged, or even old homeless men. Their plight was suspected by most as being self-inflicted, the result of bad living, bad behavior and habits, or drugs.

Most people Connolly and Franks had encountered in the judicial and law enforcement community didn't go to bed worried about them. The tax-paying citizens didn't want too much of their money being wasted on people whom they felt should be working and taking care of themselves like everybody else. The churches were trying to convert them. Few understood or wanted to understand why or how this could happen. There were also far too many Jaspers who were willing to exploit the situation. For the public, Jasper's warehouse was the face of the homeless.

As Connolly and Franks arrived at five o'clock, the annual dinner was being prepared. It was standing room only. The homeless men were their usual thankful selves, dutifully playing their part for the good folks who had come out to give them food, hats, and gloves. The discomfort on the faces of most of the volunteers was amusing to Connolly, and hugging the homeless men was particularly arduous for some, he observed.

Franks remarked, "I wonder how long they'll bathe tonight after this?"

Connolly chuckled. "Think they'll ever wear those clothes again?"

"Probably not," replied Franks.

"If only the holiday spirit persisted past December twenty-sixth," Connolly said. "It's as if all it takes to cleanse you of your sins and reserve your spot in Heaven is serving a turkey dinner to homeless people."

Franks nodded in agreement.

Most of the homeless men knew Connolly and Franks, and they pretended to be happy to see them. Only those who had recently gotten into trouble or had warrants looked away. The detectives knew who was who. They needed these men to accomplish their jobs. They had developed relationships with many of them over the years, mutual respect had grown, and they knew when to be heavy-handed with them and when not to be. The detectives knew that for most of these men, their only crimes were poverty, race, and the public's fear of them.

The detectives looked around for a homeless man wearing bangles and matching the description they had been given. As soon as they described their man to a few people, everyone they asked replied, "That's Mack Oliver."

"Mack Oliver?" the detectives asked each other.

Connolly pulled one of his longtime informants, Charles Tolbert, outside. He placed a twenty in Tolbert's hand and asked, "Charles, who's Mack Oliver?"

Jasper was at the shelter that night, but the detectives did not want him to know who they were looking for. Jasper would call anyone and everyone and expose their leads. However, the bounder was much too preoccupied to be concerned with the men's investigation – dressed as Santa and accepting donations in the Santa hat he held in his hands. The money would certainly never reach any homeless person.

"You mean Mack Oliver with the chains, man?" Charles responded, stuffing the twenty in his front pocket.

"Yes," replied Connolly, "that's the one. Is he here tonight?"

"I ain't seen him. He don't usually eat here, especially not on Christmas. He has family, I think."

"Drugs?"

"Yeah. He's on medicine, too. For a long time."

"Where does he hang out?"

"Well, he has a bike, you know, he's everywhere. He rides that bike like he's in that French race, you know. He's at Five

Points on the Southside a lot. He plays that horn at the fountain. You've seen him ain't you?"

"Yeah, of course, I've seen that guy," Connolly replied.

"Where does his family live?" asked Franks.

Charles hesitated, wondering if he would be compensated for the additional information. "On the Southside."

"Oliver is his last name?" asked Connolly.

"No, Purifoy."

"Charles, anyone know anything about a murder Friday night?" asked Franks.

"That white girl? Hell no. Nobody knows about that, man. They ain't talking about it anyway. Nobody wants that kind of trouble." Charles looked around, then said quietly, "That person would have to be crazy."

"If you hear anything suspicious, let me know. If you see Mr. Purifoy, use some of that money I gave you to use a pay phone and call me."

"Alright, chief. Merry Christmas."

"Well, Franks, we have a name," Connolly stated.

"I'll run it," replied Franks. "You gave that guy a lot of money."

"It's Christmas, and that's just a little motivation. He'll call if he hears something," Connolly explained. "I'll put someone at the fountain. Mr. Purifoy may just show up."

CHAPTER SIX

Family Night

The cold rain in Atlanta had not deterred any family members from attending the patients' much anticipated Family Night. The overflow parking lined both sides of the streets the whole length of the block and wrapped around the building. All the families were walking to the large, gated building, with some children and adults without umbrellas running toward it. All of the families packed into the large dining facility of the Atlanta Mental Health Center. The dining room was the cafeteria of an old high school that had closed many years earlier. Seventy-five families had shown up on this wet last Sunday in January. Many who had attended church earlier were still in their Sunday dresses and suits.

There were joyous greetings and hugs, and the families remarked on how much weight many of the patients had gained and how good they looked. The weight gain was often time pretty remarkable for those recovering from addiction, who now had turned their compulsive behavior to eating. The round tables were adorned with white plastic tablecloths and loaded down with the comfort food, like black-eyed peas, collard greens, macaroni and cheese, fried chicken, baked ham, buttered rolls and cornbread, and overly-sweetened iced tea that required Dr. Sam to use one part tea and three parts water before she could drink it. The aroma of all the immaculately prepared dishes was irresistible. No one, however, touched the food until it had been properly blessed. The prayers were often very extended, and tested the younger children and sinners who attended Family Night. The patients had put together a choir, and following the prayer, they would go right into song and enthusiastic praise dances. The beautiful voices echoed throughout the dining hall and filled most of the mental health center with gospel melodies of hope and deliverance. After the selection of songs, the feast would begin. The generous helpings overflowed from the plates of the attendees.

As Dr. Sam walked up to the table where Mrs. Carey and Cassius were seated, she noticed Cassius lean over and whisper in his mother's ear. "Momma, here comes Dr. Sam."

"Hi, Mrs. Carey. I am Samantha Williams, Cassius' therapist."

"Oh, I know who you are. Cassius talks about you all the time. You are just as he described."

Betsy Carey was a woman in her mid-fifties with a thin face and high cheekbones, although she looked twenty years older. She had pronounced veins on her thin hands and legs, and the outline of the veins was clearly defined through her opaque stockings. Her legs were stiff and skinny, appearing arthritic. Her once beautiful, cocoa-colored skin was now worn and leathery. She was dressed in her best Sunday clothes. She was very proper in her demeanor, pronouncing every word correctly and distinctly.

She shook Dr. Sam's hand firmly and excitedly said, "You are just as pretty as Cassius said you would be. You are the only one he trusts, you know. Tell me, you look mighty young to be a doctor. How did you get such an important job? Are you responsible for all of the patients?"

Her questions came faster than Dr. Sam could answer them. Dr. Sam had created Family Night at the center because her patients – urban, mostly black, all poor – had many preconceived notions about counseling and mental health treatment. She knew her patients were reluctant to engage in treatment readily, as were their families, because baring your innermost feelings to strangers was considered strange, unconventional and taboo. This was territory reserved for your relationship with God. Dr. Sam had long noted that her relationships with black friends had not gotten very personal until the relationship had been cultivated for many years. Only when she became very close to them did the most innocuous conversations develop, because exposing ones' dirty laundry to outsiders was particularly shunned in the black community. It was a cultural reality that could easily incubate the worst forms of abuse. As a therapist, she noted that her patients demonstrated the same reticence.

Blacks in America had long ago learned the negative consequences associated with discussing their problems, inequities or any assaults. The issues had fallen on deaf ears in the past. Reporting a crime against you that had been committed by a white perpetrator could only exacerbate the problem, and one committed by a black assailant was often ignored. There were no authorities to rectify an injustice. It was a reality in the black community that would be one of the many causes of high crime and homicide rates, as blacks took the law into their own hands, solving their conflicts not by calling the police or relying on the judicial system, but by their own vigilante justice. The means for therapy or even adequate medical attention were not available to the common African American of years past, so these did not become a viable outlet for healing in their culture. Complaining about a problem, regardless of how large, was also considered unchristian, where it was perceived that suffering was a prerequisite to make it into Heaven.

Blacks had also learned to suffer in silence, to pray about their problems, and to ask for mercy and the strength to bear their difficulties. They had developed coping skills and compartmentalization techniques far superior to their white counterparts. This silent anguish, however, was the root of many problems, physical and mental.

As laws and the social climate changed in America, many wondered why the culture hadn't kept pace – as if you only had to change a law, like flipping a switch, to change hundreds of years of cultural practice. Blacks still distrusted the law, law makers, law enforcers, doctors, white people and therapists.

Understanding this cultural reality, Dr. Sam's creation of Family Night was to introduce the idea of treatment in a non-threatening environment. It was a social gathering, with friends, food served, and a film or a lecture given, to foster casual conversation where relationships could develop. She disguised therapy as a social function, and the patients loved Family Night. They dressed up, sang and cooked elaborate dishes. Dr. Sam knew that most whites told a stranger almost anything about themselves or their intimate lives. This cultural difference at times had caused blacks to be labeled as non-compliant, difficult, guarded, or not making progress, as is often the case when one culture – the dominant culture – forces its norms and expectations onto other cultures.

Dr. Sam, although born and raised in Athens, Georgia, had received her graduate education from Brandeis University in Massachusetts, the college chosen by her parents because they felt that it would offer her the most liberal education available. Dr. Sam excelled throughout school and graduated at the top of her class. Her parents, local college professors at the University of Georgia, had high hopes for social activism from Samantha. In the Deep South, at a time when it was very dangerous to do so, her parents had openly protested the racist practices of the then-governor of Georgia, Lester Maddox. They were visited by the KKK one night for their activism. Her family remained in Georgia. Dr. Sam always said that they got a cross burned in their front yard and didn't get invited to some parties, but other than that, her Georgia upbringing was filled with fond memories.

Her mother and father never removed the cross from the yard, which for a while gained a lot of spectator attention. But, as the years went by, people hardly noticed, and eventually her father had to point it out. Dr. Sam was amazed by how the cross had become such an acceptable part of the landscape. The irony of it could not be overlooked, how other racist behaviors and symbols had also become just a part of the landscape. The cross in her parents' yard, the Confederate flag flying over the capitol building, and the practice of segregation remain in Georgia today.

Mrs. Carey took full advantage of Family Night. She loved social functions and was ready to talk.

"Dr. Sam, how's my child doing?"

"He's coming along just fine."

"I agree. I sure wish he could stay here for awhile. I home-schooled Cassius, you know. It wasn't called that back then, but that's what I did. I'm a retired library aide. They didn't let us become librarians back then," Mrs. Carey recalled.

She remembered that she had gotten the job when she was only a young girl, and it was her very first job. "My mother did domestic work for the librarian's family, and when I was a little girl, she read to me, and read and read. That's why I developed my love for literature. Then when I turned sixteen, I went to work with her at the school."

"Why did you home-school Cassius?"

"Well, he and his brother, Mark Antony, had such a tough time in school during the integration. Mark Antony was seven years older than Cassius."

"He *was* seven years older?" asked Dr. Sam.

"Yes, we lost him three years ago." Her voice dropped to a whisper. "He died of AIDS, but he wasn't a homosexual. They sentenced Mark Antony to five years in prison. They said he stole a car. They only caught him with fireworks, though. They said the fireworks were in the car. But he only served three years. He was such a good boy that they released him on good behavior. It was such an injustice. His brother going away was very hard on Cassius," she continued sadly. "I worked around dozens of children for many years and I knew how troubled he was, so I came home and schooled him. And by that time, me and the Reverend had gotten married and he didn't want me to work anyway. He said the woman's place was in the home. You know the boy was so alienated, so discouraged, so distraught."

"Mrs. Carey, they have interesting names, Cassius and Mark Antony," remarked Dr. Sam.

"Yes, I love Shakespeare. Do you like those names?" asked Mrs. Carey, blushing.

"Yes, they are nice. You said they had trouble in school and that's why you home-schooled Cassius?"

"Yes, he was the only black child in his class. They wanted to put him in a special class because I taught him to stand up for himself. They sat him in the back of the class. And when he raised his hand to answer questions with the rest of the kids, they wouldn't recognize him. The teacher never even checked his homework. Mark Antony started off in a black school, where he had been recognized, so he didn't take the negative treatment as hard. He had higher self-esteem. I took Cassius out in the fourth grade when they said he was just too disruptive. He was only nine years old. You couldn't tell, could you, that I home-schooled him? I bet you he's got a better education than anybody else you've counseled. I covered all the subjects with him – math, science, reading, history – and my boys were especially fond of literature, probably because I was. I read all the best literary works to them; Shakespeare, Chaucer, T.S. Eliot, Hemingway, Steinbeck, and Shaw. I would have them memorize characters and we would have theatre at home. They did *Hamlet, Macbeth,* and *Julius Caesar.* They were so fond of *Julius Caesar,* perhaps because they heard their names being spoken."

"He's very intelligent, Mrs. Carey."

"But my baby is very troubled, Dr. Sam. I hope you can help him."

They had left Cassius to mingle with the other families and patients as they strolled through the common areas of the treatment center, eventually settling in the old auditorium. Dr. Sam and Mrs. Carey sat in the wooden auditorium chairs of the old high school, side by side. Mrs. Carey had interlocked her right arm with Dr. Sam's left. They looked straight ahead as Cassius' story unfolded ever so carefully.

Dr. Sam told Mrs. Carey, "Cassius told me he lost his younger brother, that he died."

Mrs. Carey was quiet for a second. "He must really trust you. He never talks about that. Neither do I, except to the Lord."

"Can you tell me what happened?"

"He just slipped and fell and bumped his head. Isaac, that was his name – after the Reverend – was trying to hold onto Cassius, trying to keep him from leaving the house to do drugs. I was upstairs asleep. Cassius was always in and out of the house. Isaac knew it was going to start a fight with the Reverend. Little Isaac loved his brother so much. He was very emotional about the arguments. He was only five years old. My husband – he's deceased now – wanted to blame Cassius. Cassius wasn't his. Neither was Mark Antony. I had them before I married the Reverend. He was never close to my boys, but he gave them his name. He blamed them for everything. He even said Mark Antony should go to jail for stealing the car. But I know they railroaded Mark Antony because he was black. Cassius was only a child when Isaac died."

"He was twenty-five or so, wasn't he?"

"That's right, only twenty-five, a child. Yes, he was on drugs, but he was a good boy." Emphatically, Mrs. Carey said, "It was a mistake. I wasn't about to let them send Cassius to jail, too. We just had to lean on God, not question His judgment, and get over it. The Reverend worshipped Isaac too much. He put that child on a pedestal and he wouldn't go anywhere without him. He kept him on his lap and never recognized my boys at all. You know, we didn't have him until late in life. The Reverend didn't have any other children. He was ten years older than me and I was forty at the time we had him. The Reverend said he was a miracle and he just went on and on and on. I think that's why God took him. God doesn't like that. The Reverend put Cassius out for good after that. And he's just been wandering ever since, city to city."

"Mrs. Carey, was Isaac's death investigated at all?"

"No. But the Coroner said he had injuries inconsistent with falling, a broken rib and a punctured lung. That was all the Reverend needed to blame Cassius."

"What did you think, Mrs. Carey?"

"It was a tragic accident. Cassius wouldn't hurt his own brother. My baby wouldn't hurt anybody."

"You said your husband died?"

"Yes, he had a stroke two years ago. Cassius came to help me see about him. Cassius was feeding him when he died."

Curious, Dr. Sam asked, "How did he die?"

"He choked. We had to practically make his food into mush for him to get it down. We did all we could do. He died right there in Cassius' arms. Cassius moved away to Birmingham a few weeks after he died. I'm so glad he's home. I hope he stays this time."

CHAPTER SEVEN

The Arrest

The police had, over the weekend, questioned every homeless person they encountered. They visited the corners where they hung out, the crack houses and abandoned buildings used by the homeless. They staked out the bus station and questioned hitchhikers. Early on the morning of Monday, December 26, the Birmingham police dispatcher called Detective Connolly to let him know they had picked up Mack Oliver Purifoy.

"Anything on this guy?"

"Nothing but public drunkenness this time last year. We've charged him with the usual until you get here."

"Alright, hold 'em. I'll call Franks and we'll be down." Detective Connolly poured his usual cup of coffee and headed downtown. In the interrogation room, a bruised and disheveled Mack Oliver Purifoy awaited the detectives.

Connolly and Franks had investigated dozens of homicides over the past twenty years and remembered every one of them. Connolly's knack for knowing which direction to go during an investigation was legendary. He was rarely wrong. He could see things in the evidence that no one else saw. He was calm, rational, and exceedingly polite, which effectively masked his rigid and dogged determination. He and Franks were the consummate professionals of the old school. Their cold neutrality had earned them the respect of good cops, bad cops, politicians, and men like Draper Wallace. Franks was obsessed with protocol, police procedure, and rules of evidence – a policeman who had graduated from night law school to improve his skills as a homicide detective.

The interrogation of suspects was ostensibly professional and dignified, but Connolly saw himself and Franks at war with criminals; the good guys against the bad guys. People who were questioned or arrested by the police were the potential foes. They were all treated as if they were armed and dangerous. Neither detective knew Mack Oliver. He was not a regular among lawbreakers. He was not among the usual suspects hauled in whenever there was a crime. Mack Oliver had not run and had no previous history of violent behavior. Connolly had no premonition that Mack Oliver was his man. His immediate feelings were that Mack Oliver was mentally ill, a drug addict, and had a personality incompatible with this sort of violence. However, the forensic evidence was not in, and Connolly at times had been surprised. Franks, on the other hand, judged only evidence. He and Franks proceeded with the customary questions – questions that were intended to lock Mack Oliver into a story, trip him up, or get a confession. He had not yet been Mirandized.

Mack Oliver was not an atypical homeless man. Black male, in his thirties, tangled full head of hair, with rings one usually wears on fingers woven throughout his beard. He was bejeweled – every finger had a ring, some with more than one, all silver, and at least a dozen necklaces, all silver. Silver bangles went from his wrist to halfway up his forearms. He wore a blue jean jacket, three or four shirts, blue jean pants and sneakers. His clothes were not soiled or worn too badly. He lacked the fetid odor the detectives had come to expect from the homeless. Mack Oliver leaned back in the chair with his hands in his pockets, as Connolly and Franks entered the interrogation room.

"Can we get you a cup of coffee? Are you hungry?" asked Connolly.

Mack Oliver responded, "I don't drink coffee and I'm not hungry."

"Mack Oliver, do you know why we picked you up?"

"They said I was drunk, but I ain't drunk. I don't drink and I haven't done drugs in over a year."

"Mack Oliver, we want to ask you a few questions. You don't have to answer them if you don't want to," Connolly stated.

"But if you don't have anything to hide, you shouldn't be worried about answering them for us," interjected Franks.

"We want to talk to you about a robbery, rape and murder that were committed on Friday night, the twenty-third. Do you know anything about this?" asked Connolly.

"No, sir, I don't know anything about no murder, no rape and no robbery."

"Do you know this girl, Mack Oliver?" asked Connolly, showing him a picture of Jodi.

"Yeah, I know her."

"How do you know her?"

"She's always on the Southside."

"When was the last time you saw her?"

"She gave me five dollars Friday night."

"Do you know her name?"

"No, I don't know her name."

"Well, what happened after she gave you five dollars?"

"What do you mean what happened? I said thank you. I said God bless you. Most people around here don't give you money, especially five dollars. She's a real nice lady."

"Do you use drugs, Mack Oliver?"

"No. I told you, I've been clean over a year."

"Mack Oliver, this young lady is named Jodi Wallace."

"Yeah?"

"You say she gave you five dollars. Was that the first time you asked her for money that night?"

"No, she didn't have any money when I first asked her. She went and got some and brought it to me. She's a real sweet lady."

"She brought it to you?" Connolly sounded puzzled and suspicious. "Were you mad at her when she didn't give you any money?"

"No, she was always sweet. I never got mad at her."

"Do you get mad at other people?"

"Yeah. People treat you like shit, there's nowhere to go rest. They are always harassing you, police always picking you up for nothing – like last night they picked me up – or telling you to move on. You can't go to the shelter, you'll get sick in there and people steal your stuff. You can get better food on the street than in the shelter. Those people don't care about you. Well, some do."

"Where are you living, Mack Oliver?"

"Here and there. Around this time of year, you do pretty good on the streets. There are more folks who want to help you."

"Anything else happen that night between you and Jodi?"

"No, man, like what?"

"Well, you said she gave you money, you said thank you. What next?"

"I got on my bike and went to the house around the corner. It's boarded up. I stayed there."

"Anybody else there?"

"No, just me."

"And after she gave you the five dollars, you left and she left?"

"Yeah."

"Did you follow Miss Wallace on your bike?"

"No, I was going in that direction. I saw her walking towards her car and I kept riding."

"Did you see anybody else talk to her, Mack Oliver?"

"No."

"Did you see anyone else in the alley?"

"No man. It was dark. I just rode on by."

"Did you see her get in her car?"

"No."

Looking at Mack Oliver's countless necklaces draped around his neck, bangles on his arms, and rings on every finger, Connolly asked, "Where is your bike now?"

"They say they got it downstairs. Can I go now?"

"Mack Oliver, are you telling us that you didn't have any physical contact with Miss Wallace?" Franks interjected with disbelief and indignation. "This is your last chance. I'm tired of playing games. If you tell us the truth right now, we may be able to help you. If you don't, you're going to get 'Yellow Momma.' You ever heard of 'Yellow Momma'? That's our affectionate name for our electric chair. She's waiting on you. You killed her, didn't you?"

"No, I'm not a killer, man."

"You didn't assault, hurt, or see anyone else hurt Miss Wallace Friday night?"

"I told you, now, no."

"How did she get your bangle and your hair on her?"

"I gave her the bangle when she gave me the money."

"Why didn't you mention that earlier?" Franks was now so close that Mack Oliver could smell his morning coffee.

"I forgot."

"How did your hair get on her?"

"I don't know anything about that."

"Did you rape Jodi Wallace?"

"No."

Nothing about what Detectives Connolly and Franks learned struck them as unusual, but they were suspicious. To Connolly, Mack Oliver seemed forthcoming and confused about the whole process. Yet, the detectives also knew that Chief Canon was making his way to the station to take a look at this would-be murder suspect for himself. Connolly knew the likelihood of Mack Oliver spending the rest of this holiday in his usual way was slim, as was the case for himself and his partner.

"Mack Oliver, just a few more questions," Franks continued. "Do you know this girl?" He presented a picture of Tiffany Miller.

"Yes."

"How?"

"She was my girlfriend."

Franks and Connolly absorbed his answer. They both knew Mack Oliver's answer to that question had changed his life forever.

Connolly asked, "What do you know about her murder?"

"Nothing," replied Mack Oliver.

"Did anyone talk to you about Miss Miller's murder, Mack Oliver?"

"No," responded Mack Oliver.

"Where were you the night she was murdered?" asked Connolly.

"I was in a house we found vacant on the Southside. It still had the power on. We used to have our own house on the Southside. We stayed there together," replied Mack Oliver. "But we sold it. We stayed there a little while after I sold it, but the city bulldozed the house. She started going back out. She slipped. That drug is a monster," explained Mack Oliver.

"Anyone else live there?" asked Connolly.

"No."

"When was the last time you saw her?" asked Connolly.

"That night."

"What night?" Franks asked.

"The night she died," Mack Oliver responded.

"When did you find out Tiffany had been killed?"

"I found out the next morning when I went looking for her. Everybody was talking about it," said Mack Oliver.

"Who do you think did it?" asked Franks, suspiciously, as if Mack Oliver had done it or knew who had.

"There are a lot of crazy people out here. It might have been drugs, rape. But it's been tough without her and she has a real nice family," replied Mack Oliver.

"Where do they live?" asked Connolly.

"Avenue I," replied Mack Oliver.

"Mack Oliver, what's the Haldol for that was in your belongings?" asked Franks.

"Schizophrenia," Mack Oliver replied, matter-of-factly.

Connolly told Franks, "I think you better read him his rights."

Mack Oliver was Mirandized by Franks and booked on suspicion of murder of Tiffany Miller and Jodi Wallace.

A background check revealed that Mack Oliver was not a hardened criminal.

This was his first brush with the law, except for the public drunkenness charge a year ago. The men knew judges with worse records than Mack Oliver. But his interrogation revealed issues that would be very troubling for any defendant, and especially troubling for an indigent, homeless man. Franks advised Mack Oliver of the seriousness of the investigation and asked Mack Oliver if he had a lawyer.

Mack Oliver responded, "No."

"Do you have family you want to call and inform them of your whereabouts?"

"Yes." Mack Oliver seemed uncomfortable and scared to be talking to detectives in jail.

Connolly motioned for Franks to follow him outside the interrogation room. The two entered the viewing room and observed Mack Oliver, who sat there anxiously rubbing his head.

Franks asked, "Do you think he's our man?"

"He doesn't strike me as a double killer and rapist," Connolly responded.

Franks replied, "But the evidence is starting to stack up. Although heavily circumstantial, it's a lot of it."

"Sure, but we still have forensics to come in."

"The chief, the D.A., and the mayor are going to want to wrap this up with what we have. I have seen good cases with less," replied Franks.

"How do you see it, Franks?" asked Connolly.

"Well, I see a homeless man with mental problems, addiction. I'm sure he could have been fiending, needing money for a fix. The store owner, Alman, saw him harassing her. The girls saw him following her to her car. We found her in her car. She was clenching one of those bangles. The time of death on the pathologist's report puts him there. He has no alibi and no one who witnessed his demeanor afterwards. Tiffany Miller was his admitted girlfriend, for God's sake! It seems air tight. And, it's already been forty-eight hours. If this was someone else – and I emphasize *if* – then the trail is probably already cold. If you don't arrest him, who *are* you going to arrest? He's our man. What do you see?"

"I see what you see," replied Connolly. "But she gave him money; the girls saw that. He has no priors. Did he wake up one morning and decide to start killing people? He may have mental issues, and I know I'm no psychologist, but I don't think he's crazy enough to kill and rape a white rich kid his first time out. That is too far over the line."

"What if Tiffany Miller was his first time?" replied Franks.

"Well, both these women were brutally strangled and manhandled," Connolly said. "You read the pathologist's report. Jodi was strangled by one big, gloved left hand. It crushed her esophagus and dislocated two of her vertebrae. She was brutally assaulted, vaginally and anally. The coroner thinks he used a wine bottle. There are traces of alcohol, wine he thinks, in her orifices. No trace of semen that he could determine. This person was tremendously strong and sick," said Connolly.

"Or schizophrenic," concluded Franks.

"But Mack Oliver seems very small for that," Connolly continued. "He's five-seven and a hundred and fifty pounds at the most. If he's no psycho and did this for the hell of it, what's his motive?"

Connolly reassured Franks though, "But listen, partner, I know what he's facing and I know we've been convinced with much less. Hell, I've been convinced with nothing in the past. And I know with this much circumstantial evidence and being black and homeless with a white victim – who is the worst white victim he could ever pick on top of that – are definitely enough to get an indictment and a conviction."

"Well, we better let the chief know," a somber Connolly continued.

"Looks like we're going to beat Wallace's deadline," Franks added.

* * *

At 2:00 p.m., Lt. Jack Connolly left the interrogation room, washed his face, took an extra-long look at himself in the bathroom mirror at the station, gathered his notes, got his jacket, and took the long walk to the chief's office, reflecting on the case that has taken only two and a half days over a Christmas holiday. The twenty-year veteran was approaching retirement. He had been on the force through segregation and the city's struggles with integration. He had served beside Bo Canon all those years. He was considered by every fellow officer as the best homicide detective on the force. Although not arrogant, he was proud of the years he had worn the uniform for the Birmingham Police Department.

He didn't feel good about this case. What was missing? Was he losing his edge? Had he gotten too liberal, soft and melancholy in his old age? Did he not want to see another black man put to death – the certain reality of any black man convicted of rape and murder of a white woman in Alabama? He wanted to get it right. This was certainly not the case he wanted to end his career on. Connolly had navigated the highly politically-charged climate of the Birmingham Police Department for two decades. He had policed one of the most dangerous and polarized cities in the country. He had tried to play it straight and put murderers behind bars. However, like most law enforcement officers, he found it difficult to deal straight with criminals who had no respect for the law or human life. He was particularly disturbed by the brutal murder of Jodi Wallace. The murder of Tiffany Miller had gone uninvestigated and practically unnoticed. Its only mention by authorities would be statistical. This imbalance of outrage had come to be expected by those committing the crimes, and by the public – both black and white – the judicial system and public officials. These attitudes drove investigations, jury verdicts and sentencing. The system was the people, complete with all its prejudices and bias.

Connolly had worked for Draper Wallace all of his professional life doing investigative work for him. He had investigated business competitors, potential partners and employees of the Wallace Corporation. He had played with Jodi when she was a toddler and had given her birthday presents, and he remembered the hugs she had given him on his visits to the estate when working for her father. She felt like family. She reminded him of his own daughters and he wanted someone to pay, badly. Mack Oliver was all he had.

As Connolly entered the chief's office, the chief started smiling. He knew Connolly's routine. He knew he had barely eaten since this investigation started and that he was known to drop twenty pounds during an investigation. Connolly let his cases consume him and he knew what was at stake. Even when he thought he had his felon, he still anguished over the process. The chief knew when Connolly made his walk that he had his man.

"My dear friend," remarked the Chief, "What do you have for me?"

"His name is Mack Oliver Purifoy." Connolly proceeded to go over the two-and-a-half-day case. "At approximately ten p.m. on December twenty-third, the victim, Jodi Wallace, left the Urban Clothier, according to eyewitnesses, including the store owner who had to let her out of the store because the door was locked at ten p.m., an hour later than usual due to the Christmas holiday shopping. When Alman, the boutique owner, let her out of the store, there was a homeless man just outside the door. Mr. Purifoy fit the description. This morning, Mr. Alman picked Purifoy out of a lineup with certainty. The homeless man asked Miss Wallace for money. Miss Wallace told him she had none. Alman reported running the homeless man off. He locked the door behind Miss Wallace and returned to take care of the remaining customers. At approximately ten-oh-five p.m., Miss Wallace met two friends, who attend college with her, at the Starbucks in Five Points South. They drank coffee and talked until eleven p.m. The girls had a midnight curfew. As they were leaving the coffee shop at eleven p.m., Miss Wallace asked Miss Winters for change. She gave her five dollars and Miss Wallace then proceeded to give the money to the homeless man. Miss Winters and Miss Drover picked Mr. Purifoy out of a lineup this afternoon, with certainty. They reported that after Miss Wallace gave him the money, they walked in opposite directions, and Mr. Purifoy followed along behind her on his bike.

"Mr. Purifoy stated he did see Miss Wallace that night, that he did ask her for money, that she did give him money, and that he did trail behind her on his bike. To get from the Starbucks to the alley where Miss Wallace's car was parked would take three minutes, taking into account that one would have to cross a busy intersection. Mr. Purifoy reported that when they got to the alley where her car was parked, he just rode on by. He reported that the alley was dark, and he didn't see anyone else or see her get in her car. The pathologist put the time of death between eleven and eleven-thirty p.m., the time Mr. Purifoy and Miss Wallace would have been in the alley. Miss Wallace was found in her car at six-thirty a.m. on December twenty-fourth. She was in the trunk of her car with her neck broken by one gloved hand, according to the pathologist's report. There were splinters of wood on her neck, and her left hand, two fingers and two ribs were broken. She had been sexually assaulted, and the pathologist thinks she was a virgin. There were traces of alcohol in her orifices and blood – her blood. The pathologist thinks the assailant used a wine bottle – a chipped wine bottle. In her left hand was a bangle that belonged to Mr. Purifoy. He said he gave it to her for giving him the five dollars. The bangle could have been lost in a struggle. There was a single hair found on her right mitten, a Negro hair. The pathologist is comparing the hair to that of Mr. Purifoy. We examined his belongings and the abandoned house where he was staying. There were no belongings of Miss Wallace's and no hair or blood of hers on his belongings. No one saw him after he left the Southside who can give a description of his state of mind." Connolly continued, "In the matter of Tiffany Miller…"

"Tiffany Miller? What's she got to do with this?" interrupted Canon. "Damn, he is a serial killer."

"Technically, chief, their needs to be three murders for this to be a serial killer."

"Well, two will be close enough for the papers and the public, and who knows, there may be more. This just may be all we know about," the chief added.

Connolly continued. "Mr. Purifoy stated that she was his girlfriend, that they lived together, that they were together the evening before she was found murdered. She had excessive amounts of alcohol and cocaine in her body. She had motile sperm from three different donors, one of which was probably Mr. Purifoy. Her neck was broken in the same fashion, with splinters of wood on her neck and body as well, and she had been beaten. The matter of rape could not be determined, but traces of alcohol were found in her orifices. Her body was found behind a dumpster one hundred feet away from the location where Miss Wallace's body was found." Connolly's presentation was methodical, professional and complete, giving little sign of the personal grief he felt for Jodi Wallace.

The chief nodded. "Jack, you're a damn genius." But Connolly's lack of conviction prompted the chief to ask, "Jack, what's your conclusion?"

"A few trouble areas. One: no priors that even closely resemble someone headed towards sadistic murder and rape. Two: no motive. She gave him the money." Connolly was one of the few people whose mind would not assume the motive was the rape of a white woman and murder to hide the evidence. "Three: if he is lying, why didn't he say he saw someone else in the alley? Four: he's very small. I saw Jodi Wallace in her trunk. This person was a brute. Five: this seems like a crime of hate and revenge. And the rape – a wine bottle? It appears to be the ultimate insult. Those are the troublesome areas."

The Chief waited, knowing Jack Connolly. He had come to his office, which only meant one thing.

"But this is way too much evidence," Connolly continued, "albeit mostly circumstantial, for him or anyone probably to overcome. He was there. His bangle was in her hand, and probably his hair on her. He was seen following her. His semen was in Miller. He's schizophrenic, a drug addict, black and homeless. Penick will definitely indict. Any jury in Jefferson County is going to convict him, and give him the chair."

"What does Franks think?"

"That he's lying and guilty as hell. That the motive was robbery and rape that got out of hand. That he killed her in a panic."

"I've been doing this a long time, Jack. I've seen people on drugs do some things they wouldn't be capable of if they were clean. I've seen mentally ill people do some incredible things when they weren't medicated."

"It appears he was clean, though, and medicated. I've seen a lot of murderers. He doesn't strike me as a cold-blooded murderer."

"How much doubt do you have?"

"Some."

"Some?"

"Ten percent chance he didn't do it."

"What does your gut tell you?"

Hesitantly, Connolly responded. "That he didn't do it. I don't see it, but I'm going to close the case. Here's my report. It's free of my personal opinions."

"Good job, Jack. I'm going to send it over to Billy. This is our man, Jack. Good investigation is a process of elimination. The only thing those victims have in common is Mack Oliver Purifoy. He did it."

"I hope we're right," Connolly said. "But I would wait until the forensics come in before I took it to the D.A. for indictment."

"Well, there was no semen present in Jodi Wallace, only the alcohol. We've taken a blood sample from Mr. Purifoy, right?"

"Right," responded Connolly.

"Miss Miller had motile sperm from three different donors. You said there was probably a match to Purifoy?"

"Yes," responded Connolly.

"And there was a hair that appeared to be a black person's hair on Miss Wallace's mitten, and she was clenching one of those bangles he was wearing," the chief continued. "We need to get that crime lab to hurry it up on the hair, but I think it's fine to go ahead to Billy. We better keep Mr. Purifoy in isolation, though. We don't want anything bad to happen to him. There are a lot of rednecks locked up over there. Hell, who knows what Wallace might do."

"Maybe they should take their time on this one, sir. Know what I mean?"

"Peyton is gonna run with this," the chief surmised. "He wants the citizens to feel safe downtown. All the whites have been leaving and businesses have been leaving ever since he was elected. A black mayor, you know what I mean. They think he is soft on crime, and Wallace made him, you know. Peyton is going to feel exposed; but if this girl was black, Peyton wouldn't feel as vulnerable. It would just be another of the one hundred murders he's gotten used to in the city. This will change the city more than when we put Martin Luther King in jail. The Klan has already applied for their marching permits. Tell me what's bothering you; we've put a lot of people in jail."

"But no one I've felt might be innocent."

"I thought you said ten percent chance. Listen, Jack, if Wallace knew what we had on this guy – and he will know – and he wasn't arrested, we'd all feel a whole lot worse. We're lucky we got anybody. You did a great job. Accept your success. This is going to be good for you."

As Connolly left the chief's office, he was certain of Mack Oliver's fate. He had to get comfortable with his 10 percent uncertainty of his guilt. Everyone knew there was a difference in the way black and white crime was investigated and prosecuted, but the issue too uncomfortable and too wrong for anyone to mention. Connolly called Draper Wallace, who he had kept apprised of the investigation, and informed him of the pending indictment. Wallace indicated his satisfaction. Chief Canon phoned his boss, Mayor Castelle.

"Peyton, I want to update you on the Wallace case so you won't get blindsided by the media," began Chief Canon. "We've arrested Mack Oliver Purifoy on suspicion of rape, robbery, and murder of Jodi Wallace and Tiffany Miller."

"Great news, great news," replied Mayor Castelle. "Who is Mack Oliver Purifoy?"

"He is a homeless, schizophrenic, drug addict that we picked up in an abandoned house on the Southside. The boys did a tremendous job finding him. They searched every abandoned house and crack house in the city. We fished him out of an old boarded-up house on the Southside." The chief continued, "This morning, Connolly and Franks questioned him. He doesn't have an alibi. He was seen by a couple of the Wallace girl's friends following her to her car. He admits to this and to taking money from her. And this is the kicker, Peyton. He was the boyfriend of Tiffany Miller. We've done his pedigree..."

"Pedigree?" interrupted the mayor.

"Taken blood samples and fingerprints to see who he is and if anything matches the forensic evidence preserved on Tiffany Miller or anything we found on Miss Wallace," explained Canon. "The district attorney is going to take him before the judge in the morning for arraignment."

The mayor responded, "This ought to make Draper happy. His daughter's funeral is tomorrow. This is an important case, Bo. Are you one-hundred percent certain? 'Cause I don't want anymore shit on my face."

Chief Canon carefully laid out the evidence to date on Mack Oliver Purifoy and all the eyewitness testimony.

"Looks like you got your man, now let's nail his ass. This stuff has been on TV nonstop. The damn papers are comparing us to the Middle East. We need to get the word to people as soon as possible so they can get back to something resembling normal life," a relieved Mayor Castelle responded.

"Mayor, you're just in time for the evening news to give a press conference about this arrest," said Chief Canon. "As a matter of fact," the chief continued, "that may give the Wallaces peace of mind tonight and let the public know that we worked quickly on this case."

"Great work, chief. This should make a difference. Great job."

* * *

At 5:00 p.m., Chief Canon and Mayor Castelle walked out of City Hall and down the front steps where the Birmingham press corps had gathered. A triumphant Peyton Castelle strutted up to the microphone confidently to announce that the Birmingham police had arrested Mack Oliver Purifoy for the murders of Jodi Wallace and Tiffany Miller.

"Today, we have solved not one, but two murder cases. I want to thank the police chief for all the hard work from his department in finding and arresting this man, where his justice surely awaits him. I can only answer a few questions because we don't want to jeopardize the integrity of the case and the impending trial. But I can say that the citizens of Birmingham should feel safe that they can shop downtown and carry out their normal activities," the mayor stated. "Mr. Purifoy will be arraigned before the Honorable Judge J. B. McPeake tomorrow morning. The city still mourns the death of Miss Jodi Wallace and our heart-felt sympathies are with the family as they lay their daughter to rest tomorrow. I know that the whole city mourns, and we can find some solace that an arrest has been made. Now I will take a couple of questions."

"Mayor, when was Mr. Purifoy arrested and where?"

"He was arrested last night in an abandoned house on the Southside, near the crime scene."

"Are there any other suspects?"

"No."

"Can you give us a description of Mr. Purifoy?"

"Mr. Purifoy is a homeless, vagrant black male in his early thirties."

"Was it related to drugs or robbery?"

"What's he being charged with?"

"Robbery, rape, and murder."

"Is this case related to the Tiffany Miller murder?"

"Yes. I can't take any further questions at this time. Thank you very much," Castelle answered hastily.

"Chief, are you confident you got your man?"

The chief turned back to the microphone, leaned into it, and, with his eyes fixed on the press cameras, stated, "Absolutely."

CHAPTER EIGHT

Retribution

Beginning to feel the effects of his Haldol wearing off and unable to get any medication until seen by the jail psychiatrist, who was out of town for the holidays, Mack Oliver waited. His mind began to wander as he tried to make sense of all the instructions the officers were giving to him. His diagnosis of schizophrenia had been made five years ago, but it had been managed easily with medication and without cocaine use. Mack Oliver's mother had died from heart failure the previous December – his only relapse in five years – and his father preceded her death five years earlier.

"Time to make your call, Purifoy."

December 26 at 7:00 p.m., and now stripped of all his jewelry and wearing his white jail suit, Mack Oliver made his one phone call.

"I didn't know who else to call," said Mack Oliver in a grim, hoarse voice. "Mack Oliver, that's fine. I saw what was going on on the news tonight. How are you?" replied his comforting and longtime therapist, Dr. Lincoln Drake.

"I didn't do it. I would never hurt anyone," replied Mack Oliver.

"Mack Oliver, we don't have to talk about it over the phone."

"They said I need a lawyer. I don't have one. I don't have

any money. They won't give me my medicine. You think you can help me get a lawyer? Help me out?" pleaded Mack Oliver, desperately.

"Sure. They reported on the news that they are arraigning you in the morning at nine a.m."

"Yeah."

"Well, I will see what I can do about a lawyer, Mack Oliver, but I know that the court, too, will appoint you one. I'll see what I can do. Hang in there," Lincoln said to his patient. "I am sure they will give you your medication soon, Mack Oliver. Don't talk to anyone about what you did or did not do until you have a lawyer, okay?"

"Okay."

"And I'll be in the courtroom in the morning and see if there is anything I can do. Remember how you told me you could escape for hours at a time by playing your horn or painting? I want you to think about playing your horn and painting. The time will go by very quickly."

"Okay, Linc."

"I'll see you in the morning."

✡ ✡ ✡

There had been countless arraignments at the courthouse over the years, but no one could remember any arraignment that had attracted so much media attention or so many officials as the arraignment of Mack Oliver Purifoy. He appeared before the efficient court of the Honorable J. B. McPeake promptly at 9:00 a.m. on December 27. He was the first to be arraigned that day. The court saw no need to keep anyone important there to hear the mundane hearings of petty thieves and drug offenders. People also needed to have time to leave the courthouse and get to Jodi Wallace's funeral by one o'clock.

The *People vs. Mack Oliver Purifoy* demanded the presence of the Jefferson County District Attorney himself, William Penick III. To describe the charge, he planned to be deliberately and unusually verbose for his arraignment audience, which included the mayor, the council, Chief Canon, Connolly and Franks, and two dozen other city and state officials, and Draper Wallace with his legal entourage. The prosecution had even reserved seats for the family of Tiffany Miller. Wallace was now getting his first look at a wild-eyed, bearded, homeless Mack Oliver. His mind drifted to all the money he had helped raise and donated to build the Catherine Fairchild Center. He felt betrayed now by Fairchild, who had advocated for the homeless. He thought how much of his own money had gone to house and treat and feed his daughter's killer. He wished Mack Oliver and all homeless people dead and felt foolish and sick inside that he had ever given a dime to help them.

It was standing room only, the way Billy Penick had hoped it would be. The press was inside the courtroom, overflowing into the halls and outside the building. Lincoln Drake observed from the furthest rear pew. In the state of Alabama, there were no public defenders. In the absence of legal council, which is often the case for the city's indigent and homeless, the judge appointed counsel – and possessed broad discretion. The attorneys that had to make a living this way were not considered the best, and the best attorneys had not run to the courthouse to volunteer to be appointed by J. B. to defend Mack Oliver Purifoy. J. B. considered the pool of lawyers he always had and decided to appoint Cecil Pitman, known by all his acquaintances as Piti.

Piti, at fifty, by all accounts was an ambulance chaser with a well-known drinking problem. From what J. B. knew of this case, it was simple and straightforward. The killer had practically been caught red-handed. Not even Piti could screw this up. This case should be settled with Mack Oliver begging for the mercy of the court not to get the death penalty. J. B. also didn't want to ruin a good lawyer by having him defend a guilty, homeless, drug-addicted, double murderer. That attorney's career would be seriously jeopardized in Alabama. He also was not going to allow any lawyer from up north to make a spectacle of his courtroom defending Mack Oliver.

J. B. believed in the integrity of the system and thought it beyond reproach. Heinous crimes had been committed against an upstanding family. A legitimate, professional investigation had taken place. The accused had been legitimately and fairly charged. And now, a jury of his peers would hear his case in a dignified manner. The reporters would tell a story of high drama in the evening papers and on the evening news of the five-minute arraignment.

"All rise for the Honorable J. B. McPeake."

After confidently seating himself, and in the most exaggerated of southern drawls, where no word in the aristocratic Southern dialect ends with the enunciation of the letter R, the judge's raspy voice resounded, "Y'all be seated."

The clerk read the docket.

"Is the prosecution heah?"

"Yes, ya honah," replied Billy Penick in full bloom, his speech equaling J. B.'s in rich dialectic custom.

"Is the defense heah?"

"Yes, suh, ya honah," replied Piti nervously.

"What's the charge of the People?" asked J. B.

"Ya honah, we the People charge Mack Oliver Purifoy Jr. with the robbery, rape, and murdah of Miss Tiffany Miller." Billy looked over at Tiffany's family. "And with the particularly brutal robbery, rape, and murdah of the eighteen-year-old Jodi

Wallace," he concluded, looking over at Draper Wallace in dramatic style.

"Mr. Pitman, how does the defendant plead?"

Piti looked at his client who, after two days without his Haldol while in jail, was decompensating rapidly. He stood there in shackles with two deputies beside him. The small, mellow Mack Oliver now looked like an agitated, aggressive, and menacing accused killer. Piti had only known his client for an hour. Mack Oliver had threatened to kill at least three other people during that time in his new lawyer's presence. Piti had quickly determined the best he could hope to do was make a plea bargain with the prosecution, in hopes of saving Mack Oliver's life. But he needed time, a psychiatric evaluation, and he needed to speak to the prosecution.

Nervously he stammered, "Ya, ya, ya honah, not guilty."

Quickly, Billy Penick responded, "Ya honah, we request due to the capital offenses and the potential for flight that the defendant be held without bond."

"Piti?"

"Well, ya honah, this is the first time my client has ever been charged with anything like this. He has no previous record of violent behavior."

Cutting him off, Penick rebutted, "How many times does a person have to be charged with capital murdah? He's a vagrant. He could disappear in the night to never again be seen or he could murdah again."

J. B. responded, "Bail denied." He looked over the courtroom, and then settled his eyes on Piti and a dazed Mack Oliver Purifoy. "The defendant is guaranteed a speedy trial, and this community is deserving of the same. Therefore, the trial date is set for February twenty-fifth, sufficient time for the prosecution and defense to prepare their cases. His gavel sounded. "Next case."

Billy Penick III, D.A., named after his father and grandfather – both lawyers and legendary – grew up as "Little Bill," despite the fact that he was now six-feet, six-inches tall and weighed two hundred and eighty pounds. His father, Billy Jr., was six-eight. Little Bill was a graduate of the University of Alabama School of Law. While at Alabama, he had played football for a National Championship team coached by none other than Paul "Bear" Bryant, one of the greatest football coaches that ever lived and an icon in Alabama. Billy Jr. had played for the Bear as well, and no quarterback at Alabama had ever run for more touchdowns.

Little Bill was not as talented a football player as his father. He played quarterback like his father, but never got in the game unless it was the last seconds of the fourth quarter and Alabama was way ahead. But that was plenty for Little Bill. He would go in, take the snap, and let the defense pile on. He might get two snaps before the clock ran out. Little Bill, though, had an excellent attitude and spirit. What he didn't possess athletically people overlooked because he was so gung ho. He was a bigger cheerleader than anyone on the sidelines. He loved the University of Alabama, and he loved football, he just couldn't play the game. His pedigree was excellent, however. The coaches thought there must be football greatness inside him somewhere. He was six-six and two hundred and fifty pounds in college. He looked so intimidating in that uniform, and his daddy was the great Billy Jr. But for four years, greatness never came.

After law school, Little Bill continued the family legacy by following his father and grandfather into the law profession. He joined the D.A.'s office right out of college and excelled. What he could not accomplish on the football field, he more than made up for in the courtroom. Little Bill had the perfect demeanor and presence to be an effective Alabama prosecutor. He even lost his old nickname; he became William Penick III and just Billy to his friends. But as Billy's convictions began to pile up, he got a new nickname from his fellow prosecutors: "Conviction Bill." He thought his success was 80 percent his brains and hard work and only 20 percent his name and where he lived. He had the percentages backwards – his name and his culture had made him.

Billy entered the courtroom very dapper by any standard. By Southern standards, he was a sight to behold – and at his size, he was hard to miss. He wore highly polished alligator cowboy boots to accentuate his height and remind all that he was "one of y'all." He wore a small-brimmed cowboy hat and, in the winter, assorted topcoats with matching scarves. When he entered the court room, he kept the whole ensemble on until he got to the prosecutor's table, then disrobed very slowly. First he placed his hat on the table, then the scarf, carefully folding it. Gloves were removed one finger at a time and placed together on top of the scarf. The triple-X sized topcoat was folded in half and placed in the chair reserved for his ensemble. When seated at the prosecutor's table, his long legs were crossed at the ankles and stretched under it, protruding far beyond the other side, with those cowboy boots highly visible. Billy commanded the courtroom. He was one of the community's favorite sons. He was their standard-bearer. Billy understood Alabama's history. He understood its culture, and when his people looked at him, they felt proud. Surely his famous name and presence helped him, but Billy became D.A. because he won cases. And with memories fading, Billy was now remembered as a great Alabama football player who played on an undefeated team coached by the legendary Bear Bryant.

Billy had earned his nickname "Conviction Bill" when he was prosecuting a case and his opening statement and closing arguments ended with the two sentences, "This man is guilty, and the evidence shows it and if it weren't true, I wouldn't say it. The only appropriate verdict is guilty."

The door to the deliberation chamber had barely closed before the jury convicted. No one wanted to face Billy Penick III in the courtroom in Jefferson County, Alabama.

Billy Penick and J. B. McPeake belonged to the same country club. The club had a one-hundred-thousand-dollar admittance fee that was waived for the right kind of applicant. For the wrong kind of applicant, if the fee didn't dissuade you, there would be some other admittance criteria that you did not meet. The country club had never had a black member; however, only blacks were employed as caddies, waiters and doormen. All the visible help was black. No whites could be seen doing manual labor and menial tasks, as that would ruin the scene that had been so carefully orchestrated. The black waiters were especially dazzling to watch. Wearing black coats, white shirts, and black bow ties, most had salt and pepper hair. Young black men never waited tables; the experience was too intimate for the white patrons to feel comfortable with a young black male. The dining room was grand, spectacular in architectural detail and ambiance. The exceptionally well-mannered black men attending the tables would take the members to another time – a better time. After an experience at the club, its members would be renewed in their commitment to protect and defend their way of life bitterly, whether at the ballot box, in business, in education, in church, or in the courtroom.

Billy and J. B. weren't racist. They wouldn't convict or charge a man that they thought was innocent just because he happened to be black. They wouldn't frame anyone. However, they knew that 80 percent of the violent crimes that came before them involved black defendants. Billy and J. B. thought every one of them were guilty. They prosecuted them aggressively and gave the maximum sentences. As white men of means, they didn't think that what they had achieved in life and their status had anything to do with their skin color. Hence, they also did not think that the plight of black people had anything to do with their skin color. The result was an unconscious conclusion by Billy and J. B. that the situation these black defendants found themselves in had absolutely nothing to do with their race or resources.

J. B. McPeake was by all accounts a hanging judge. He sentenced at the upper end of the sentencing guidelines. He was in his late fifties, with snow-white hair and pale skin. His hands were exceptionally clean and extremely soft. He had a stiff jaw, a stern look, and perpetually smelled of cherry pipe tobacco. He made anyone before him regretful they had gotten involved with the judicial system. Criminals lost all bravado before J. B. He had a Bible on his bench and would often quote the Good Book during sentencing. He was a portrait unmistakably Alabamian and considered himself a defender of all things right, Christian and Southern. He desperately defended the way of life that he thought was being encroached upon.

The courthouse where J. B. reigned was the Hugo Black Court House, named after the only member of the United States Supreme Court who was from Alabama, and the only member of the Supreme Court who was a known member of the Ku Klux Klan. The courthouse was built to intimidate. The exceptionally high judge's bench, the marble and mahogany interior, and the granite exterior would frighten litigants as they walked up to and entered the ominous building. One's stomach felt as if one was being led to the edge of a cliff on a windy day. The awesomeness of the structure was to remind all that no one was bigger than the law.

CHAPTER NINE

The Defense

Lincoln Drake remained seated as Mack Oliver was escorted from the courtroom and all the spectators cleared out to assemble on the courthouse steps as the district attorney, the chief of police, the mayor, Draper Wallace, and other luminaries departed. An obvious show of unity, and all for Mack Oliver Purifoy. As a befuddled Piti gathered his belongings and headed for the exit, Lincoln approached him.

"Mr. Pitman, I'm Dr. Lincoln Drake." The six-foot two-inch black man in a full-length overcoat scared the hell out of Piti. He didn't know if he was NAACP or Black Muslim, but Piti wanted nothing to do with him.

"I'm sorry. Who are you?"

"I'm Lincoln Drake. I treated Mack Oliver Purifoy, your client."

"Doctor, you say?"

"Yes. Lincoln, please."

"You say you treated him?"

"Yes. I am Mack Oliver's psychologist. I treated him for addiction and mental illness for the last five years. He's been in monthly therapy sessions the past year."

Piti shook his head and said, "So, he is crazy."

"No, no, he's not crazy at all. But listen, Mack Oliver asked me to help him and, considering the circumstances, I think I should talk to you about him." Following Piti into the hallway,

Lincoln continued, "Mack Oliver is decompensating because he hasn't had his Haldol and Cogentin."

"Haldol and Cogentin?" Piti's eyebrows raised.

"Haldol is an antipsychotic, Cogentin is for the side effects the drug causes."

"Side effects?" Piti shouted.

"Mack Oliver is a paranoid schizophrenic."

"Shit, that's terrific. I knew something was bad wrong with him. Hell, he was threatening the guards. I was afraid he was going to threaten J. B. That would have gotten him fried today – at least made the news. Hell, but he looked bad enough just sitting there and saying nothing."

"Mack Oliver has been stabilized for five years and I can assure you he's not violent."

"He threatened to kill three people in front of me. He's been held on double murder charges. Am I hallucinating, too?"

"Like I said, without his medication, he is psychotic. The medicines are typically withheld until the police have a psychiatric examination performed on the inmate and they determine what these medicines are and if they are legitimate. But he's not on them now."

"And what if he wasn't on medication the nights those girls were murdered?"

"When Tiffany Miller was murdered, he was on his medications. He discussed the loss in therapy."

"When was the last time you saw him?"

"Last week. During this time of year, he comes to the center weekly. Triggers."

"Triggers?"

"Christmastime, mourning the loss of his mother. His mother died at Christmastime. Those are triggers for Mack Oliver. He was doing well. There were no signs of drug abuse or psychotic behavior last week."

"You say a week ago?"

"Yes."

"Well that's good. How long does it take for him to go crazy if he doesn't get the medicine?"

"Well, there are many factors which determine that. Depending on the severity of the illness, someone with schizophrenia can decompensate within seventy-two hours. For someone like Mack Oliver, forty-eight hours at the most."

"Maybe we can get an insanity plea. Save his life."

Lincoln fixed Piti with a questioning look, "So you think he did it?"

"It doesn't matter what I think, only what I can prove."

"I don't think the Mack Oliver I know is capable of murder," Lincoln added without conviction.

"Have you had a lot of experience with serial killers, doctor?" Dropping his voice to a whisper, he said, "I know he's your patient, but let me tell you what they got on him. A storeowner saw him harassing her. They have a bangle from his arm in the girl's hand. They think they have his hair on her. It's a Negro hair anyway. He even says he was there. They think there is a semen match from him in the Miller woman."

"She was his girlfriend," stated Lincoln.

Piti broke his whisper for a moment. "The woman was a prostitute. She had a lot of boyfriends. Listen, not to mention," Piti whispered even lower, "well, I don't mean any disrespect, but the man is homeless, he's black, one of his victims is a white girl, eighteen years old. Hell, she might have been a virgin. She's the damn daughter of Draper Wallace."

"It sounds like you have already given up."

"I am a realist. This is Alabama. I want to keep this boy alive if at all possible."

"What about proving his innocence? Have you heard his

side of the story, Mr. Pitman? Let's get him stabilized. I know the jail psychiatrist. I think I can get in touch with her. Perhaps I can accompany you when you meet with him next."

"That will be tomorrow. The judge has given us two months."

"Why don't I contact Dr. Farah tonight and get her to call in the medication for Mack Oliver, and maybe something to calm him down?"

"Listen, that's fine but you let me do the lawyering. We've got to be realistic with Mr. Purifoy."

"Sure."

"We are scheduled for nine a.m." Piti held out his hand.

Lincoln returned the gesture and shook hands, but then replied, "I'd like to talk to you about Mack Oliver."

"I have a little time before my next appointment," replied Piti. "I'm going to John's for a late breakfast. You want to join me?"

"John's Restaurant, around the corner a couple of blocks?" asked Drake.

"Yeah. Walk with me?"

"Sure."

As they walked, Piti confided with excitement, "This is the biggest case I have ever had. Draper Wallace's daughter, and a serial killer."

Lincoln interjected, "Alleged."

"Yeah, yeah," replied Piti. "Well, this is the biggest murder trial that's ever happened here anyway. Everybody's on edge. No one wants to piss off Wallace."

Lincoln asked, "Do you think Mack Oliver can get a fair trial?"

Piti remarked, "Fair? Hell no it won't be fair. The system isn't fair. Wallace is a damn billionaire. Billy is gonna try the case himself. Wallace has a dozen lawyers and private investigators and cops working for him, and the defendant is homeless, black and crazy. And he's only got me. Fair? Shit."

"Can you move the case to another county, city? A change of venue?" asked Lincoln.

"You think that's gonna help Mr. Purifoy?" replied Piti.

"Birmingham is the most liberal city in Alabama and it ain't liberal."

Lincoln added, "Maybe in another city people won't know Mack Oliver or the case so well."

Piti replied, "There isn't a frog in Alabama that doesn't know Draper Wallace or his pretty little girl. Or the homeless, black man that…that is accused of killing her. And even if I was stupid enough to ask, J. B. wouldn't grant it – or any other judge – and it would only piss him off. That wouldn't help us."

The two-block walk was starting to wind Piti, and the downtown exhaust fumes weren't helping either. But his robust size was the real problem. Southerners weren't accustomed to walking. They drove everywhere and the city wasn't congested enough to make parking a problem. They also ritualized eating and long walks weren't that compatible with their overindulgence. As they approached the restaurant, Lincoln was losing confidence with Mack Oliver's court-appointed defense, and his first impression of him was lingering in Lincoln's mind. Piti was born with an oversized head and an extremely thick neck that made his chin disappear. His head was nearly as wide as his shoulders and made up a disproportionate amount of his five-three height and two hundred and fifty pounds. The shirt he had chosen to impress J. B. and awe the prosecution was at least a size too small, and there was an inch gap at the collar that he tried to camouflage by tying an extra big knot in his tie and pulling it way up. The tie he'd chosen did not look well thought out and the buttons at the midsection of his shirt strained to stay buttoned. His wrinkled summer suit was cotton and tan in color. Piti wore only thin summer suits regardless of the weather, as his girth made him uncomfortable and prone to sweating. He had sweated a lot before J. B. that morning and his thin, receding hair was now stuck to his neck.

* * *

Cecil Pitman knew the law in Birmingham and Alabama. He had lived in Alabama his whole life. An occasional trip to Biloxi or Gulf Shores was as far as he had ever ventured. The floating casinos in Biloxi were his favorite pastime, and he went to Gulf Shores; not for the beach, but the Florabama, a local nightspot that never closed, had great bands, sometimes karaoke, and a bartender that poured tall drinks. To Piti, it was paradise.

Piti, however, was likable and much smarter than he acted or looked. His drinking had curtailed his legal career and almost got him disbarred when he was representing regular folks. Piti had accepted his lot and J. B. used him often for the homeless indigents. He had been able to scrape out a decent living that way.

Piti waved to the hostess as they entered the restaurant. "Hey, Gail."

Gail gave him a big smile that grew when she saw Lincoln. "Good morning, Piti. Table for two?"

"Very good food here, Dr. Drake," Piti said as they sat down.

"Yes, I know. I've eaten here often."

"Never seen you. I'm starved. I was so nervous this morning I couldn't eat."

Lincoln thought that must be a rare occasion. He suspected

that it hadn't kept Piti from drinking, however. There was a faint smell of bourbon that Lincoln's much experienced nose could detect emitting from Piti's breath and pores, despite the fact that Piti had tried to mask it with mouthwash and Old Spice. He also noticed a few spots Piti had missed during his shave.

Their waitress greeted them as enthusiastically as the hostess had. "Good morning, Piti."

"Good morning, Becky. Me and my friend here are gonna have some breakfast."

Becky poured Piti his regular cup of coffee. He had already drunk his water, and, after requesting permission, Lincoln's.

"Coffee, sir?" Becky asked Lincoln.

"Yes, please."

"Do you gentlemen know what you're gonna have?"

"Go ahead, doctor?" offered Piti.

"Just toast, please."

"Jam?" asked the waitress.

"Sure." Excusing his light breakfast order Lincoln added, "I had cereal earlier."

"Piti?"

Piti wasn't unsure about what he wanted. "Bacon, three eggs over easy, potatoes, toast, and a side of grits and apple butter."

The restaurant had thinned out after the early breakfast crowd. John's with its quaint old-fashioned atmosphere was a favored spot for the downtown lawyers. Becky quickly returned with the order. Lincoln slowly buttered his toast, waiting for a good break between Piti's preoccupation with getting his apple butter on his toast just right and blending butter into his grits. Lincoln couldn't help but notice that Piti's fingers were so fat that they all looked like thumbs.

Lincoln began, "Mr. Pitman, I think if I told you about the

real Mack Oliver, that might help you formulate your defense strategy."

"Yes," Piti agreed, chewing. "Who's Mack Oliver?"

Lincoln picked up his toast and took a small bite, chewing thoughtfully. "I met Mack Oliver five years ago when I arrived at the Catherine Fairchild Treatment Center. I am the chief psychologist at the center. Mack Oliver was an intriguing case. He had an out-of-control crack cocaine problem and the initial onset of schizophrenia at that time. He was preaching in the streets and hallucinating. His father was a chronic alcoholic who died prematurely of cirrhosis. He had been tremendously physically and emotionally abusive to Mack Oliver and his mother. Mack Oliver would describe how his father, a steel worker, would be drunk by the time he arrived home after payday on Friday evening, if he came home at all. He would be broke by Sunday. The music blared from the shotgun house. B.B. King and Etta James played over and over. You could smell the gin from the street. The neighbors avoided passing by the house to prevent confrontations with Mr. Mack Purifoy. 'Big Mack' they called him. For two days, the tall, slim Big Mack with blood-gorged eyes and usually a nylon T-shirt would march in and out of the house arguing with people, real or imagined, waving his pistol and vintage service rifle from the Vietnam War. He would pass out for an hour or two, and then begin again.

"He would alternate assaulting Mack Oliver and his mother, Dorothy. Dot and Mack Oliver would try to keep him inside, try to get the guns, hold him down. He would choke Dot and throw her around, kick her if she fell down. When the cops drove by the house, Mack would put his guns just inside the door and sit on the porch with his arms folded, as if nothing had happened. As soon as the cops turned the corner, he would start again, with his anger focused on whomever he thought might have called them. Usually, that was anyone who was brave enough to walk by the house. 'Did you call the police? I'll shoot your damn brains out.' They would hurry by the house. However, he never hurt anyone, except Dot and Mack Oliver. Mr. Purifoy was probably bipolar or schizophrenic, as well, and obviously badly addicted.

"Every Sunday, Dorothy Purifoy would take Mack Oliver to church. She was humble, and a dedicated wife and mother. As the years went on, her depression caused her to put on more and more weight. As they left the house on Sunday morning, Big Mack would throw things at them and turn his music up exceptionally loud, straining the speakers. 'You ain't no damn Christians,' he would shout as other neighbors left for church. He would hurl insults, 'Damn hypocrites. That preacher is a damn whoremonger. Dot, you better not bring any of those bastards to my house. You hear me?' Dot would pray hard during the service. Without fail, when she and Mack Oliver returned home, Big Mack was passed out and broke. Dot would search his pockets for what was left to pay bills and buy groceries. Big Mack would wake up Sunday night embarrassed and apologetic. He would cry and beg his wife and son for forgiveness, and they always obliged. He was a tolerable man Monday through Friday. But he deteriorated pitifully over the years and died at fifty. The day of his funeral was the first time any church folks had ever come to his house.

"Mack Oliver didn't have much of a chance. He had inherited his father's mental illness and addiction. Big Mack's abuse of Mack Oliver had left the small-framed boy shy and awkward and suffering from post-traumatic stress disorder. Mack Oliver's withdrawn demeanor and learning disability that was a result of his environment landed him in special education classes where he was not well educated. Only until his mother introduced him to the saxophone and the school introduced him to art class was his intelligence realized. But by then, and with the circumstances he found himself in, nothing became of his artistic talents. He was not well educated after high school and he could only find menial work. Big Mack finally threw him out of the house and Mack Oliver remained homeless until he wandered into Fairchild one day looking for food and shelter.

"Once he was clean, his schizophrenia properly diagnosed, and medicated, he became a different person – an incredibly intelligent, funny and talented person. Last December, Mrs. Purifoy died of complications related to heart disease. She had gotten severely overweight, and after Mack Oliver was stabilized, he cared for her remarkably well. Mack Oliver relapsed when she died; but, amazingly, he quickly got it back together. I was proud of Mack Oliver. He used only once during that episode and came into the center. He got clean again and has been doing fine since that period. That was a year ago.

"Mack Oliver is also an extremely gifted artist. He paints and sells his artwork on the Southside by the Storyteller Fountain at Five Points. He also plays his saxophone on the corner. I think it adds to the unique culture of the Southside, and he can make a couple of dollars to live on as passersby throw change in his box. Mack Oliver on his bike, with that horn slung over his back, has become a staple of the Southside. The bike is adorned with practically everything he owns. Pictures of his artwork are pasted over the spokes of the bike. He probably feels pretty lost without it right now. He has always wanted to work for his money. Many homeless people will put their hand out and gratefully accept whatever they are given. Mack Oliver wanted to play his sax, sell you a painting, or give you a hand-made bangle for whatever money you gave him."

"The Wallace girl had one of those bangles in her hand," interjected Piti, who had managed to consume most of his breakfast in the time Lincoln had been talking.

"I'm sure Mack Oliver gave her that for any money she may have given him," replied Lincoln.

Piti nodded, "The report says she gave him five dollars."

"That would have been quite generous. I'm sure he was very grateful," remarked Lincoln. "Mack Oliver also receives disability compensation. I don't think he would have had a money motive."

"How do I convince a jury of that, doctor? He lives on the streets and he's poor. How could he not want money?"

"The money he makes is enough for him."

"The public will never understand that," replied Piti. "What if his motive was rape? The rape of a young white woman. The jury might think he killed her just for the hell of it because she was white and rich."

"Has that ever happened?" asked Lincoln, discounting the idea.

"White people think it has," retorted Piti.

"Listen, I've treated murderers, rapists, sociopaths, antisocials, and psychotics. Mack Oliver does not strike me as a killer or a rapist. The person who did this is much sicker than Mack Oliver. That person had an extreme hate for these victims."

Piti's voice rose, filled with agitation. "He may not be the man, but do you understand that everybody will believe he is? He looks like what they think dangerous people look like. He was at the scene. They don't have to prove his guilt. I have to *prove* his innocence. That's the way this works. I am touched by Mack Oliver's story, and honestly, there are big holes in the prosecution's case. You can see them, I'm sure, but I am unsure that even a hole big enough to drive a pickup truck through it will be enough to convince people he didn't do it. I've lived in Alabama all my life and I know a jury will convict and recommend death for this evidence, however circumstantial and filled with holes. Their fear will fill the holes – and Billy Penick is an expert at riling up and putting fear into a white jury. He will ask, 'If Mack Oliver didn't kill both those girls, who did?' I know how to raise reasonable doubt, but I can't deliver miracles. The cops have closed the case, doctor. The jury will think that means guilty."

Lincoln calmly asked, "Is there anything?"

Piti gave a shrug of frustration. "I'm still thinking. The investigation only lasted two and a half days. There was so much pressure to get someone fast, and the girl is being buried today. The mayor, the chief, Wallace, the public – they all wanted something before then. Maybe it was someone else. Maybe another one of your homeless people."

"I read that Miss Miller and Miss Wallace were both assaulted with wine bottles and traces of wine were in their orifices."

"Yeah. Sick ain't it?"

"Mack Oliver never touched alcohol because of his father's alcoholism and abuse."

Piti gave a sarcastic laugh. "Hell, I'm convinced. Now you only need to convince every other white person in Birmingham."

"Do you think there will be any blacks on the jury?" asked Lincoln.

"Nope. Billy will strike them all," Piti said.

"Isn't that illegal, to strike someone because of race?"

"Who said that would be the reason he gives? Happens all the time. And I think most blacks will think he's guilty, too. They just won't want to kill him." Piti had become impressed with his breakfast companion. "How did you get to be a doctor? I mean, what kind of a doctor are you again? Where are you from?"

Piti's opinions were colored by the fact he had not traveled outside the state often, and usually blacks he had encountered were on the other side of the law – accused murderers, thieves, drunks, rapists, and petty criminals he was defending before J. B. Many could not read or write. They were always poor. Piti had never had a conversation with anyone like Lincoln Drake, although he would only have had to travel a few blocks in any direction to meet others like Lincoln. But his world and their world seldom interacted on an intellectual basis. Piti was curious. He thought, *This fellow seems smart.*

Lincoln had encountered this often. He called it "The Audition." He, as well as other blacks, had considered it an obligation to educate and represent blacks well when these occasions arose, as they too often did. Many felt like they were in a constant state of "auditioning." He could seldom relax in public, and was always perfectly groomed, prepared to make a good initial impression. Perfect haircut. Perfectly shaven. White teeth. Crisp shirt. Coordinating tie. Tailored suit. Highly polished shoes. Impeccable speech and manners. In addition, he had been blessed with movie-star looks and a smooth walk that the hostess and all the waitresses at John's observed.

As he had done many times before, Lincoln obliged to answer the questions. "I was born in Alabama. I grew up here in Birmingham and I went to college in California, at UCLA."

"How did you get way out there? Where did you go to high school?"

"I went to Mountain Brook High."

"Mountain Brook? So you're one of those rich...I mean, so you're rich?"

"No, absolutely not. It was a bit of an unusual circumstance. My father worked at the country club. He eventually ran the whole dining room. My mother was the head of the domestic help at the McPeake estate."

"As in J. B. McPeake?" asked Piti.

"Well, his mother and father."

"The banker, right?" asked Piti.

"Yes."

"He was good friends with Mr. Wallace," Piti noted.

"Yes, Jedidiah McPeake."

"So, how did you end up at that school?"

"We lived in the carriage house on the estate, so we lived in the district. My mother insisted, and Mrs. McPeake gave her anything she wanted. When old man McPeake said the Brown decision demanded it, no one was going to argue with him. I was the first. Rich people knew that desegregation laws wouldn't affect them. How could blacks integrate a multi-million-dollar neighborhood or a country club with a one-hundred-thousand-dollar admittance fee? If they can't afford the neighborhood, they can't go to the school. They can't afford the restaurants that rich people eat in anyway or shop where they shop. They don't live near their churches.

"Wealthy whites weren't worried about integration. Poor whites worried about it because politicians, who would use anything to keep the voters stirred up, were always driving that wedge between blacks and poor whites. The rich whites thought it was entertaining to have me at their school. It broke the boredom and was the topic of much debate, I guess. There were a few of us that went through back then.

"Before the buses were integrated, I asked my father if

he thought it would happen. He replied with a very calm, 'Of course.' Rich whites don't care if poor whites have to sit by blacks on a bus. The rich people didn't ride the bus. Regardless of Klan marches and all the irate speeches by politicians, after they had their say, in the end the rich whites were going to say integrate the buses. They needed the labor at work on time and didn't want out-of-state investors being turned off. The Dr. King-led boycott of the buses brought that reality to rich whites. My father asked me a rhetorical question once. 'Now son,' he asked, 'do you think the country club will ever be integrated?'

"My parents, Jefferson and Genevieve Drake, had to carry themselves in the most dignified manner, living at the McPeake estate. My father was extremely proud, and there seemed to be a mutual respect between himself and Jedidiah. Jedidiah was proud to have a man like my father working for him. The dining room at the club was run flawlessly. My father's proficiency, smile and gracious manner endeared him to his employer. Even back then, he was known as Mr. Drake. Jedidiah McPeake loaned blacks money when others would not. He understood the untapped financial potential in the black community. The one bank he inherited from his father became many banks, and the most powerful bank in the region. When others eventually saw the potential, they tried to sway the blacks over to their banks, but only had marginal success. Most blacks by that time had identified with McPeake. Of course, all that would change later. McPeake visited my parents' church. He sat close to my father, and before the service and afterwards, he would gregariously – for all to see – embrace him. My father knew he was marketing, and of course he was a willing participant. Both men got a lot from each other."

Lincoln was compelled to share a story with Piti that had

always intrigued him, about his father and about the silent power many blacks wielded.

"My father told me a story once about a time when a grocery merchant called him a boy. The merchant catered to blacks in his chain of stores across Alabama. My mother and father had frequented his stores for years. One day while they were shopping, the grocer felt they were taking too long observing the fruit. He said to my father, 'Move along, boy.' My father, of course, was deeply insulted, and they never shopped there again. Three years later, Jedidiah – who had over the years loaned the grocer money to expand his business – asked my father if blacks were still using his stores, and if he thought they would continue to be loyal to the chain. The grocer was in a financial crisis and needed more money from Jedidiah to stay in business.

"That comment the grocer had made to my father three years earlier haunted him. My father was not one prone to forgiveness, and he told McPeake that blacks were very unhappy with the grocer's products and the grocer's treatment of them, and were leaving for more appreciative merchants and better quality goods. But in reality, my father was the only person who had left. Although Jedidiah didn't tell my father why he was asking, he knew and added, 'Anyone who loans him money better be willing to give it away, because they won't get it back.' Jedidiah smiled with pride at my father's treachery. Jedidiah felt that beneath the skin, blacks were just like whites, an obvious but radical belief then. He liked being proven right. The grocer lost his stores. Jedidiah foreclosed on him. He found a new buyer. Blacks got a more appreciative merchant, Jedidiah made a lot of money, and my father got his vengeance."

Piti got the message.

The black men who worked at the club knew everything that was going on in the city. They knew the deals, they knew who was sleeping with whom, who was losing money, who was making money. The whites talked as if the blacks weren't present, or as if these issues just didn't matter to blacks. They were wrong. They did matter. Jefferson Drake was a powerful man because he understood this reality. Genevieve and Jefferson accepted their status in life. They wanted Lincoln to have all the opportunities they did not. When Lincoln wanted a summer job, Jefferson would not let his son work at the club. Lincoln begged for his father to let him park cars or bus tables. Jefferson refused. He remarked, "I do this so you won't have to. You're going to be somebody." He made Lincoln study all summer. At the time, Lincoln thought it was unfair and cruel. Jefferson didn't want Lincoln to only compete with whites. He knew that for his son to be recognized at all, he needed to be much smarter, which required more sacrifice, and he also didn't want Lincoln with a lot of spare time on his hands that might get him into trouble. Lincoln recognized his father's brilliance now. His parents saved most of their money to ensure that Lincoln had it better.

"When my mother said she wanted me at Mountain Brook High, Mrs. McPeake didn't deliberate about it for a second. 'Sure,' she said. My mother thought it would be harder than that, but Mrs. McPeake wasn't about to lose my mother to what she referred to as the parvenu that were moving into Mountain Brook. The old money crowd didn't steal the others' house ladies. Domestic help like my mother was highly coveted."

"The parvenu?" asked Piti.

"Yes, that's her rich and polite way of saying new money wannabes," explained Lincoln. "I ended up at UCLA because my parents wanted me as far away as possible."

"Alabama isn't so bad, is it?" But as soon as Piti asked the question, he realized, *I wouldn't want to be black in Alabama*. "Well, why did you return?"

"My parents had sacrificed for me all of my life. They are older now. They need me." Lincoln didn't know Piti well enough to tell him that his father had cancer and that was the major reason he'd returned. "I'm tremendously blessed to have them as parents. They are the reason I'm a doctor – a psychologist, by the way. They are the reason I received the education I have. I never had to work to pay for even a single book in college or graduate school because of them. Few blacks have had such good fortune. I was accepted and respected in California. Driving my convertible down the coast one day, I thought, I've got to do more than this with my life. I closed my practice and I made some money off of it, too. I moved back five years ago. I got an offer from Catherine Fairchild to work at her center as the chief psychologist. She has since passed away. But no one served the homeless, the poor and the disenfranchised more earnestly."

"Yes," agreed Piti. "I worked with her often. Many of my clients were treated at her center. So that's how you got to the Fairchild Center?"

"Yes. Mack Oliver was one of Catherine's favorite patients. I don't think he's capable of murder, Mr. Pitman."

"Do you know J. B.?" asked Piti, looking for any help he could find.

"Not well. He's twenty years older than I am. He knows my parents well, of course, but J. B. made his own way. He didn't want to just run the family business. His older brother runs the bank now. My father is closer to him. He still banks there."

"I wouldn't have thought J. B.'s mother and father would be so liberal," stated Piti.

"Who said they were liberal?"

The meeting had lasted longer than either man thought it would. Piti had met a man who had articulated to him that blacks were as human as whites, for better or worse. This observation had escaped him all of his life. Piti now had a client he was starting to believe in, but he still couldn't help but think that if it went to trial, Mack Oliver would be sentenced to death. Lincoln also knew that if another suspect wasn't found, Mack Oliver would be condemned for who he was, not for what he did. The homeless were the new alienated, the feared. The signs that once read No Colored had been replaced with attitudes that said No Homeless. The homeless were male, female, black and white, adults and children. But when people thought of the homeless, they thought of the 70 to 80 percent who were black. They thought of drug-addicted, mentally ill black males. They thought of Mack Oliver. They didn't want him in their city, their neighborhood. They didn't think he was their responsibility to help. They thought he was dangerous and that he should be locked up.

Lincoln beat Piti to his pocket to pay for breakfast, and the men left the restaurant. They made the walk back towards the courthouse where they both had parked. Only poor people rode the bus in Alabama, and there were few buses to ride. Visitors who were used to public transportation systems and rail lines in other cities were often shocked. Everyone in the South drove.

As the two men approached their cars, Piti asked, "Are you going to the funeral? You folks are practically neighbors."

"Yes, my father knew Mr. Wallace. He was a regular at the club, and my mother planned on accompanying Mrs. McPeake. I planned on going with them. What about you?"

"You better believe it. I'm already going to be hated for representing Mack Oliver. I need to do everything I can to keep some sort of standing in the community. Hell, who won't be there?"

As Piti drove away, Lincoln contemplated and observed downtown Birmingham. He did not have a good feeling about

Mack Oliver's chances or Piti's commitment to proving his innocence. Dr. Lincoln Drake was no stranger to the Alabama judicial system. He had had many patients who were parolees or on probation. He had to integrate many back into society. He was also aware of the inequities that existed with the judicial system that gave black men unusually long sentences and disproportionately sentenced them to death. Lincoln became a psychologist to better understand why men made the decisions they made. He was particularly interested in why the black and underprivileged communities were so prone to crime, violence, and self-destruction, to behaviors like drug and alcohol abuse. Why were their families broken and their communities crumbling? Why were homeless men and women walking the streets as outcasts of society? What was eating at the souls of this community? The attitudes that permeated America about blacks and the poor were especially pronounced in the South. To be black and poor – or the poorest of the poor, the homeless – was especially condemning. Why was there such condemnation, such hatred, such fear?

When Lincoln was accepted to UCLA, it was a source of tremendous pride for all of his family. He was not just the first to graduate college, he was the first to attend college. His parents both cried when they set foot on the college's campus. It wasn't just that Lincoln was going away to college, but that they had never seen that side of a college campus before. Their son had always more than accomplished their aspirations for him. As they left Lincoln on the campus and made the long train ride back to Alabama, they were filled with joy and high expectations. And Lincoln would not disappoint them.

Lincoln's exceptional intelligence earned him perfect grades through school. He graduated magna cum laude from UCLA. He earned a bachelor's degree in Political Science, a master's degree in Business, and a dual doctorate in Psychology and Business. Lincoln's charisma would earn him acceptance in California from the moment of his arrival. The very things that had been hindrances in the south – his obvious good looks and his brains – had earned him more than full acceptance in the Golden State. Amazingly, he found himself fitting in and most on the campus looked at him as no different from anyone else. His golden skin color may have even given him an advantage. He was shocked to see black men being heralded as heroes and called smart. They were affluent, they were business people, and they were dating white women openly. Lincoln could hardly go to sleep at night and could not wait to get up in the morning. And only his Southern friends could understand his sense of freedom and jubilance.

However, Lincoln never lost sight of his parents' upbringing, and no one ever had to remind him that he needed to study and make good grades. He always felt the obligation of having to prove himself. Lincoln's euphoria would not begin to wane until the last year of his master's program, when he began to work on his Ph.D., and as his freedom began to not be such a novelty and preoccupation. He thought more of all those he had left behind – his parents, family, and friends, black and white. Even those where the social relationships were awkward because of race. As a psychologist, he knew that one's culture was a strong driving force that guided decision-making. It was fascinating how one's culture might keep some people in the desert under a scorching sun, and where water and food were scarce – or in areas prone to hurricanes, earthquakes, or tornados – and how one becomes accustomed to these conditions, and how one preferred them after a while. So it was with Birmingham.

CHAPTER TEN

The Quiet Drive

By midmorning on December 27, all of Birmingham was reading the morning edition of *The Birmingham News.*

Slain Daughter of Birmingham Billionaire, Draper Wallace, Funeral Today

Joanna Dee Wallace, 18 years old, who was brutally raped and murdered on Birmingham's Southside while shopping, will be laid to rest at Canterbury United Methodist Church in Mountain Brook at 1:00 p.m. Miss Wallace, the youngest of Draper and Millicent Wallace's four children, was a graduate of Mountain Brook High School. She was a freshman at The University of Alabama and a member of the Crimson Cabaret Dance Team. The brutal slaying of the youngster has sent shockwaves through the community. The district attorney's office will arraign a homeless man today for not only the rape and murder of Miss Wallace, but also for the rape and murder of Miss Tiffany Miller that occurred on the Southside more than nine months ago. Those close to the investigation say that eyewitness and crime scene evidence that includes DNA evidence, places the alleged double murderer at the murder scenes of both women. Residents and merchants of downtown Birmingham have been moving

> from the area for many years. The crime rate in the city has soared over this time, ranking Birmingham as one of the worst cities in the nation when it comes to violent crime. The growth rate of surrounding cities and suburbs are booming due to migration of Birminghamians to these areas in search of better schools and safety. Many believe that there is a rift between City Hall and Chief Bo Canon's police department. Mayor Castelle's attempts to bring more accountability and fewer resident complaints against the police department, according to some police officers, has tied their hands and created an atmosphere of lawlessness downtown. More than six months ago when Mayor Castelle was questioned by concerned citizens at a city council meeting, he responded that there is escalating crime all over the nation, and he felt it was wrong to single out Birmingham. This led many to believe he had accepted the rising crime, the murders, rapes, and robberies, as an inevitability, which has weakened his standing in some polls. The mayor's critics site apathy and corruption as the problem. His supporters say white flight from Birmingham has nothing to do with crime, but is due to the uneasiness with the "blackening" of the city.

The editorials were extremely harsh. One prominent physician wrote, "This is an indictment of the current administration and the administrations of the past twenty years, for ignoring the social issues that would cause such obvious decay." He compared Birmingham to other historical great cities that had succumbed to greed, corruption and immorality.

A businesswoman described downtown Birmingham as "being under siege by troops of homeless men whose menacing behavior and crimes have been ignored for years."

The atmosphere in Birmingham was one of shock and outrage as with the mourners who gathered at the large Methodist Church to pay their respects to Jodi and a family in despair. The sanctuary was filled to capacity, with many gathered in its expansive hallways.

Jefferson finished his morning paper and stood in the bay window of the dining room of his Titusville home, waiting for Lincoln to arrive. The pansies were in bloom just below the window, the thick beds of flowers framing the window and the front of the brick porch. The manicured lawn was divided by a brick driveway, with well-tended holly bushes lining the drive from the road to the house. Jefferson enjoyed the times he, Genevieve and Lincoln spent together, even though the occasion for today was tragic – the funeral of Jodi Wallace. Jefferson always enjoyed showing his son off. The success of a man, Jefferson felt, was measured by the success of his children, and Jefferson felt extremely successful. He was getting anxious, though, because, he didn't want to be late. He knew exactly what time they had to leave in order to drive to Mountain Brook, pick up Mrs. McPeake, and then get to the church, park, and be seated. He had plotted the entire trip in his head and knew within minutes how long it would take.

The Drake home in Titusville was now a lot more expansive, including a study, a large kitchen, a den and two additional bedrooms, due to many renovations made to the small, two-bedroom, one-bath house they had purchased eighteen years ago. The Titusville neighborhood was the most affluent neighborhood for blacks when it was first planned and constructed. The neighborhood was also one of the few built for blacks. It wasn't a Birmingham neighborhood that turned black after whites left when blacks started to move in. Jefferson could not bring himself to purchase in a neighborhood that whites were abandoning. He and Genevieve looked in Bush Hills and Norwood, once thriving white communities. But the experience was so humiliating that they couldn't buy in either of the communities. They looked at the houses and listened to the excuses that the whites gave as to why they were leaving. They knew there were only two reasons: the black family that had moved in down the street and the black kids that had integrated the school. Jefferson passed. He never regretted his decision.

He had lived in the carriage house at the McPeake estate for ten years, saving every dime he made at the club and working for Jedidiah when he wasn't at the club. He paid cash for the house because if he borrowed the money to buy it, he would have had to use McPeake's bank because he worked for him, liked him, and thought it would have been ungrateful to borrow from someone else. And Jedidiah probably would never have forgiven him. He wasn't against borrowing, but he didn't want McPeake to know how much he paid for his house. That was his business and he didn't want Jedidiah or Lily McPeake in it. Living at the McPeake's had afforded Lincoln a first-class education and Jefferson the position of "Big Man" in his community, a name his relatives called him when they visited them in Dothan. Jefferson's position was highly coveted.

The carriage house had been finely furnished with items from the mansion that were placed there by Mrs. McPeake or purchased by the Drakes as she tired of them or when she just wanted a new look. These items of furniture were now at the Drake's Titusville residence. The all-fabric pieces were covered in well-fitting transparent plastic covers to preserve them. Gold upholstery tacks lined the edges of the furniture, and plastic runners were placed over the Persian rugs. Genevieve's excessive fastidiousness made visitors feel like they had to be careful in the house, sitting just so. No one slouched and many wouldn't even sit down. They all walked carefully over Genevieve's rugs, being sure to stay on the plastic runners. Jefferson even had plastic put over the velour seats in his cars. Leather would become popular years later. He drove only Cadillacs, and paid cash for every one he had ever owned. The Sedan de Ville, dark green with lighter green interior, was his current one. He always picked up his new Caddy in Detroit, right off the assembly line, and drove it all the way back to Alabama, gloating the whole way.

When the family went to Dothan, kids would follow the car. When the relatives introduced Jefferson to people, they would say, "This is my cousin" or "my brother. He's a 'Big Man' in Birmingham." When the family was introduced, they were introduced as "Big People." Jefferson never went to high school, but no one would have known it. He had read most of the books in the McPeake library and he read both the morning and evening editions of *The Birmingham News.* When he traveled, he picked up a newspaper in every major city to read later. He made Lincoln send him copies of *The Los Angeles Times.* He even read Lincoln's college newspaper.

Jefferson loved to read, but told Genevieve when she complained about him reading so much that he read to be good at his job. He conversed with the club's regulars, learning everything about them; their anniversaries, their birthdays, children's birthdays, and bar mitzvahs. When members needed information about the city or any other subjects, they would ask Jefferson. Jedidiah used Jefferson as a resource if he was contemplating lending someone money. He would ask, "Jefferson, that fellow Jones, have you read anything about him?" If Jones had ever been in the paper, even if it was a real estate sale, Jefferson remembered. He also knew any gossip passed around by the employees at the club. He knew all their secrets, but never divulged them, except to Jedidiah. Jedidiah talked openly in front of Jefferson about all of the bank's business – mergers, acquisitions, and foreclosures. Absorbing every detail, Jefferson invested accordingly. He never knew if Jedidiah wanted him to hear. To openly talk of these details to Jefferson would probably have been illegal, and, at a minimum, unethical. Nonetheless, Jefferson paid close attention.

Perfectly attired in a black suit, crisp white shirt with French cuffs, highly polished black Florsheims, and a white pocket square placed perfectly, with his white hair cut close, Jefferson stood erect with military bearing, now on the front porch, agitated as Lincoln arrived. The showroom-polished Sedan de Ville was out of the garage; the engine on, purring quietly, with exhaust emitting from the tail pipe, giving an indication of the frigid temperature. The front end was pointed towards the road, making the car appear as anxious as Jefferson. Lincoln parked on the road and he walked up the drive, sensing his father's frustration. Lincoln was on time by anyone else's standards, but he knew his father and anticipated the scolding.

"Son, we mustn't be late."

"Pop, we won't be. How are you doing?" Lincoln asked, trying to change the subject. But it didn't work and never had.

"Fine, son, and you?" Jefferson responded rapidly.

"Pretty good."

"It is not only that we shouldn't be late. I'd like to be early.

Mr. Wallace is a man of stature. He deserves for us to be early. On time is late."

They walked into the house, Lincoln first, his father in tow, still using every opportunity to train Lincoln. Genevieve was in the living room, looking royal, her fair skin contrasting against her black dress and dark mink stole.

"Mother, you look beautiful." Lincoln leaned down to kiss his mother's cheek as she blushed.

"Thank you, son."

Jefferson's deep voice interjected, cutting short the pleasantries. "They say blacks don't respect being on time. The Drakes are always early."

Genevieve ignored him. "Son, you look quite handsome today," she said, restoring congeniality.

"Thanks, Mother."

"It's going to take five minutes just to get Mrs. McPeake in the car," Jefferson's inpatient voice echoed in the room.

Genevieve and Lincoln knew Jefferson all too well, and that arguing wouldn't help. They knew he would be over his episode in fifteen minutes or so.

Five minutes into their journey as Lincoln drove the Sedan de Ville with his father sitting beside him, Lincoln was ready for another subject.

Jefferson remarked, "This is a tragedy." Sadly, he added, "Everyone at the club is in mourning. This was the saddest Christmas we've had in all my years there."

From the back seat Genevieve agreed, "It is truly the work of the devil."

"The only consolation to this family is that they have the killer," Jefferson added.

Lincoln sat quietly, unable to bring himself to tell his father that he knew the alleged killer, didn't think he had done it, and planned to help him.

Jefferson, looking disgusted, added, "Why did it have to be a black man? Lincoln, this isn't one of your homeless people, is it?"

The question accelerated Lincoln's heartbeat. He decided not to respond and looked away slightly.

"Lincoln, I asked you a question. That homeless man in the paper, do you know him?"

Lincoln cleared his throat. "Yes."

Genevieve said, "It's not his fault if he knows the man. He treats those people."

But Jefferson now looked right at Lincoln, trying to sense what Lincoln wouldn't tell. "Well, that's right, that's right. It's not his fault that he knows him." Then, pleading, he asked, "But son, you're not going to get involved in this in any way, are you? What you're doing, trying to help these people, is noble and all. I mean, we raised you that way. But from what I read in the paper, what they have on this guy is pretty compelling. He might as well have left his photo and phone number at the scene. And this is Wallace's daughter. He's a friend of ours."

"A friend of ours, Dad?" Lincoln asked curiously.

"The man sent you a high school graduation gift and every time you earned a degree at college he sent a gift. He even offered you a job," Jefferson said tersely.

"Listen, Dad, I know, I know. But what if he didn't do it?"

"What if who didn't do it?" Jefferson asked, shocked.

"Mack Oliver Purifoy. What if he didn't do it? It's all too convenient, too quick. I think they rushed."

Jefferson, sounding bewildered, replied, "Too convenient? Too quick? It's a blessing that the killer was dumb. He didn't cover his tracks well. He was probably high on drugs. The news accounts say he's schizophrenic and had to be chained in the courtroom. I saw the picture on the front page. He wanted to kill everyone in the courtroom. And remember whose daughter he killed. He will never leave that jail, not alive anyway. Getting mixed up with this could ruin your whole career – everything we've worked for."

Knowing that he couldn't discuss what he knew about Mack Oliver with his father, Lincoln just listened as the quiet Caddy rolled through downtown towards Highland Avenue. Jefferson noted the crumbling inner city and the homeless people and vagrants they passed along the way.

"Lincoln, if someone had hurt you, I don't know what I would have done. That man is lucky he made it to jail. I would have…"

Genevieve interrupted, "Jefferson, idle words, idle words. You should be careful what you say. You will speak those things to truth. God does not abide idle talk."

"Genevieve, I would have…"

"Jefferson," she said, with a warning.

"Dad, wouldn't you want the right man punished?"

"Son, you're just too close to this. How much evidence would it take for you? This man was bound to kill someone sooner or later. Homeless, crazy, on drugs. The Miller girl was his girlfriend and no one did a damn thing about it when he killed her. Not the cops, not the black community, and certainly not the politicians or the courts. No one cared. That's the lesson here. Ignore the problems in the black community and they'll spread. I don't want you ruining your career and reputation dealing with this. The man is a bum and is going to get what he should get – 'Yellow Momma.'"

"Dad, what if he never had a chance? And I mean this seriously when I say it." Lincoln could keep silent no longer. "Not everyone had the benefit of having a Jefferson Drake as a dad. Where would I be without you? Seventy to eighty percent of these guys have no father and live in unimaginable poverty, you know that?"

"Son, you give me way too much credit. I wasn't sitting beside you in the classroom at UCLA. You did it. Magna cum laude," Jefferson smiled with pride at his son's accomplishment.

"Dad, every day at UCLA I saw your face in the next chair beside mine." Jefferson and Genevieve laughed.

"Son, there is no excuse. Blacks or any other group only have themselves to credit or to blame. That's the way it is today anyway. There's no slavery, no laws that prohibit blacks from achievement or from attaining the American dream. It's not the way it used to be. Just look at George Washington Carver, Booker T. Washington, Martin Luther King Jr. My parents were born on the hills of slavery. I've fought against Jim Crow all my life in Dothan and Birmingham, Alabama, of all places. I worked in the fields from sun up to sun down, picking cotton and peanuts and velvet beans. Have you ever seen cotton? Do you even know what a velvet bean is?"

Lincoln thought to himself, *Yes.* He'd been to Dothan many times and his father had said the same thing every time.

But Jefferson wasn't through. "If you get the velvet on you from those beans, it will rub the skin right off of you. I had to drop out of school after the eighth grade to work and help support my brothers and sisters. When I joined the Army during

World War II, it was a relief to get out of the fields. Being a tanker was easy compared to that cotton field and those velvet beans. I served under Patton, a complete racist. I drove a tank in the Black Panthers Battalion. I've got shrapnel in my neck for my efforts. My country gave me a Purple Heart and a Silver Star. This is my country as much as it was George Washington's or Thomas Jefferson's. I fought for it and I own it. There was nothing – no Klan, no rednecks or Jim Crow laws – that was going to keep me from being a man or making sure that you achieved your dreams.

"Look at these people today." As the car passed the shelters and the homeless on the streets lining the sides of the buildings, Jefferson gestured to them disapprovingly. "Where's their dignity? These drugs and crime, living on the streets, not respecting their women and families – that's a choice. What they are doing hurts us all. Who is forcing them to use crack and drink and steal and kill? It's their own fault. I could have made the choices they made, too." The car was silent for a moment as Jefferson took a break.

The Caddy had left the gray, smoky streets of Birmingham and was now entering the lush greenery and the winding, smooth roads of Mountain Brook.

Lincoln looked at his father. "Dad, you said that if something had happened to me when I was a boy that you don't know what you would've done."

"That's true. You are my responsibility. I love you more than I love my own life."

"What if homeless people feel that kind of loss every day, and have that desperate feeling every waking moment?"

As the Caddy pulled into the long driveway of the McPeake estate, Jefferson asked, "Are you listening to me?"

Genevieve, knowing that God would guide them through

this issue as he had led them through all others, acted as if she had not heard a word of the conversation.

CHAPTER ELEVEN

The Funeral

Despite Jefferson's fears, the Drakes and Mrs. McPeake arrived early at Canterbury Methodist Church for the most regretted day in recent memory among the hundreds of mourners. Jodi's sister eulogized her. Her older brothers also made remarks about their youngest sister on this uncharacteristically cold afternoon. The temperature hovered around freezing, and the inclement weather felt appropriate for the mood inside the sanctuary.

No one could remember a murder of any Mountain Brook child. The particularly offensive nature of this murder had shocked and enraged the community. The dozens of classmates, sorority sisters and college friends who had known Jodi were in attendance. Even her first grade teacher, music and dance teacher, and tennis coach were present. The president and chancellor of the University attended, as well as senators, congressmen and judges, including J. B. McPeake. Numerous lawyers, including William Penick and Cecil Pitman came to pay their respects. The mayor of Birmingham, the mayor of Mountain Brook, the council members, and every notable citizen and family of Birmingham all took their seats side by side. No occasion had ever brought so many of them together.

Reverend Winslow remarked that the light drizzle of icy rain, the dark clouds that had settled in over Mountain Brook and the distant thunder seemed to indicate even God's dissatisfaction with the tragic loss of the life of an innocent child. Those familiar with the Wallace girls knew of their close relationship and were deeply affected by Vicki's steely strength. Most wept openly. Millie Wallace was held up only by Draper's support, his arm her anchor through the entire ceremony. Draper Wallace cried, Jefferson Drake stared, and Genevieve and Lily McPeake held hands, sharing tears that didn't let up for an hour. From Lincoln Drake's rear observation point of the sea of black-clad attendees, he could sense the overwhelming grief and anger. He, too, had an eerie, sick feeling in his stomach. Each swallow was difficult. He knew now, even more so, that every soul in attendance at Canterbury would be emboldened to do something about this tragedy, to severely punish anyone responsible.

Lincoln was in agreement with their sentiment, but feared that the shock of the crime had led to the arrest of the wrong man. Still, he couldn't help wondering if he had missed something about Mack Oliver. Were the police, prosecutors, and newspaper right? Was Piti right? Was his father right? Would anything he thought about Mack Oliver make any difference? Lincoln's mind sorted through the five years he had known Mack Oliver and all the experiences the man had shared with him that had shaped his life. One incident stood out as Lincoln sat quietly on his rear bench and pondered Mack Oliver's fate.

* * *

Big Mack Purifoy was already upset with Mack Oliver after Dot told him she had to go to the school because Mack Oliver had been suspended for fighting the day before. But when his coworkers ribbed him about the beating Mack Oliver had taken at the hands of Curtis Jackson, the twelve-year-old bully who had been held back twice and was in Mack Oliver's fifth grade class of ten-year-olds, Big Mack was mad. Some of the men had poked fun at him since lunch about Mack Oliver not being a bad ass like his old man, and that he was skinny and short and stuck under his mother so much he might even be a sissy. The men stopped, though, when Big Mack grabbed one of them and threatened to throw him in the pit where they melted and formed iron ore.

The Purifoy family lived in a small, shotgun house in a community adjacent to the Alabama Cast Iron Pipe Company, where Mack worked – close enough for the families to smell the chemicals used at the plant. Their clothes could only be hung out to dry on the weekends, when the plant was mostly shut down, because the coal soot covered everything outside Monday through Friday. The families used the plant whistle at twelve noon – lunchtime – and 3:30 p.m. – quitting time – as guides for activities. Mack Oliver had been conditioned to hate the whistle blows. In the summer, the noon whistle meant Big Mack had thirty minutes for lunch and might come home. It took only five minutes to walk from his work to the house and back again. The 3:30 p.m. whistle meant he was definitely on his way home, except for Fridays.

Mack Oliver was normally sure to be away from the house when Big Mack arrived. He would return home after Big Mack was well fed and sleepy. But that day, Dot had him on punishment for fighting and he couldn't leave. So he hid in his room hoping Big Mack wouldn't notice him. However, Mack was determined to notice him, and was livid. He walked down the middle of the street headed towards the house, pulling Curtis Jackson along behind him. Curtis had been called "Spot" all of his life by everyone in the small community because of a skin disorder that made the skin on his face, hands and legs varying shades of light brown, dark brown and white in a jigsaw puzzle pattern. He probably had it all over him, but he never took his shirt off in public and rarely wore shorts. His spotted appearance and stocky build made him quite scary to younger boys, and the butt of a lot of jokes told by older boys, which had turned him into a bully.

Mack Oliver told Lincoln that the fight at school had started because Spot had witnessed the water meter reader cutting off the Purifoy's water because Big Mack had not paid the bill. The Purifoy's water, gas and electricity were turned off chronically during Mack Oliver's childhood. Dot was not allowed to work because Big Mack was so jealous. He could see the house from his worksite and made sure Dot didn't even come out on the porch. Most days she just sat on the window box, looking through a small opening in the curtains, chain-smoking and drinking coffee. The heavy doses of caffeine were a needed stimulant to help with her depression and lack of energy. Dot had been a very attractive woman when she was younger and a much better catch than Big Mack deserved. He was afraid he would lose her, so he kept her in the house, beat her and called her fat to keep her self-esteem low. He allowed her to attend church, but she could not play the piano that she loved or sing in the church choir because Big Mack felt it would draw too much attention to her and give her the "Big Head." Dot never left Big Mack, not even once during their entire marriage of thirty years. When he was too sick to physically abuse her as he succumbed to cirrhosis, he abused her verbally. He was mean to the end. Dot's short-lived freedom came when Big Mack died.

When Spot witnessed the meter man turning off the water, he told everyone, "The Purifoys have no water." Spot then started to tease Mack Oliver. He had called him "Stinky" for a week, until Mack Oliver couldn't take it anymore and told Curtis, "The stink will wash off when the water's back on, but those leopard spots won't."

Everyone laughed and Curtis decked him. Before Mack Oliver could get up, Curtis got on top of him and started beating him. The principal suspended them both.

When Big Mack headed toward the house with Spot, people started to gather. When he got to the front yard, he shouted, "Mack Oliver, get your ass outside."

Mack Oliver had told Lincoln that his mother went to the door first, and was astounded by what she saw.

"Mack! What are you doing?"

"Woman, don't you get in the middle of this. This is between me and my son. Purifoys don't take ass whippings." He shouted louder, "Mack Oliver, do you hear me calling you? Get out here now!"

Mack Oliver, who was terrified, left the corner of his room where he was hiding from Big Mack and walked out onto the front porch of the small house.

The houses in the neighborhood were only ten feet apart, so everyone who was home had heard Big Mack's command and had come out on their porches as well. Mack Oliver was shaking and so was Spot, Big Mack still holding him steady by the collar. His shirt had come out of his pants and he was missing a shoe. Big Mack was greasy from working at the plant all day. He still had his safety helmet on, and had his lunchbox and gloves in his right hand. Spot was squirming in his left.

"Mack Oliver, get down off that porch and come in the grass."

Mack Oliver slowly walked down the rotting steps of the porch and into the front yard, which was mostly dirt and rocks, but Big Mack still called it grass.

Big Mack said menacingly, "I heard a dirty, filthy rumor."

Mack Oliver's shaking voice answered, "What?"

"That you let this little spotted idiot kick your ass. Now that's not true, is it?"

Mack Oliver mumbled, "Yes, sir. It's true."

Big Mack bent down, grabbed Mack Oliver by his collar and hissed very matter-of-factly at him, "No, it's not." He then yelled for everyone to hear, "That was round one! This is round two!"

Mack Oliver looked at Spot, who was at least twelve inches taller and a whole lot heavier. Spot was twelve and big for his age and Mack Oliver was ten and little for his age – and Spot had a lot more experience fighting.

Big Mack squeezed Spot's collar so tightly that he couldn't breathe. Big Mack looked Mack Oliver in the eyes and whispered, "You're a damn Purifoy and if you don't whip his ass, you're gonna get two ass-whippings today."

Big Mack let Spot go. Mack Oliver put his hands up, but Spot was on top of him. Mack Oliver was punched at least a dozen times before Big Mack pulled Spot off. Now Big Mack was even madder. "Round three!" he shouted at Mack Oliver.

Dot yelled from the porch, "That's enough, Mack. Mack Oliver, get in the house."

Then, Spot said, "Shut your fat mouth, bitch." The comment sent Mack Oliver into a rage.

Mack Oliver had told Lincoln that he didn't know what came over him, but when he got through with Spot, Spot was crying and Big Mack was running in circles saying, "That's my boy! That's a Purifoy! He beat his spotted ass. You saw it! You saw it." He picked Mack Oliver up and carried him inside the house triumphantly. That was the proudest Mack Oliver said his dad had ever been of him. From that day forward, people would say Mack Oliver was as crazy as Big Mack.

The extremely opposite worlds of Jodi and Mack Oliver

had collided disastrously. Jodi Wallace's funeral would not soon be forgotten, and neither would her accused murderer, Mack Oliver Purifoy.

CHAPTER TWELVE

Eminent Domain

Lincoln and Piti had agreed to meet at 9:00 a.m. on the twenty-eighth of December. Lincoln had tossed and turned most of the night, playing the events of the last few days over and over in his mind. Lincoln was a gifted psychologist, and from what he knew of Mack Oliver and his diagnosis, he could not put together any scenario that would result in Mack Oliver being the perpetrator of this crime. Not as long as he was sober and medicated. But even so, Lincoln wondered if he had been conned by Mack Oliver. He wondered for the first time if his skills were as good as he thought and others had told him. Had he missed the signs of a cold-blooded double murderer right under his nose? Was it his ego that wouldn't let him accept the fact that Mack Oliver was a cold-blooded murderer who had killed two women? What would that say about Lincoln? His profession? The other homeless men he treated?

He grilled himself. Was Mack Oliver a rapist? Did the rape get out of hand? Had he fantasized about Miss Wallace in a psychotic episode? Had he killed Miss Miller in a fit of psychotic jealousy and rage? He lived with her, slept with her. Rape and murder on the street didn't make sense. And why now? But all the evidence that pointed to his guilt was way too much to explain away. Mack Oliver had shown no signs of any behavior like this throughout his life.

Lincoln wondered if he was too close to Mack Oliver. Had he become more than a patient? A friend? Was Lincoln trying to rationalize something that was beyond rationalization? Psychotic behavior? Was he relying on his heart and gut, and not his brain?

Lincoln went over the evidence in his head. Mack Oliver was at the scene of the crime with no alibi. He had asked Jodi for money. He had followed her. His hair was there on her clothing, and she had his bangle. He called Miss Miller his girlfriend. Was that a delusion? She was a street hooker, after all. His semen was found inside her the night she died. He had no alibi for his whereabouts that night either. Had he just lost it, the way he had on Curtis Jackson when he was ten? And, most disturbing of all, if it wasn't Mack Oliver, there was a monster roaming around that no one was looking for.

Lincoln was anxious to get to the jail, a short distance from his downtown loft. He arrived early and waited for Piti just inside the door, beyond the metal detectors. Although the jail had been renovated over the years, it was still unmistakably a Birmingham jail – a place that housed people unfit to live freely among the law-abiding public. Although Lincoln was a well-adjusted, upper middle class doctor, he felt vulnerable around the police and jails. He had been taught to fear and distrust law enforcement, as most blacks had. The stories of shooting unarmed black men, planted evidence, beatings, dogs and racism of the past were permanently etched in the back of their minds. He wondered how the small, schizophrenic Mack Oliver was fairing behind bars. He stood there uncomfortably, waiting for Piti to show up, hoping he would not be late. He kept waiting for one of the policemen to ask him what he was doing or frisk him. No one did. No one said a word. Most were smiling, drinking coffee, and joking around with each other as visitors and coworkers came through the doors. When Piti arrived, everyone knew him and just waved him through. He didn't have to empty his pockets or go through the regular routine. He didn't have to pass through the metal detectors.

"Good morning, doctor."

"Good morning, Piti."

"I saw you at the funeral, doctor."

"I saw you, too."

"Were those your parents?"

"Yes."

"Was that your mother sitting with Mrs. McPeake?"

"Yes."

"She looked white."

"She's not."

"Quite an ordeal, wasn't it? Did you go to the Wallace house afterwards?"

"I dropped my mother off there with Mrs. McPeake. Only selected guests were invited."

"That's something. Did you read the paper yet, doctor?"

"Yes."

They began walking toward the visiting area, Piti talking nonstop. "He would have been better off killing Helen Keller. I mean, they have already tried and convicted our boy. How the hell are we supposed to get a fair and impartial jury after all of this? Well, I don't know if it would matter anyway. Did you see that mob yesterday? They want blood. It's the whole damn state against me, you and Mack Oliver."

As the elevator door opened, Piti sensed Lincoln's discomfort and said, "Take it easy. I'm on your side."

"Mack Oliver may have some clues," responded Lincoln.

They waited in the conference area for Mack Oliver to be brought down. The room was filled with inmates, some meeting with family. Others were talking to lawyers – some white, some black, but all in cheap lawyer suits. There were only one or two white inmates, but all appeared extremely poor, with bad teeth, scars, tattoos and hopeless expressions. Some people were crying, some arguing. There was a distinctive jail smell. The floor was scuffed from all of the activity, and the metal chairs and tables were worn and banged up from frequent use. The guards were particularly large and emotionless.

When the shackled Mack Oliver was brought into the room, Lincoln was shocked. He looked like the Mack Oliver from five years earlier.

The guard remarked, "Be careful with this one. He's violent."

Piti asked in an alarmed tone, "Is this how he looks on medication?"

Lincoln stated flatly, "They obviously haven't given him any." Mack Oliver had a bruised face, disheveled clothes and a swollen upper lip.

"What happened to my client?" Piti asked the guard.

"He's been out of control. We had to isolate him, but he still tried to get to some of us."

Lincoln said, "May I speak to the nurse? I'm a doctor."

The guard, feeling as if he should comply, responded, "I'll get her."

Turning back to Mack Oliver, he said, "Mack Oliver, its Lincoln. You recognize me?"

Mack Oliver squinted to focus his eyes and then gave a half-smile. "How could I forget you? What's up, Linc?"

"You remember Mr. Pitman."

"Yeah, my lawyer."

"Do you know where you are?"

"Hell, I'm in jail, man."

"Do you know why you're here?"

"They're saying I killed Tiffany and a white girl. I didn't do it. Did you come to get me out?"

"Mack Oliver, were you given your medication?"

"No. Can't you tell? But I'm hanging on."

"Any thoughts you can't get rid of?"

"Yeah."

"Like what?"

"Hurting one of these damn guards, man. I'm not used to this shit."

Piti watched the exchange between the doctor and patient and was at a loss. How could he have ever thought he could mount a defense for Mack Oliver? The situation was clearly hopeless.

The jail nurse was brought into the room. Lincoln realized with relief that he had worked with her before.

"Carla, I phoned Dr. Farah last night about Mack Oliver. She said she would order the meds and you would give them to him. What happened?"

"Can I talk to you outside?" Carla said, not wanting to talk in front of Mack Oliver and unsure of who Piti was.

"I'm Cecil Pitman. This is my client," Piti stated indignantly.

"Then you can come, too, sir," Carla responded. The three exit, leaving Mack Oliver in the conference room, chained. Nurse Woods informed Lincoln and Piti that Dr. Farah had not directed her to give Mack Oliver the medication. "Considering the circumstances, she didn't think it wise to do anything but strictly follow the guidelines."

Incensed, Piti interrupted, "You mean she found out that he's being held on suspicion of murdering Draper Wallace's daughter."

Lincoln added, "I've known Frances for five years. This is customary. What's her backup plan? Can he see another doctor?"

"Dr. Drake, Dr. Farah wants to see him herself at the regularly scheduled time when she returns. This is a critical case. She said you'd understand."

"When does she return?" asked Lincoln.

"In two weeks." Carla hesitated. "I'm sorry, there's nothing more I can do."

As she departed, Lincoln shook his head. "Mack Oliver will be in full-blown psychosis by then, and the trial that will decide if he lives or dies is in less than two months," he said.

Lincoln and Piti were desperate. Piti felt the pressure of a looming murder trial. He had hoped that he would plead this case, but Lincoln had worked on his emotions. He now felt that they were being foolish, and the only responsible option was to try and save Mack Oliver's life, plead guilty and hope J. B. would give him life in prison.

"Listen, the game is over. This man is going to die if we don't grow up. I'm not going to be a part of this. He's going to get fried if we don't plead this case. And let's hope Billy will go for it."

Lincoln looked at Piti and stated, "You haven't asked him if he did it. Ask him. Are you afraid he is going to confess? Never mind, I'll ask him."

Piti, unsure of his client's guilt, held up his hand to stop Lincoln. "I don't think that's a good idea."

But Lincoln had already stepped back into the visitation room and seated himself across from Mack Oliver. Piti hesitantly followed.

Lincoln leaned forward, caught Mack Oliver's gaze and held it firmly. "Mack Oliver, did you kill Tiffany Miller and Jodi Wallace?"

Tears began to roll down Mack Oliver's face. "No, man. I didn't kill anybody. You know that."

Piti looked at Mack Oliver with defeat and added, "Mack Oliver, if we plead your case, I may be able to get you life in prison. If we don't, I fear that with the evidence that is present, the jury will convict and recommend the death penalty for you. I'm sure the judge will then sentence you to death."

"What do you mean, plead my case?"

"We would have to admit that you're guilty."

"I'm not guilty. You want me to admit to something I didn't do? I'm not going to lie. I didn't do it."

Lincoln looked on as Piti stated again, "I think it is an uphill fight, with the odds against you."

Mack Oliver turned to Lincoln. "Linc, what do you think?"

Piti looked at Lincoln, regretting that he had ever allowed him to join him.

Lincoln believed Mack Oliver was innocent and didn't think that he deserved to spend another hour in jail, but was reluctant to answer. This was Mack Oliver's life, but he was the closest thing Mack Oliver had to family. That's why he was there. That's why Mack Oliver had called him, he thought. Both his parents were gone. Mack Oliver had no brothers or sisters, or any extended family that anyone knew about. Lincoln felt that Mack Oliver was his opposite. They were born near the same time and grew up in the same culture, but Mack Oliver had pulled the short end of the stick in every way. But he had a pure heart. Piti would never understand, most wouldn't. But Lincoln did.

Mack Oliver caught his eye again. "Lincoln, what would you do?"

"It's not my life, Mack Oliver."

"But what would you do? What would you do if it was your life? If you were accused of crimes you didn't do and was in jail for them? Would you just say you did it? Because I'm homeless I should say I killed people that I didn't kill? Lincoln?"

Lincoln looked at Piti and then at Mack Oliver. As soon as he looked at Piti, Piti knew what Lincoln was going to say. Lincoln grimaced and his jaw tightened. His eyes focused. He showed glimpses of the anger he kept bottled up, but rarely expressed. He looked deep into Mack Oliver's eyes and said, "I would fight."

His firm answer, however, wasn't as confident in his head because he knew that by the time Dr. Farah returned, Mack Oliver would have deteriorated to the point of not being able to assist in his own defense. He explained to Piti what would happen to Mack Oliver's mental status, but Piti couldn't imagine it getting any worse.

Piti suggested taping Mack Oliver – having him answer questions and hoping it would be admissible. Although Mack Oliver wouldn't have been subjected to cross examination, J. B. might make an exception and allow it, considering the circumstances.

Lincoln, though, had another idea. He knew that Mack Oliver's best hope was for the real killer to be found. He had studied the thoughts and behaviors of sociopaths and criminals. He was no private investigator, but he knew that he had to find a killer that no one else was looking for.

Piti remarked in a defeated tone, "Mack Oliver, I need to ask you more questions. You're going to have to concentrate. We'll get the medication soon, but we need to get your story as soon as possible so we can start your defense. Let's start with Tiffany Miller. You said Tiffany was your girlfriend What do you mean by that?" Piti asked, positioning the tape recorder between himself and Mack Oliver.

"You've never had a girlfriend, Mr. Pitman?"

Pitman sighed, "Okay. Where did you meet?"

"We met in treatment at the Catherine Fairchild Center. We've been together five years – well, were together five years. We had an apartment, but when my momma got sick, I moved in the house with her because I had to take care of her. I tried to keep the apartment, but I was never there, so me and Tiffany decided to just move in to my mother's house. But my mother died last Christmas."

"What did you do then?"

"We stayed at the house. My mom left it to me. I was now the man of the house. It felt funny being in charge. My mother had enough money to buy the house, from the insurance money she got when Mack died."

"Mack Oliver, what was your father's full name?"

"Mack Oliver Purifoy Senior."

"Your mother's?"

"Dorothy Ann Purifoy."

"What was your address?"

"Twelve-oh-one, Eleventh Avenue South. We were doing good, but we had to sell the house."

Lincoln, who knew Mack Oliver's background and believed in his innocence, felt that Mack Oliver and Piti were acquainted and would be fine together. He interrupted the questioning and told Mack Oliver to keep talking. He reminded him that Piti was there to help, and that he was sure everything would be fine. As he left, Piti stepped outside the room with Lincoln, where Lincoln informed him that he was going to see what he could do about the medication and return some phone calls at his office. He asked Piti his thoughts about going over the psychiatrist's head, but Piti said that he'd get nowhere with the chief and the jail administrator. He told Lincoln he'd had many clients at the jail and had dealt with similar roadblocks.

But Lincoln had another idea. He suggested getting an appointment with Peyton Castelle.

Piti remarked, "You know him?"

"Well, kinda."

"Yes, he's black. That's good," remarked Piti.

Lincoln told Piti he'd call him tomorrow, and left the two alone at the jail.

He went to his office and returned calls, retrieved Mack Oliver's medical record and reviewed it for any possible clues. He called Mayor Castelle's office, and was told that the mayor would return his call and likely schedule an appointment for the following week, January fourth.

Piti returned to the room with Mack Oliver to resume his questions, and had to interrupt Mack Oliver in song. He was singing a verse over and over that Piti didn't recognize.

"Mack Oliver?" Piti looked around, making sure he wasn't talking to someone else. "Are you up to continuing? I have just a few more questions."

"Sure, man, I'm fine. This is better than being back there."

Going back to his yellow legal pad, Piti asked, "You were saying that you had to sell your house. When did this occur?"

"Last March."

"When did your mother die again?"

"Last December, the day after Christmas."

"So, you were in the house with Tiffany for three months?"

"Yes."

"So you sold your house in March. That's the month Tiffany Miller was found murdered, wasn't it?"

"Yeah, man. Somebody killed my girl. She went back out, started using drugs. We got too much money. But I can't blame her – I used, too, when my momma died. I went back into treatment for a little while. Then I was fine. But she started getting itchy once we got that money. Next thing I knew, she had spent all our money. All that money, up in smoke. Gone"

"How much did you get for the house, Mack Oliver?"

"Man, they gave me ten thousand dollars cash." Mack Oliver was obviously impressed with the sum, but Piti thought it sounded extremely low for that part of town.

"Mack Oliver, why did you sell your house?"

"Had to. But that's okay; I got a lot of money for it."

"You had to?"

"The city was eminent domaining it. They bought a lot of houses."

Piti scratched a note to follow up on the sale of the house and the eminent domain issue.

"Well, where did you go when the house sold?"

"We stayed there for a couple of weeks, then went back to the streets. We sold the house on the third of March. The money was gone by the thirtieth. Tiffany was killed the next day."

As he was answering the question, Piti thought that when you got past Mack Oliver's appearance and the awkward looks and gestures he made because of Haldol deprivation, he seemed intelligent, forthcoming and likable. But Piti was a little scared. He had witnessed Mack Oliver upset and, without the benefit of Lincoln calming him down, he didn't know if Mack Oliver would flip out again or not. And Mack Oliver was sweating more than Piti. Piti knew he sweated because he was fat, but he didn't know why the slim Mack Oliver was sweating so much, and in December. He certainly didn't like the way it made him look. Piti decided to ask his questions more rapidly.

"Mack Oliver, how did you find out about the death of Tiffany Miller?"

"I went looking for her that morning. She had left that night and didn't come back. We had found a vacant house that was for sale the night before that still had the power and water on. She was excited, but she didn't show back up. That morning, I went looking for her. Everyone at the fountain said she was dead. Man, I just broke down. I went to where they said she was, but she was already gone. They had already taken her away. She didn't deserve to be treated like that. They put her behind a dumpster. I gave her momma my whole April check. I wanted to bury her right. She was a good girl."

"Check?"

"I get a disability check for my schizophrenia."

"Anybody see you at the house, Mack Oliver, the night Tiffany was killed?"

"Well, we were hiding. We didn't want anybody to know we were at the house. That's breaking and entering, man. But Cynthia and Cassius came by for a little while."

"Who are Cynthia and Cassius?"

"They lived with us for a while at my mom's house when she died."

"Why didn't you mention their names to the police?"

"I don't mention my friend's names to the police."

"Where are they now?"

"I don't know."

"What are their last names?"

"Cynthia Bates and Cassius Carey."

"Did the police ever ask you any questions about Tiffany?"

"No."

"Did anybody ever talk to her family?"

"Not until now. They're telling them that I did it."

"What will her family say?"

"I don't know. Somebody killed her. They might think it was me."

"Who do you think killed her?"

"She might have owed somebody money for drugs, or it might have just been a sick dude. But she was real sweet. We called her 'Dimples.' I don't know how anybody could have done that to her. She never hurt nobody. She'd give you anything. She just couldn't leave that stuff alone, those drugs."

"Mack Oliver, the police say she was a prostitute. Is that true?"

"No, man, she wasn't a prostitute. She just did what she had to do. It was the drugs."

"You were together sexually the day she left?"

"Yes."

"You ever hit her?"

"No."

"Were you jealous that she was sleeping with other men?"

"No."

"But you said she sold her body. You weren't jealous or angry?"

"No. It wasn't like that. It was the drugs. She was a good person."

Piti looked at his notes of the time line and the fact that there were motile sperm present from three donors, one of which he was now certain was Mack Oliver. Tiffany's and Jodi's bodies were found within one hundred feet of each other. Both had been strangled and assaulted with a wine bottle. But Mack

Oliver's story was plausible and sincere. Piti was surprised to find that he believed him.

"What was the reason you were on the Southside the night Jodi Wallace was killed?"

"Everybody was there. People give you more money at Christmas. We all hung out at the fountain. There are a lot of artists there, and people treat you better over there."

"How much money did you get that night?"

"I got forty dollars that night, man. It was a good night, except for this."

"Mack Oliver, do you ever drink wine, or any other alcohol?"

"No, man. I wouldn't touch that stuff."

"Why not?"

"I saw what it did to my daddy and how it made him treat us."

"What do you think happened to Jodi Wallace?"

"Probably the same dude that killed Tiffany."

"Well, I think that wraps it up." Piti packed his legal pad and pen into his worn briefcase, along with his tape recorder. "Mack Oliver, I am going to be checking in on you. Do you need anything? Cigarettes?"

"I don't smoke. I need my medication."

"We're working on it."

Piti knew he had his work cut out for him, but the evidence that connected his client was circumstantial. He had to follow up on the story of the selling of Mack Oliver's house and the eminent domain issue that just didn't add up. Piti had lived and worked in Birmingham all of his life. He knew every judge, lawyer and detective in the city. He had worked with Jack Connolly and Vincent Franks, who investigated the murder of Jodi and arrested Mack Oliver. He wondered how convinced they were of Mack Oliver's guilt? He decided he would give Connolly, whom he knew very well, a call. But first, he wanted to do a real estate search at the courthouse.

Piti had gotten energized about his case. He had not had a drink in three days and he wanted to make it this time. He had attempted to quit often, but had never gone this long. He stayed busy. He had been at the jail for three hours and now it was lunchtime. He grabbed a bite to eat from the corner hot dog stand and then made his way to the courthouse. He decided to drive this time. As Lincoln wasn't with him, Piti reasoned that there was no need to walk and try to impress anybody. His lunch consisted of three hot dogs – one slaw, one chili and one kraut – a bag of chips, and a large sweet tea. He ate one of the hot dogs and finished the chips while at the stand. He took two hot dogs with him to eat at the court house while he performed his search.

At the courthouse, the transactions of the sale of Mack Oliver's house were easy enough to locate. On March 3, Mack Oliver Purifoy sold real estate to Roy Ezell for the sum of $10,000. A search of Roy Ezell showed he had made fifteen real estate purchases within sixty days of that period, for a grand total of $450,000. The city had purchased the property three months later in June for $1.5 million dollars. Mack Oliver's property was sold for $75,000, probably $40,000 more than it was worth and a whole lot more than Mack Oliver received. Not a bad profit for Ezell. The address listed was in Nashville, Tennessee. Who was this lucky millionaire? Mack Oliver had said his property was "eminent domained," but Roy Ezell was not the City of Birmingham. He was just a private citizen from Nashville. Piti finished off his other hot dogs quickly, staining many court documents and his shirt in the process. He had leaned back in the rickety courthouse chair, thinking that the arrest of Mack

Oliver Purifoy might turn out to be bad not only for Mack Oliver, but for others, as well.

CHAPTER THIRTEEN

The Confession

Cassius's demeanor was different than it had been January 25. A full week had past since his last counseling session with Dr. Sam. In fact, he had changed drastically from their first meeting. The withdrawn person that avoided eye contact and was somewhat passive and regretful seemed, remarkably, to be replaced by a confident person with an exaggerated macho walk and a very arrogant aura. Cassius' lean frame, although not considered tall, seemed very powerful. He was compact with tight muscles, athletic and awkward at the same time. His handshake was extremely firm, and the firmness had progressed over the past several weeks while in treatment. His hands were wide, and powerful and rough. Cassius had well-groomed hair and a well-kept appearance and nice teeth. He appeared both confident and self-conscious. His eyes were a deep brown that hid the pupil, with barely any sclera showing on the sides of the iris. They were cold and piercing, but tried hard to connect.

Cassius was looking forward to his therapy session with Dr. Sam at 4:00 p.m. He felt she was the only person at the center smart enough to understand him. He knew many therapists before her had anguished at the thought of counseling him, and he had proudly reduced many to tears and fear. He felt Dr. Sam and he had developed a close relationship, and he had paid particular attention to his physical appearance that day. His attitude over the past several days was jovial, drastically changed from the past several weeks. This was Cassius' fourth try at inpatient treatment and he had never completed an entire stay.

Cassius' education, due to his mother's home-schooling, was much more advanced than his high school equivalency diploma indicated. He was well read with an advanced education in literature and history. But his innate intelligence led to his false perception of importance and his personality was laced with an aura of haughtiness. These traits, mixed with his antisocial behavior, had inevitably been a disastrous combination in past treatment attempts with inexperienced counselors.

The treatment centers he frequented were free of charge and devoid of any fluff and frills. Most were small, non-profit centers with limited budgets. The public funding and donations they received were just enough to provide the most basic of treatment, with many employing recovering addicts with limited training as counselors. Others who worked for such low wages were novices, recent college graduates and graduate students. Although they were very effective with most addicts, those like Cassius – with complicated mental health issues and severe addictions – were beyond their scope of expertise. In fact, they were beyond the expertise of most.

Lots of research had been done on addicts, producing plenty of literature, but often the research findings and the treatment practices at the poorly funded centers were not integrated. Cassius had slipped through the cracks. Mismatched treatment, frustrated therapists and his severe illness had him in and out of treatment for years with no progress.

The Atlanta Mental Health Center was not unlike the many other centers around the nation that treated the mental illnesses and addictions of the uninsured, poor and homeless. The patients did the cleaning and cooking. They slept on military-style narrow beds that were usually in rooms with several other patients. This at times could be helpful, as the patients provided each other support and supervision, but it could also be very hazardous. Background checks were not performed on the residents, and when the centers were astute enough to request medical records from previous centers, these frequently arrived long after the patient had departed – if they ever arrived. Consequently, each treatment episode was a new beginning between the counselors and patients.

The centers could rarely afford security and could not lock the doors, so ill intentioned community residents where these centers were located could access the buildings. Industrious patients found it easy to leave in the middle of the night without the knowledge of the night staff, which in most cases was one or two people at a time. The centers' scant funding and the population they served allowed them a pass when it came to serious expectations and scrutiny. But it was these treatment centers that treated those most involved with crime and the judicial system, the chronically homeless, and the most severely addicted.

Dr. Sam had joined the Atlanta Mental Health Center for this very reason. She was an advocate and a gifted clinician who could have worked anywhere for much higher wages. Her colleagues had often asked her why she worked where she did and treated this element of society – the poor, mostly black drug addicts. "Aren't you afraid? Especially working downtown?" She was as perplexed as to why they didn't understand as they were as to why she was there.

Cassius had come to the center on Christmas Eve. He was fortunate to be able to get right in without a wait. But because it was Christmas, most who needed treatment felt they would wait until after the holidays. The center often had a flurry of people seeking treatment in January after overindulgence during the holidays and the New Year's resolutions that followed. Cassius had not been able to eat breakfast or lunch, looking forward to his early evening session with Dr. Sam. He was on time, lathered in cologne, and presented his best behavior. He sat anxiously in the waiting area for Dr. Sam.

Dr. Sam was en route to the Atlanta Mental Health Center from a fundraiser across town. She found herself fighting the I-85 traffic to make it to the downtown center in time for her appointment with Cassius, her only appointment that evening. As she arrived, Cassius got quickly to his feet.

"Cassius," stated, Dr. Sam, somewhat taken back by his eager appearance, "come on in. And how are you today?"

"I am doing great, Dr. Sam. I feel much better. And how are you?"

"Just fine. I have heard good things about your progress this week from the treatment staff."

The Family Night conversation with Mrs. Carey had given Dr. Sam even more insight into her patient. There were also many challenges. Cassius had just under a month left in inpatient treatment. Only the most motivated patients continued their treatment after this period. Dr. Sam assessed that Cassius would need intensive treatment for some time. He was addicted to alcohol and crack cocaine, and had admitted to using other drugs. He showed signs of post-traumatic stress, was antisocial – the depths of which Dr. Sam was uncertain – and Cassius had shown the initial signs of being one of her sickest patients.

At Cassius' last session, he was preoccupied with keeping what was bothering him a secret. Who did he want to hide it from? Dr. Sam did not think it was his mother, his only family member left, who seemed to be his chief enabler and thought he could do no wrong. His mother said he had just returned to Atlanta after a stay in Birmingham. What had been the catalyst for his entering treatment on Christmas Eve? What had he left in

Birmingham? What were his feelings surrounding the death of his brothers and his step-father? What were the circumstances surrounding his biological father that his mother had not mentioned? Cassius was unemployed and homeless. His issues were plentiful and complex and would require years of treatment to progress. But how long would he stay? What was his commitment and motivation this time? These were the questions Dr. Sam had about her new patient.

In the hour they had before them, Dr. Sam wanted to pick up just where they had left off the previous week. She had done a good job of creating a therapeutic environment in her small office. Cassius reclined in the side chair, relaxed, and put forth his most masculine and charming persona. He had put the last session far out of his mind and was unprepared for Dr. Sam's initial questions.

"Cassius, last week we talked about the loss of your younger brother. Have you thought more about that since our last discussion?"

"No, not really." Cassius looked away.

"No? Last week you said that the thoughts were giving you trouble and kept you awake at night."

"It comes and goes," responded Cassius. "Last week was one of those times."

"What tends to make you think about it?"

"Times like now. Something might remind me of him, people bringing it up, like you."

"Last week you wanted to get something off your chest and we ran out of time. I want to give you the time you need to talk about that night. The night your younger brother, Isaac, died."

The charm and the laid-back attitude had disappeared from Cassius' demeanor, but he was coaxed very effectively by Dr. Sam's style. After a pause, he proceeded hesitantly. "I was having one of those weekends. I had a job here in Atlanta. I was doing pretty well. I was a carpenter apprentice. The wood – the shaping, sanding, the pounding, making something out of nothing – was nice. I really enjoyed it. Hours could go by and my mind would be totally clear and at peace. The carpentry required great precision, which meant I had to concentrate, and that took my mind off of everything else. And I think the noise from the saws and the hammer drowned out every other noise that I had in my head. I don't know, the Reverend had set me off, as usual. Always criticizing, always putting me down. He'd graduated from the seminary, you know. They called him the Reverend Doctor. He thought he was big shit. Thought he knew everything about the Bible, like God had put him in charge. Day and night, every day, he preached mainly about me and my older brother and made little cracks about how he had saved us, gave us a home, and made my mother respectable. He didn't think we could pick up on it, but I knew what he meant, and so did my mother. He was such a damn hypocrite. On the one hand, he preached forgiveness. On the other hand, he criticized and condemned my mother. You know, always preaching about fornication and having children out of wedlock."

"How did you know that was about your mother?"

"Come on, I could see through that shit. He always suggested that her having us out of wedlock was wrong. Every little thing we did, he said it was sin. God was displeased with what my mother had done. He compared us to Bathsheba and David's children."

"Bathsheba and David?"

"They're in the Bible. He said God cursed their children because of David's and Bathsheba's sins. I guess me and Mark Antony were supposed to be cursed. My mother just went right on. She never said a word - never raised her voice, never disagreed. Just went about being the dutiful wife."

"Did you resent that?"

"I don't know how she could sleep with a man who thought she was trash. Who thought her kids were a mistake and never should have been born."

"So it made you mad?"

"Yeah. Real damn mad. I mean, we were fine before him. She thought we needed a father. Maybe we did, but not him. He bought us a nice little house. He said we didn't appreciate him. Made us call him 'Father.' My mother served him like he was a king, calling him the Reverend and her pastor. She cooked every day, three times a day, and brought his food to him. She tucked his napkin in his shirt. She brushed his hair, pulled off his shoes and rubbed his feet every day. She even ran his bath water and washed his back every damn night. He said all of that was in the Bible; that was what she was supposed to do. I never found that in the Bible, but the Reverend said it was there. That Bible was something. All he did was complain. Complained about her, us, every damn thing. But he put on a good show on Sunday. She should have left, but she just took it. Mark Antony hated him, though. And he hated Mark Antony, too. Mark Antony never would call him Father. He used to preach about Mark Antony; the homosexuals this, the homosexuals that, it's an abomination, a sin."

"Was Mark Antony gay?"

"Who knows? Maybe. The Reverend said he was. Maybe the Reverend was gay. Everything that happened to my brother, the Reverend said he deserved it and was being punished. On Sunday, though, he would get in the pulpit and preach like he loved us."

"Your older brother went to prison, your mother told me."

Cassius had tears in his eyes that he wasn't about to let fall, and obviously was emotionally affected by the thought of his brother going to jail. "He was innocent. He spent three years in prison for something he didn't do." Shaking his head, he said, "The Reverend seemed happy. He could say he was right about Mark Antony. The wages of sin. He kept preaching about it, over and over."

"How did your mother take it?"

"She took it hard. We went to the prison every weekend to see him, just me and her. The Reverend never went. But my mother never said a word to the Reverend about what he had said about Mark Antony. Never said a word to him. Not to his face anyway. You know they said he stole a car. No one saw him take the car. No fingerprints. He had never been in trouble before. The police said since he had the fireworks that were inside the car, he must have stolen it. But we were together that day. We found the fireworks on the side of the road. He was only seventeen years old. They would have sent me to prison, too, if I had been old enough. They just came to the house one day and got him. He never left jail from that day until three years later. He never said a word. Never complained. He was a good person. The Reverend didn't even allow him to move back into the house when he got out."

"How did that make you feel?"

"I hated him. I was angry every day."

"How did it make you feel about your mother?"

"I don't know." Cassius appeared uncomfortable with critical thoughts about his mother. "I don't know. I love my mother."

Dr. Sam was quiet, allowing Cassius time to process his thoughts.

After a moment, he added, "I don't know why she would choose him over us."

"What makes you feel like she made a choice?"

"She slept with him every night knowing how he felt about us." Cassius hesitated for a moment, then continued, "But after he had the stroke, she changed. She got stronger. I think she saw he wasn't God."

"Your brother died?"

"Yes, I watched him wither away to nothing. It gave the Reverend even more to preach about. The Sunday after my brother died, he preached about homosexuals again. That old abomination sermon, and the wages of sin is death, he loved to say. Everyone in the church 'Amen'ing. My mother sat there and cried. I've hated God ever since."

"Why do you hate God?"

Cassius contemplated for a moment. "Well, the Reverend worked for Him. He said he was chosen by God. If God liked the Reverend and would choose him, that's not my kind of God. He also let my brother die. He chose the Reverend over Mark Antony."

"What makes you think God chose the Reverend over your brother?"

"Because the Reverend lived and my brother died."

"What if the Reverend was wrong about God? Should you take his word about God, and who God is or what God wants?"

Cassius responded, "Maybe he could have been wrong about God the way he was about Mark Antony, huh?"

"What about you, Cassius? Was the Reverend wrong about you?"

Cassius didn't answer, and still had not directly addressed

the question about what happened to his younger brother. Dr Sam brought him back to that moment.

"We were talking about the weekend Isaac died. You said your stepfather criticized you."

"Yeah." Cassius shook himself out of his reverie. "I had come home excited about having passed my apprentice exam. It was on a Friday evening. I was telling my mother about how well I had done on the test. He just butted in, said that I was too smart to be a carpenter, that I should go to college and could do better. He said that was a dead-end job for dummies. We got into an argument and I left the house. My mother and Isaac tried to stop me, as usual. I went straight to the crack house and spent my whole check, and then started using credit when the money ran out. I didn't come home until the next night, Saturday, the same night the Reverend prepared for his sermons. When I got to the house, my mother met me at the door and ushered me upstairs. But I wanted to fight with the Reverend, so I went back downstairs. I remember seeing my mother and my little brother watching television. The Reverend was in his study; the French doors open, him behind his big desk with his Bible and his pen and paper, looking over his glasses. When he saw me, he rolled his eyes with the same disgust he used to look at Mark Antony with. So I asked him what he was going to preach about tomorrow. He said the prodigal son, a story about a son who defied his father and had to lose everything and eat with the swine before he learned better. But his father was a good Christian man and welcomed him home. I knew he was talking about me, but I said, 'You know, I wish you had discovered that sermon before you put my brother out.' The Reverend was angrier than I had ever seen. He didn't like being challenged. He told me to get out. He started swearing uncontrollably. It looked like he was going to have a stroke then. I just laughed. I went out again for more crack, more and more all night. Borrowed more money. Sold my carpentry tools. I probably used more that weekend than I ever have. Maybe I was depressed. I had been thinking about Mark Antony and my real father."

"Do you know who your biological father is?"

"No, my mother never talked about him. I never pushed. I didn't want to hurt her. But there was always someone in the neighborhood who wanted to tell us about him. Inevitably, we would hear wisecracks about who he was. But if he didn't want to be part of us, I didn't want to be a part of him. I couldn't help thinking, though, how different my life might have been without the Reverend in it and I had been with my real father. By Sunday night, when I returned home, I was out of my mind. I remember very little about that night. I've tried over and over again to recall the whole night, but I can't. I remember coming in and thinking I was there to stay. But again, something came over me and I had to go back out. My mother, though, had had enough and was trying to keep me home. The Reverend wasn't there, so I promised my mother that I was going to stay in. She went back to bed. I tried to sneak out and Isaac heard me. We were in the kitchen. He just popped out of nowhere. He was trying to keep me in. I was trying to get to the door. I remember his little hands holding my coat as I left. When I returned that night, the cops were everywhere and my brother was dead. The Reverend swore I did it. My mother told the cops that when I left, he was fine. She said he fell down the stairs and bumped his head. He broke a rib and punctured a lung. The Reverend said I was angry at him and killed Isaac, that I had resented my brother because of him. I loved my brother. But I did resent the Reverend. Things were never the same after that between the Reverend and my mother. He threw me out after that and I could never return to the house. I don't think I could have killed my brother. I just can't remember. Maybe I lost it. I don't know.

I went into treatment after that. My first time. I thought I had had enough. I thought I would never do drugs again. After a while, the reason I thought would make me never use again – the death of my brother – was now the new reason I had to use."

"Was there a police investigation?"

"The Reverend asked them to look into it. After they talked to my mother, they weren't that interested."

"What about the coroner's report?"

"What do you mean?"

"Your mother said the report said his injuries were inconsistent with a fall."

"I don't know what that means."

Samantha noted that Cassius showed few signs of grief about Isaac's death.

"How do you feel about your brother's death? Do you blame yourself?"

Quiet for a moment, Cassius responded with a barely audible, "Sad. And yes, that's true, I blame myself."

But Dr. Sam's mental note was that there might be other issues keeping him up at night. It didn't seem to be the death of his younger brother.

"When did you return home?"

"Many years later. The Reverend had had a stroke, and my mother was caring for him. She wanted me to come home. I was hesitant about returning for a longtime. I didn't want to take care for him, not after the way he'd treated us."

"But you did go home."

"My mother needed the help. But he was no different than he had been before. In some ways, he was worse. He seemed angry that he was in that condition. He would mumble and still condemn everyone. He talked about Isaac every day. I knew he did it to hurt me."

"Why do you feel that his every action he took was an affront to you personally? Could he have legitimately missed him?"

"I doubt it. You don't know him like I did. Even with his right side paralyzed and him drooling all over himself, he still thought he was better than everyone else. My mother continued to wash him and feed him. I guess it was no different for her. That was all she had ever done in the past anyway. Well, maybe it was even a little better for her."

"Why do you feel it was better?"

"She was just so content – wiping his mouth, wiping his ass, reading the Bible to him all day. It made me sick to watch."

"Did you still hate him?"

"Yes, even more. He was still punishing us. I think he enjoyed making us clean his ass. His left hand wasn't that bad off."

"Your mother said you were there when he died."

"Yes, I was."

"How did that make you feel?"

"What do you mean?"

"I mean you were there when your stepfather died. Your mother said he choked to death. To watch a person die like that – how did it make you feel?"

"I don't know."

"You don't know?"

"What are you looking for?"

Dr. Sam pressed him now. "What is the truth about how you felt?"

Cassius seemed relieved to confess to Dr. Sam, "He got what he deserved. I was glad. He tormented us for years and he had no sympathy when Mark Antony died. He finally got what he deserved. Are you satisfied now, doctor?" Dr. Sam sat quietly, and after a moment, Cassius added, "I know what you're thinking."

"What am I thinking?" responded Dr. Sam.

"You're thinking, 'I wonder if he did it.'"

"That's interesting the way you put that, Cassius."

"I didn't do it. I didn't kill him. I just didn't save him. He was eating like a pig. I let him eat." Sarcastically with a slight smile, he added, "When he started choking, I just didn't know what to do. And when the choking sent him into cardiac arrest, I was really stumped. I don't know Heimlich or CPR, so I just panicked and couldn't even dial nine-one-one, not fast enough anyway. But I managed. But when they arrived, there was nothing they could do. Now, that doesn't put you in any compromising situation, does it, doctor? I know that we have patient-doctor confidentiality and all. I didn't tell you I was going to harm someone or myself, and I didn't tell you I committed any crime, so are we okay?"

Cassius was enjoying turning the tables on Dr. Sam. Dr. Sam's questions had made him feel uncomfortable and vulnerable, and he was desperately trying to restore a power balance. He had worded his comments very carefully. Dr. Sam showed no signs of intimidation. Her calmness impressed Cassius, who had effectively learned to use intimidation to get what he wanted.

She responded, "So after your stepfather died, you moved away?"

"Yes, I did."

"Where did you go?"

"Birmingham. I got a job there as a carpenter. I got in treatment, too."

"Cassius, you only have a little over three weeks remaining in treatment with us. I want to increase your therapy sessions with me. How do you feel about that?"

"You think I need a lot of help, huh?"

"I want you to be able to take full advantage of what we can offer you."

"More time with you? Okay. Sure."

"I think we are at a good stopping point today."

Dr. Sam's assumptions about Cassius' diagnosis of being antisocial had proved to be correct. His medical records from previous treatments still had not arrived, although most had rarely been helpful in the past. Samantha knew that Cassius' lack of insurance and indigent status limited him getting the intensive mental health treatment he needed. She wanted to take full advantage of having Cassius at the center and wanted to maximize the short time he had left. She had effectively masked her shock about Cassius' comments and the fear she felt as he talked. The disturbed mental health of her patient was starting to unfold. She looked forward to Mrs. Carey's visit on Family Night this coming Sunday, February 5.

CHAPTER FOURTEEN

Downhill

Peyton Castelle had planned his career effectively. He had risen to the pinnacle of political power in Alabama through a combination of intelligence, charisma, and outstanding political acumen. He had worked for both Democratic and Republican administrations. Many said he was so effective because he lacked ideology. Peyton had no political agenda other than being elected. He wasn't so committed that a persuasive argument couldn't change his mind about any issue. "The Chameleon" many called him. He could bring his black supporters to tears with his civil rights rhetoric, and could even stir up whites with his message of self-responsibility. He was black and had to woo voters from both sides of the political spectrum to be elected. The slight majority of the voters in Birmingham were black, but many didn't vote.

The promise of jobs and opportunity was attracting more and more blacks to Birmingham, and, as they came, more and more whites left for the suburbs of Hoover, Homewood, Vestavia, Alabaster and Chelsea. They were on the verge of pushing the boundaries of metropolitan Birmingham to Montgomery in the south and Huntsville in the north. Peyton found himself in an unenviable position. He was the chief executive of a large, falling city. Like all others, it ran on tax revenue. The taxes were the city's fuel. It came from business and individuals. The size of that tax revenue determined how the city would look, what the police protection would be like, and the kind of schools it would have. Birmingham was losing its tax base. It was losing middle class whites and blacks. The population of Birmingham had dropped by one-third from the sixties to the present day. The businesses that were located downtown were leaving for other cities in proximity to Birmingham, where the population was whiter and richer. The result was a crumbling Birmingham with poor schools on academic watch, with crime among the worst in the nation, and where nearly half the city's homicides went unsolved.

Peyton looked much older than his fifty-two years. He had all the pressures of being in the wrong place at the wrong time. He was a compromiser, with no ideas of his own for the city, but a thousand ideas and initiatives that belonged to others. This lack of conviction left him trying to please everyone and had caused ulcers, depression and deep wrinkles. Still, the mayor managed to include a morning jog in his daily ritual. He was wound so tightly that he ran three to four miles each day. He gave the appearance of being a very busy man. His calendar always full. He was, however, a likable man. He had no position that people could find to dislike him for. Unfortunately, he legitimately saw all sides of an issue.

That particular January 4 morning, just days following the funeral of Jodi Wallace, he was wound tighter than he had ever been before. As he ran through the city, he counted the vacant buildings that had been left by businesses moving over the mountain, one after another. Most of the steel mills had shut down some time ago. The city was rising to the top of every bad list and sinking to the bottom of every good list. He had watched how Birmingham, a once large and fast-growing city with promise, had fallen far behind its neighbors, such as Atlanta and Nashville. The largest, most prominent city in Alabama was on its way to not being the largest city and losing its dominance.

As he approached the Southside, his pulse accelerated even more than the brisk run was responsible for as he ran past the alley where Tiffany Miller and Jodi Wallace were murdered. He lost his breath and had to cough to get his rhythm back. He made a left off 20th Street onto 11th Avenue South and passed the Storyteller Fountain. The homeless were already huddled around the fountain at just after six o'clock. It was so cold that morning the wind was cutting to the bone. The mayor wearing shorts, was wound so tightly he felt nothing. The more than one hundred murders that had occurred in Birmingham during the past year had become an acceptable and ugly part of the reality of inner-city living. Fifty-four of the one hundred and five murders in Birmingham were unsolved that year.

Many whites of every ilk had broadly supported Peyton. His landslide victory included Blacks, Whites, Jews and Gentiles – mainly because of Draper Wallace, who liked Peyton's form of politics, easily influenced and pandering to big business. He also felt the city's image needed improvement. The old image of Alabama was bad for business. Many of his critics predicted the rise in crime and the state of the schools if he were elected. They were right in the sense that the Castelle election was an avalanche in the slide of Birmingham, but the problems were due to the abandoning of the city by the white and black middle class and the businesses that followed them.

Peyton, who had desperately sought his job, wished anyone else had it on this cold morning. Although no people in passing cars or walking pedestrians said anything, Peyton felt as if they were throwing eggs from the cars and the pedestrians were spitting on him as he ran past. He felt that he had let his supporters down; that he would be judged for the murder of Jodi

Wallace alone; that her murder would be his only memorable legacy. He was right that this event would define him. He took consolation in the fact that Mack Oliver was behind bars. He'd gotten a look at Mack Oliver in the courtroom and thought he was guilty. His anger at Mack Oliver the day of the arraignment was at the top of the list, behind Draper Wallace's. Mack Oliver was black, homeless, and a criminal, everything Peyton thought was the impetus for whites leaving the city. Why couldn't Mack Oliver have chosen a black victim? Why the hell did he have to choose a white victim? Why the hell did he have to choose Jodi Wallace?

Peyton's anger, however, was because he saw Mack Oliver's actions as threatening to his political career. This was the prism Peyton saw everything through. He had seen himself with a cabinet position in a presidential administration within ten years. Many had felt he was on the short list for Secretary of Housing and Urban Development. His future was in jeopardy, but he had to be careful. He had broad support in the black community. The community had long feared the police, for good reason. The attacks on him for being hard on the police and the label of being too liberal had helped him in that community. But he was in a jam. If this had been any other person, he could blame it on the senseless violence that most major cities were experiencing. But he couldn't trivialize Jodi's death and offend Draper Wallace. The key to white support was Draper. If he lost him, he lost the support of the country club elite, their money, and their votes. If he went too far on police crackdowns on the Southside and downtown, he would be seen as folding to the fears of bigots and he'd lose black support.

This particular morning was also worrisome because Lincoln Drake had asked for an appointment to see him. He had thought about letting him talk to an aide, but Jefferson Drake,

Lincoln's father, had been an ally. He wanted to maintain his support, which was critical in the black community and among country club whites that Jefferson knew oh so well. Peyton was also familiar with the story about the grocer that Jefferson had helped to bankrupt. Lincoln had told the mayor's assistant that the topic was Mack Oliver Purifoy, an inmate at the city jail awaiting trial for murder, who didn't have access to his medication.

The mayor had chosen 21st Street on his route back to City Hall from the Southside, to take advantage of the downward slope and to avoid the heavily traveled 20th Street. As Castelle headed downhill, his thoughts were of his optimistic views when he was first elected to the mayor's office and the path his career had taken. He was now planning his exit strategy and salvaging what was left of his political career. Regardless of his best efforts, the city was in decline by any objective measurement. However, he – like all politicians – put a positive public spin on issues that he knew had no positive aspects.

In politics, your deftness at the game determined who would win and who would lose. His public persona of Birmingham was unflappable, but privately he wept. Escalating crime, poorly performing schools, several city bureaucrats facing charges of accepting kickbacks, and two city council friends facing charges of conspiracy and corruption. Had he been complicit in creating this atmosphere at City Hall? He had long known about the corruption, as had his predecessors. Just like them, he did nothing. He accepted the graft as normal practice. The necessary nod and wink it took to get things done. He was unsure of how high the investigation would reach. He was certain he had not broken the law, but politics often aren't about truth, but rather appearance.

Lincoln Drake requested to meet Mayor Castelle as a last resort. He was at a loss. He had gotten nowhere with Dr. Farah at the jail concerning Mack Oliver's medication. Mack Oliver had decompensated to the point that he was experiencing a full-blown psychosis. He was hallucinating, ranting, and in his psychotic state was saying that he had killed Jodi Wallace. He was in isolation and on suicide watch. His legal defense had been unable to meet with him for the last week. When the psychiatrist returned, the medications would surely be given, Lincoln thought, but time was of the essence and a murder trial was looming. The jail administrator and the police chief both reported to the mayor. Lincoln thought a phone call from the mayor to the jail would get Mack Oliver the medications.

Lincoln was on time for the 7:30 a.m. meeting. As the mayor's assistant escorted Lincoln to the mayor's office, Castelle had slipped on a royal blue, cotton jogging suit over his shorts and sweatshirt. The pants had a white stripe down the outside of each leg and the jacket had a white stripe down the outside of each arm. The word "Mayor" in white letters was embroidered on the left side, just over the heart. Castelle was drinking coffee, black. He would not have breakfast that morning. He looked much older than Lincoln had remembered. His hair was now gray, but he still possessed the campaign poster looks and disarming smile.

As Lincoln entered the office, Castelle removed his bifocals and came from behind the large, African mahogany desk that had been overtaken by mounds of paper. The office looked worked in. Lincoln had always been impressed by the mayor's accomplishments. He was someone Jefferson Drake liked because he had worked hard, not made excuses, pulled himself up from a challenged youth and background, had finished college and become a major political player. Jefferson had spoken highly of him and Lincoln had grown up with Castelle as one of his role models. Peyton served in the legislature, worked for two governors, and was now mayor. Many thought he would go on to Washington.

As Lincoln greeted him with his right hand outreached and the customary, "Good morning, sir," the mayor opened both arms, embraced Lincoln and said, "I was so proud of you when you received the donation from the country club at Christmas." After pausing for a moment and smiling, he added, "But what do you think that Gala cost?"

"My dad said a couple of million," Lincoln responded quickly.

"A couple of million for one party, on one night. It must be nice." Both chuckled. "I haven't had a good talk with you since you were a kid. You look just like your father. You're a good-looking fellow. Your father has kept me up to date on all your great accomplishments. So, you decided to come back and live among us country folks?" the mayor said jokingly. It had been twenty years since they had seen each other. Lincoln was a teen-ager. "How's your father?"

"He's fine, mayor."

"And your beautiful mother?"

"Just fine."

"I need to get over there and see them. It's been way too long." It had been three years since he had visited their home. It was during the campaign. The last time he'd had a conversa-tion with Jefferson was at the mayoral inauguration. "Sit down, Lincoln. Tell me more about what's going on."

"Mayor, let me thank you first for agreeing to see me. I know you're busy."

"A friendly face does me good every now and then, Lincoln. Don't see many from this position. Everybody is mad at me about something."

"Sir, I wanted to talk to you about Mack Oliver Purifoy. He is being held in the City Jail."

"Yes, I'm familiar with him." Just hearing the name of Mack Oliver Purifoy caused the mayor's blood pressure to rise. Lincoln took note of the animosity he heard in the mayor's voice and his angry face. "That fellow is being held for the murder of two citizens."

"Yes, he is. The reason I wanted to talk to you is that his medication is being withheld pending an evaluation by the jail psychiatrist."

"What's the problem?"

"She happens to be on vacation and won't return for another week. Mr. Purifoy's trial is approaching. His lawyer can't meet with his client to discuss his defense."

"Lincoln, what's this got to do with you?"

"I know Mack Oliver and wanted to talk to you about this on his behalf. Mack Oliver has a mental illness and without medication is incapacitated. Considering the circumstances, he is being denied a fair trial because he won't be able to defend himself."

"Lincoln, I'm not a doctor or a lawyer. That's an issue for them. I am here to protect the citizens. This man has been arrested for killing two people. People are leaving Birmingham for his actions and those like him."

"But we don't know if he did it or not. That's what the trial is for, sir. If he did kill those people, he should be punished. But wouldn't you agree that the only way to know what really happened is to have a fair trial?"

"Everyone wants a fair trial, but I'm not going to get involved with what the psychiatrist does. I'm sure she is just trying to be extra careful. Remember, we have had an investigation, an arrest, and an arraignment. He's being held without bond because of the circumstances. We'll have a trial soon, in less than two months I understand. My getting involved in this case could only make things worse. I'm everyone's mayor, Lincoln, even those who didn't vote for me. I have a responsibility to this city. It needs tax revenue, and that comes from businesses and people. What would you have me do, forsake all for one homeless man? A vagrant, a murderer? Well, an accused murderer."

"You know, mayor, it wasn't long ago that there were other citizens whose rights just didn't matter, who were expendable. Protecting someone like Mack Oliver protects us all. I remember when you were the one making that argument."

"I remember, too, but things are a whole lot different from this vantage point. Things change."

"Mayor, what have we come to? I remember when we were the people who despised the cronyism, the greed, the injustice. We were the people left out of the board room, the political decision-making. We were the throwaways, the unimportant. The homeless are just the latest in the lexicon. It means the same thing. I remember when you ran for office – the ideas you espoused had everyone so optimistic. You say you're everyone's mayor. What about the homeless? If you want the businesses and the residents to come back, you've got to do something about this problem. You can't just wish they would go away. You need a substantial strategy. Those around you telling you to turn a blind eye are not serving you well."

"Son, I haven't thrown you out yet in deference to your father, but who do you think you are that you can come in here and talk to me like that? You have no idea what it takes to keep this city running. We're giving millions of dollars to programs for those people."

"The people you give the money to, do they even have to prove the money gets to the poor? Have you ever walked inside Jasper Thrash's shelter you're giving a million dollars to? Are you concerned about the rumors of where the money is going?"

"Lincoln, the people don't want it. They don't want their money being spent on people that won't go to work and help themselves. I work for them."

"I wonder where we would be if other leaders in the past only gave the people what they thought they wanted? Doesn't government have to protect the rights of those who are powerless? Shouldn't you be their voice? Shouldn't you want to make us great, not just give us what we think we want?"

Their voices could be heard outside the office and Teresa, the mayor's long-time secretary, had ushered everyone to another office. In twenty years, she had never known Mayor Castelle to show such emotion.

"Lincoln, that's naive. The city government, the judicial system, and the economic powers are at war. There was a time when all three worked together, as fingers on the same hand. With the population becoming more and more black and electing leaders who look like them, a rift has occurred. Now, you have city government in conflict with the judicial system and the economic powers that drive the city – a clash of cultures. Your vision, my vision; I just don't know if we'll ever get there. I hope we get there." The mayor looked around his office at all the memories, and then out his window that overlooked downtown. "Lincoln, you know this city almost never happened. There was a cholera epidemic that nearly wiped it out at its birth. Then, the Jim Crow laws, the civil rights demonstrations, the dogs, the hoses, the bus boycotts, the bombings, the National Guard at the schools just to ensure that blacks could get an education. Those things almost killed it during its adolescence. It's had a rough birth and a rougher upbringing. Maybe she's all grown up now. She's a little different from what some of us hoped she'd be. Maybe she's outgrown me. Maybe she's outgrown a lot of us."

Peyton Castelle had given up on Birmingham. His actions were what he thought was best for him in the long run. His reputation had only been hurt by becoming mayor. His term had weakened his chances of getting a cabinet post. His dream of being addressed as Mr. Secretary was fading. He was depressed and half listening to Lincoln's tirade. If he had heard him, his ego would have cut Lincoln off about ten minutes ago. Whatever ideas and ambitions Peyton had for Birmingham were long gone. He was going through the motions. He resented those he blamed for derailing his dreams. His anger now aimed at Mack Oliver Purifoy. Castelle thought he represented the crime, the ugliness of the city that he was being blamed for.

The murder of Jodi Wallace had drowned another story that appeared in *The Birmingham News* over the Christmas holiday season that would have surely made the front page and the evening news were it not for her death. Part of Peyton Castelle's preoccupation during Lincoln's visit was with the news that the FBI was going to investigate the veracity of the charges made by the newspaper. *The Birmingham News* had informed him that a follow-up story would be run the next day. Longtime Birmingham journalist, Jacob Levin, had reported that two city councilmen, close allies of Peyton Castelle, and three bureaucrats linked as supporters of Castelle's, had accepted bribes from a construction contractor, Long-Hinkley, who had renovated several city office buildings at what were thought to be inflated prices.

Long-Hinkley Construction was a competitor of the Wallace Corporation, and one that would learn of the uncanny luck of the Wallace Corporation firsthand. Many suspected that the anonymous leads about the corruption were the work of the Wallace Corporation. The paper never named Castelle as a recipient in any bribe. However, in most cases, when describing the individuals involved, it described them only as a friend of Mayor Castelle's, a person close to Mayor Castelle, an associate of Mayor Castelle, or a supporter of Mayor Castelle. The trips, the cash, the property that had allegedly been given to the officials – it was all so blatantly corrupt that Peyton would bear the brunt of the criticism. But his troubles had only begun.

CHAPTER FIFTEEN

Lunch at the Drakes

Birmingham had settled into a cold winter by mid-January. Two weeks had passed since Lincoln last saw Piti. Both men had visited Mack Oliver during that time, making sure he was getting the care he needed and talking to him as much as was feasible about any additional information he had thought of that would be helpful for his defense, but nothing significant ever came out of these visits. Castelle made the phone call to the jail to release the medication. Mack Oliver had started to get his daily doses of Haldol and Cogentin, and Dr. Farah and Lincoln had met and reconciled.

Lincoln felt frustrated as time ticked away, while Piti searched for Roy Ezell for two weeks. He tracked him from one job and residence to another. He'd lived in Mississippi, Georgia, and Tennessee, all within one year. He needed help in finding Ezell, and his friend Connolly had agreed to meet with him. Maybe he could give him some advice on how to locate Ezell. Piti was hoping he could persuade Connolly to find him. Lincoln thought this was an interesting development, and without any other direction to go in, he thought Piti's obsession with Ezell was just as good as anything else and was the best thing they had for now.

Piti had no office and worked out of his car and his house, where he lived alone. His small cottage was in a nice area in the suburb of Homewood, but his house stood out because it was not well kept. Graying and flaking paint, once white which was now at least fifty years old. Overgrown grass and the hedges grown up to the windows. The windows were cloudy and dusty, not allowing much sunlight in. That day, Piti and Lincoln agreed to meet at Piti's house because Piti's car was not working, an all-too-common occurrence. Piti also knew that if he got Lincoln over, he could get a ride downtown for his lunch meeting with Connolly at his favorite restaurant, John's.

As Lincoln arrived in the neighborhood, he was surprised that Piti had chosen such a quaint little area. The neighbor's houses, although small, were all well kept with yards that showed that the people who lived in the houses cared. But as Lincoln pulled up to Piti's house and saw its state of disrepair, he thought, *He is definitely a redneck.* But Lincoln was fond of Piti. The two were going to compare notes and assess their progress. Making his way to the door, Lincoln soon discovered that the inside of the house was worse, despite Piti's attempt to tidy up. The house was overcome by newspapers, files, and at least a month's worth of empty Chinese takeout containers and pizza boxes. There was a fishbowl on the mantle with two fish that resembled swimming cockroaches. However, Piti was very polite and hospitable. Lincoln cleaned an area to sit on the worn brown couch, the fabric completely worn off the arms, and the two began to talk.

When Piti mentioned Mack Oliver's two additional roommates, the names sounded vaguely familiar to Lincoln. Where had he heard those names before? He made a note of the two names and placed the note in his pocket to check on later. They concluded their two-hour meeting and Lincoln agreed to take Piti to his noon meeting at John's, but he had a meeting of his own.

Jefferson and Genevieve had invited him over for lunch, something the family did monthly. Lincoln was looking forward to seeing his parents. Genevieve was preparing chicken salad, her own recipe that included pecans, raisins and pineapple. Genevieve boiled her chicken, only the white meat, and diced it in very large chunks. She served the chicken salad over a bed of pineapple wedges and lettuce with club crackers. The dish was Lincoln's favorite, and he would be on time.

The antique wooden table was formally set in the kitchen with a combination of fine china and rare porcelain delftware that had been an anniversary gift from Lily McPeake. It was a large room, with a row of five floor-to-ceiling windows allowing lots of sunlight into the space. The large round table sat in a nook. The back porch and well-manicured back yard were visible through the windows. In the summer, the windows framed the blooms of the hydrangea bushes and lilies that circled two oak trees that Lincoln said reminded him of his parents. Genevieve also had a small garden where she grew her own vegetables. She grew peppers that she used to make extremely fiery pepper sauce, which suggested her Cajun heritage. Jefferson preferred the sauce that way. Her cupboard was stocked with at least twenty Mason jars of it. She grew cherry tomatoes for salads and large tomatoes that she stewed and fried. Mint grew in thick bunches; it was used as a garnish and for her mint tea, another of Lincoln's favorites. The aroma of the garden was heavenly in the spring and summer.

Jefferson, who had been at work since 5:00 a.m., had come home for this monthly tradition. He had more time now to do this sort of thing. He remarked that the club was much different now than when he first started there, less pomp and circumstance. The new crowd wore golf shirts and shorts. The ties and jackets for lunch and dinner that were once required every day were now only required on certain days and special occasions. But the old money still preferred to dress up, clinging to the old traditions. Most of the members were also less demanding and with less discriminating tastes. Jefferson had added pizza and meatloaf to the menu. His job, too, was now less demanding and him having it less of a novelty. He, too, missed the old days.

Genevieve still went to the McPeake estate weekly. She was still on the payroll, but she only oversaw the other domestic help. Her primary role now was to keep Mrs. McPeake company. She continued to be the one who took Lily shopping, and accompanied her on occasions such as the funeral of Jodi Wallace. Jedidiah had left Jefferson a sum of money to make sure his wife was cared for properly and never forgotten. He said the children would put her in a retirement home and forget about her. He didn't want his wife to have to leave the home she loved until she died. Jefferson hadn't wanted to accept the money, but McPeake had insisted. He told Jefferson that he wouldn't be around and this was advance payment. He said his children – although millionaires, because of him – would be too cheap to pay Jefferson. Jefferson accepted the money and kept his word, but never disclosed the amount to anyone. The money given to Jefferson by McPeake had caused a rift between Jefferson and J. B. that had taken years to mend.

Jefferson was reading his morning newspaper as Lincoln and Genevieve laughed and talked. He broke the laughter with, "Lincoln, another one of your homeless people is in the paper today." Lincoln had not read the paper this morning, he read the evening paper. His father read both.

"Did you see it?"

"No, sir, I didn't."

"Here in the Metro section, the city's first murder this year, Jasper Thrash. Found in his house bludgeoned to death. He had probably been there a week. The neighbors smelled something. They hadn't even missed him at the shelter. Didn't you know him?"

"Yes, kinda." Lincoln, perplexed, thought to himself, *This can't be linked to the other murders, can it?*

Jefferson had turned the page. Moments later, he said, "I sure hope Peyton isn't mixed up in this stuff that is going on with these bribes and Long-Hinkley Construction. They are giving him hell in the paper, though. Jacob Levin has an article about it every other day. Somebody down there at City Hall has got to be feeling pretty nervous. The FBI is investigating. Some people at the club already think they've got the goods on them. Jacob has really made something out of himself – like you Lincoln."

As soon as Lincoln heard Jacob's name, his mind started to think about his childhood friend. Although the Drakes lived in Mountain Brook and he had gone to Mountain Brook High, they still lived in a carriage house and the people in Mountain Brook stayed clear of Lincoln. The only family that had invited him to their house and treated him like an equal was the Levin family, a Jewish family. He had been sure they knew how he felt. Jacob also spent hours at the McPeake's with Lincoln and had dinner many an evening in the carriage house with Lincoln and his parents. They had considered each other best friends. He had thought of Jacob often, but their schedules had not permitted them to spend time together or even to speak to each other for five years, not since Lincoln first returned home and they had enjoyed a brief reunion. They were still fond of each other.

The Drakes were also fond of Jacob, and Jefferson had especially liked Jacob's father, Eli, because he was a Jewish man who had succeeded in Alabama. Jefferson respected people who overcame great obstacles and didn't make excuses. But Lincoln also remembered that his father had forbidden him from playing with Jacob at the club, although he was probably the only kid whose parents hadn't forbidden him from playing with Lincoln. Black and white children playing together had made some members uncomfortable, even if it was Jefferson Drake's kid. Jefferson told Lincoln that some guests had complained. The atmosphere of the club was perfectly orchestrated – Jefferson had helped to make certain of it.

The Drake lunch lasted about an hour and Lincoln and Jefferson were both on their way back to work. Genevieve meticulously cleaned her kitchen and placed the leftovers from lunch in neat containers in the refrigerator for Jefferson's dinner. Uncomfortable with sitting for long, she poured herself another glass of mint tea and began to prune her indoor plants.

* * *

Piti was just settling into his lunch across town with Connolly. Connolly had nibbled on a club sandwich and mostly listened to Piti talk about Roy Ezell and the eminent domain issue. He watched as Piti finished a lunch of fried chicken, mashed potatoes, collard greens and fried okra, and many glasses of sweet tea. Piti was not surprised to hear that Connolly was not 100 percent convinced that Mack Oliver was the assailant, but Connolly told him that was not unusual. But, he added there were no other suspects. There was more on Mack Oliver than anyone else they knew and the evidence they had on him was enough to convict many others. The odds that it wasn't him were very small. Piti had intrigued him, however, and he also wanted to find Roy Ezell. Connolly knew that Wallace would not want any stone unturned.

Piti told Connolly, "I've looked everywhere for this guy and I can't find him. He's lived in Mississippi, Tennessee, and Georgia. He's had half a dozen jobs."

"Maybe he doesn't want to be found," remarked Connolly. Then calmly he added, "But we can find him. If he's on earth, we can find him."

Piti did not give the names of Cynthia and Cassius to Connolly because he saw no significance. Connolly and Piti's meeting had been off the record. Connolly told Piti to give him one week and he was sure he'd know the whereabouts of Roy Ezell.

Connolly asked, "Jasper Thrash, you've worked with him, right?"

"Yeah, the shelter guy?"

"Found him dead yesterday. Bludgeoned at his house in Norwood. It's in the morning paper." Connolly unfolded his paper and placed it on the table in front of Piti.

"Shit," was Piti's only comment.

"First one of the year," remarked Connolly. "He'd probably been there a week. The neighbors smelled something. His dogs wouldn't stop barking; two black and tans inside."

Piti imagined the scene of Jasper Thrash's morbidly obese body lying unfound for over a week, with two unfed hound dogs cooped up inside.

"I'll call you in a week or so," said Connolly as he left.

Piti finished the article and then read Jacob Levin's article about the Long-Hinkley Construction bribes.

The New Year Begins Like the Last Ends: Birmingham's First Murder of the Year Linked to Homelessness

Jasper Thrash, homeless shelter operator, was slain in his home in the Birmingham suburb of Norwood. Police found Thrash in his house after neighbors had complained of barking dogs and an odor. The sixty-year-old Thrash was apparently bludgeoned to death. The murder weapon, a baseball bat, was found beside the body. The authorities stated that the body had probably been there a week or more. He had not been reported missing. Shelter workers reported it was not uncommon for Thrash not to report to work for weeks at a time. He may have known the assailant, according to authorities. There were no signs of burglary and nothing seemed to be missing from the house. Thrash's wallet was still in his pocket. Homeless men from the shelter are being questioned. Violence in Birmingham continues to climb, with particularly brutal murders, and Birmingham is now among the top ten cities for homicides. One hundred and five murders occurred in Birmingham last year. The last was allegedly committed by a homeless man, Mack Oliver Purifoy, who remains in jail for the murders of Jodi Wallace, the daughter of billionaire Draper Wallace, and Tiffany Miller, a homeless woman. Both crimes committed on Birmingham's Southside. The trial is set for February 25.

FBI Investigates the City Government and Long-Hinkley Construction

The FBI continues its probe into possible bribes related to city construction contracts. Long-Hinkley Construction, which was hired by the city to complete renovations of the city's administrative offices, is being questioned on the extremely high cost of the renovations and the inferior quality of the work. Experts

> estimate the city was charged at least three million more than the renovations were worth. Those close to the investigation report that three city bureaucrats and two councilmen, supporters of Mayor Castelle, are under investigation. Indictments are close, according to one source. Many wondered why Long-Hinkley Construction was chosen over Wallace Construction, whose bid was 25 percent less than Long-Hinkley's. Two longtime city employees have been placed on administrative leave. Castelle's administration has been dogged by rumors of corruption and incompetence since he took office. Castelle denies any wrongdoing or any connection to the investigation at City Hall. His approval ratings are the worst of any mayor in the city's history going into an election year.

The editorials in *The Birmingham News* were scathing of the Castelle administration. A teacher who had visited the downtown shelter at Christmas with church members called Jasper Thrash a great Alabamian who had dedicated his life to serving the homeless. "This is a great sin that a person like this would die this way. That someone who had given so selflessly to the poor would be slain in his own home and left there with dogs for over a week is sickening to me. The egregious lack of gratitude and immorality shown by these people, who are surely the perpetrators of this crime, exposes a moral decay that seems to have permeated the City of Birmingham. The Castelle administration has ruined the schools and run off businesses and now hard-working, decent people aren't even safe in their homes."

A banker wrote that he admired the courage of the articles

by Jacob Levin, who exposed the corruption at City Hall. "This utter lack of respect for the law and base greed will be the destruction of the financial stability of Birmingham. Legitimate business will not participate in such a corrupt system. Taxpayers will move to areas with more trustworthy city governments. The creditworthiness of this city will plummet and its inability to acquire low-interest money will bankrupt it. I have never written an editorial before and this will be my last for this city. I, too, am leaving."

CHAPTER SIXTEEN

The Family Secret

By the first week in February, many more patients were at the Atlanta Mental Health Center. With the holiday season over, many had found their way to the center with hopes of changing their lives. This Sunday evening drew their hopeful families as well. Betsy Carey arrived early, and there was barely enough room in the dining room to hold everyone. It was the middle of winter and the food was especially heavy. Cassius squirmed during the long prayer, given by the crying minister grandfather of a patient. Mrs. Carey wore a black dress and white pearls with a white handkerchief with intricate lace pinned to her right chest and a small silver ornamental wreath with the word "Usher" engraved on it pinned on her left chest. She remarked that it was her Sunday to usher and this was her usher dress.

February being Black History Month, the patients had prepared skits that were acted out to perfection. With the right opportunities, Dr. Sam thought many would have been excellent thespians. The few white families and patients in attendance appeared uncomfortable and unsure of how to respond. Eventually, they were stirred up by a first-week patient, Leon Allen, and his rendition of Martin Luther King's "I Have a Dream" speech with "We Shall Overcome" being sung at a whisper in the background. Everyone had goose bumps and many were brought to tears and to their feet. It set the tone for the evening and motivated other patients to try and top Leon's performance, with their readings of Marcus Garvey and Malcolm X. One female patient could even hit the high notes of Mahalia Jackson. Many family members wanted to speak with Dr. Sam. There was never enough time.

Cassius was more guarded that night, but with all the excitement and ample female family members to keep him preoccupied, Dr. Sam was able to have some time alone with Mrs. Carey, who was eager to resume their conversation. Dr. Sam was anxious as well because Cassius lived among other patients and her staff and she needed to know if he was dangerous. The parolees and those on probation, regardless of their past crimes, were usually more compliant than any other patients, the threat of prison tempering their behavior. The criminal who had no experience with the judicial system was much more unpredictable. Cassius had never been arrested. She had discussed Cassius' case with her senior staff and administration superiors, but she had wondered all week whether Cassius was a parricide killer or a bragger. She hoped Mrs. Carey was what she appeared to be and not a mother who had suppressed the knowledge of Cassius killing her five-year-old son and her husband.

With very proper and polite speech, she greeted Dr. Sam, "Dr. Sam, it is a pleasure to see you again. The program tonight was outstanding and so educational for the patients. Their eyes are filled with joy and excitement. I am so proud."

"Thank you, Mrs. Carey. It is good to see you again, as well. Is this your first talk with Cassius this week?"

"Oh no. He calls every time he's allowed to use the phone."

"And how do you think he's doing?"

"He was troubled at the beginning of the week. He was carrying on about the Reverend. He has never said such things to me. He said I should have left the Reverend, that I should not have taken him out of school, that I was overprotective and controlling. Me? I gave my children everything. I gave them all of me. What more could I have done?"

Noticing that Mrs. Carey was emotionally affected by Cassius' phone calls and accusations, Dr. Sam allowed Mrs. Carey time to process her own questions. Moments went by as they heard the choir sing songs that helped to conjure up latent emotions.

Dr. Sam asked, "Mrs. Carey, did you ever talk to Cassius about his biological father?"

"Oh, as much as I thought was appropriate. I wanted him to develop a relationship with the Reverend."

"Did the Reverend want that?"

"I wanted to protect my boys. They were special. It wasn't their fault. It wasn't their fault. I had to protect them. They had so much going against them. When Cassius met you I was so hopeful. He had never talked about anyone the way he talked about you. You can do what I couldn't. Don't you understand, Dr. Sam?"

The deep anguish in Mrs. Carey's eyes was a look Dr. Sam had seen before. She knew intuitively what Mrs. Carey was about to share. Turning to grasp both of Dr. Sam's hands in her hands and looking into her eyes to the soul, Mrs. Carey whispered to Dr. Sam, "Mark Antony and Cassius' father was my father."

Dr. Sam sank on the inside to the point where she heard no other sounds. She could feel and hear her own heart pound in her chest, feel her blood circulating through her body, and feel the hum of her inner ear.

"I had to protect them. Who else did they have? They could never know. You are the fourth person on earth to know. My father, my mother, me and now you. Both my parents are gone. This is between me and you and the Lord now."

Before that moment, Dr. Sam could have thought of no scenario that could have explained Mrs. Carey's denial and blind protection of Cassius. She now understood perfectly. This mother had sacrificed all to try and cleanse herself of her guilt and her perceived sin. She was the victim of the ultimate betrayal by her father and mother. Nothing would allow her to betray Cassius. Tears began to flow down the cheeks of both women as they embraced. At the end of the night, Dr. Sam looked over the sea of families interacting and talking to the mental health center staff. She pondered the deep complexities of all their family issues, and what twist of fate had brought them to the Atlanta Mental Health Center.

CHAPTER SEVENTEEN

The Wiregrass

After lunch with his parents, Lincoln returned to his office, but he was only able to go through the motions of work, as his mind was on one patient, one being held on double murder charges at the Birmingham jail. The one he felt powerless to help. He had been so effective, he thought, in helping others. Had he been fooling himself? How could Piti come close to beating Billy Penick with a hanging judge like J. B. McPeake running the trial? Did Piti even know the law? Piti was smarter than him he thought, though. At least Piti knew they couldn't win. Lincoln couldn't help but think his own arrogance had pushed him into thinking they could.

Lincoln leaned back in his office chair looking at the ceiling, swiveling his chair from side to side. He was surrounded by numerous awards, citations and diplomas, and all the right books that should adorn the office of someone of his accomplishments. He'd read them all. He was supposed to be smart. He leaned forward and put his elbows on his desk, crossed his arms, and put his head down for a moment.

Then he remembered the note that he'd written the names of Mack Oliver's roommates on. He reached into his pocket and read the names aloud: "Cynthia Bates and Cassius Carey." Then he called for his secretary, loud enough for her to hear him through the door, electing not to use the intercom. "Pam?"

She quickly came to the door. "Yes, sir?"

"Check and see if we have medical records on these people." Pam took the note and quickly retrieved the medical records on the two. "Thank you, Pam."

He reviewed Cynthia's record first. She had completed inpatient treatment May 1 of last year. She had entered treatment on April 2 addicted to crack cocaine and had attended support groups sporadically since that time. He closed the record and opened the very thin record of Cassius Carey, who had been admitted to treatment April 2 and discharged April 5. He had been addicted to crack cocaine and alcohol, and had stayed only three days before he self-terminated treatment. He thought he vaguely remembered Cynthia and remembered seeing the medical record of Cassius. He knew now why the names had sounded familiar.

Lincoln closed the records and called to Pam once more. "Put these away, please. I have a meeting across town that will keep me out of the office for the rest of the day. I will be late in the morning. Do I have any appointments?"

"Not until after lunch."

"Cancel those too, please." Pam, who knew Lincoln well, looked as though she had figured something out. "I'll see you tomorrow," Lincoln said.

Within moments, Lincoln was on his way to Highlands Bar and Grill, located in Five Points South adjacent to the Storyteller Fountain, with 11th Avenue South running east and west between the two. He would make the drive through downtown Birmingham in his vintage Mercedes roadster, a college graduation gift from Jefferson that had once been owned by Jedidiah McPeake, and park on 19th Street. Highlands was on the corner of 20th Street and 11th Avenue South. Although there was ample parking in front of the restaurant that night, and the restaurant offered valet parking when there was not – which most patrons used regardless – Lincoln parked two blocks away. He wanted to walk the route that would bring him past the spot where Jodi Wallace and Tiffany Miller were slain. The dumpster that had hidden Tiffany's body was still there.

Lincoln did not remember meeting Tiffany Miller, but she too had taken advantage of the free drug treatment and mental health counseling offered to homeless people at the Catherine Fairchild Center. As he looked at the spot of her death, he wondered how their paths might have crossed in the hallways, dining rooms, and classrooms of the facility. The spot where Jodi Wallace's body had been found was still lined with bouquets of flowers. Lincoln walked the alley several times before continuing his journey toward Highland's. He faced the reality of how unlikely the odds were for one person to be dating one of the victims, and for the same person to be last seen with the other victim, and for both bodies to be within one hundred feet of each other. The arrest of Mack Oliver made sense to him now. But how was Mack Oliver involved in these murders?

He emerged from the dark alley facing the Pickwick Hotel on 20th Street between 10th and Magnolia Avenue, and headed south toward 11th Avenue. There would be many homeless people and other pedestrians congregated on the corner. He came to the corner, made a left, and crossed over to the north traveling side of 20th Street. There sat the Storyteller Fountain in the middle of Five Points, the area so named because it was the exact point where five streets and avenues converged. The roads seem to be pointed in every conceivable direction.

The fountain had been sculpted by a local artist, who combined the anatomies of humans and animals to reveal the kinship between animal and human behavior. A bear's head on a dog's body, a rabbit, a turtle, a dog, and frogs, and other animals all in a semicircle facing a figure that had a goat's head and feet but a human body and hands, who seemed to be reading a story to the other animals. Although the sculpture had nothing to do with the occult, many not familiar with the artist thought it did and the sculpture attracted all kinds of admirers. Some had the darkest of dyed black hair, black nails, black mascara circling their eyes and dark clothing. Others with mohawks and tattoos, and every conceivable part of their bodies pierced. Some were probably students from local colleges. There were wood and iron benches surrounding the area and many homeless people sitting and standing there, some selling paintings or any other items they thought they might get money for. Others were just sitting there and starring into space.

As Lincoln crossed the street, many recognized him. They yelled his name repeatedly, "Linc! Linc!" He waved a hand as he headed toward the entrance of Highland's. He used to be able to see Mack Oliver play his saxophone through the window, but that night Mack Oliver was missing, replaced by two drummers, each with a single Cuban-style drum, both appearing to be homeless, one black and one white. The passersby obviously did not think they were very good, as their box had only a dollar in it that was probably their own to encourage others to chip in. The Storyteller Fountain was in view from Highland's windows with Highland United Methodist Church its backdrop. There would be dozens of homeless men and women in Five Points that night, Lincoln's favorite part of Birmingham. He didn't feel like he was in Alabama, as Five Points was rich in varied culture. The neighborhood had attracted the artist, the activist, the homeless and many good restaurants and bars, including Lincoln's favorite – Highland's.

The staff at Highland's recognized Lincoln. He was a regular. The restaurant's food was superb. He was seated near the windows where he preferred, and started the evening with their oldest Macallan, his favorite single malt scotch. He ordered it neat and it was served in a thick, beveled glass that felt good in his hand. The drink was much needed and he finished it quickly. The attentive waitress was back with another before he finished the last sip. Her timing perfect for Lincoln, that night anyway. He ordered the filet and a bottle of one of the house's select wines. Although he had not been cognizant of it before, he noticed that there were many black people in the restaurant, but he was the only one not working there. His eyes visited each table. The patrons were among Birmingham's most affluent citizens, and waiting outside the window were their exotic foreign cars. Yet fifty feet from his window gathered the poorest citizens of Birmingham. The patrons in Highland's easily spent three hundred dollars per table for their dinner that evening, yet those huddled at the fountain in the forty-degree weather in the middle of winter had not seen that much in a month.

He had never felt more appreciative of Frank Fleming's Storyteller Fountain. The kinship between human and animal behavior seemed indistinguishable. Lincoln was taken back to the time he first encountered a homeless person, as a young boy of ten in Dothan, Alabama. He had begged Jefferson and Genevieve to let Jacob Levin accompany them to Dothan for their summer vacation. Jacob had asked them as well, and both had pleaded with the Levin's to let him go. The Drake family had been in Mountain Brook for only two years, and Jefferson had purchased his first Cadillac. Jacob, who never left city living, was mesmerized by Lincoln's stories of country life and adventure. Jacob had never seen a cow, a horse or a pig up close. He was about to see them everyday for a week.

Lincoln credited the trip to Dothan for the career path he ultimately followed. Grandma Drake lived in Dothan with many uncles, aunts and cousins. His grandmother had lived through the Depression and two world wars. She had, for the entire time Lincoln had known her, worn a cloth soaked in menthol around her waist. She had developed pleurisy from exposure during the Depression and thought it was the only thing that alleviated the excruciating pain. She also had rich tales that Lincoln loved to hear, such as when she and her family lived in a Hoover Hotel for more than six months during the Depression. Lincoln later learned that a Hoover Hotel was a cardboard box the poor had to use for housing – aptly named after President Herbert Hoover. Grandma Drake would forever loathe Herbert Hoover.

For as long as Lincoln could remember, Passion Drake had also left food on her screened porch for the hobos, another habit that developed from the Depression. Whatever was prepared for dinner for the family on Friday, Saturday and Sunday nights, travel nights for the hobos, was served on a tin plate, along with a beverage, usually lemonade, and placed in an iron pail with an iron lid over it. She then kept the porch light on, letting them know this was a friendly house. The hobos that passed the house on their train journeys on these travel nights found refuge at the Drake's. Monday through Friday evenings were workdays, but Friday night through Sunday night, they stopped and claimed the meals. On Sunday night, the workers were arriving in Dothan seeking the work on the peanut farms in the wiregrass country. On Friday and Saturday night, they returned to the distant cities they had left. No one was allowed on the porch after the food was set out. Grandma Drake thought it robbed the travelers of their dignity if you sat there and stared.

Awakening on the scorching hot plains of south Alabama in July, Lincoln and Jacob spent the morning chasing chickens and riding goats. Then, filled with watermelon, pomegranates and persimmons that Grandma Drake had grown herself, the boys were sitting on the porch when they heard Lincoln's cousin, Andy, yell, "Linc! Jake! Do you want to go jump the tracks?"

"Jump the tracks?" Jacob asked.

"Yeah, come on!"

The three boys started running as fast as they could down a field of graze land, just outside the back door of Grandma Drake's croft, toward the distant whistle of a locomotive engine. Andy, two years older, led the way, with Lincoln and Jacob close on his heels.

"Hurry, we're gonna miss it!" Andy cried out. "Run! Run, Linc!"

"Come on, Jake," Lincoln said.

All of them were laughing, although Jacob didn't know what was in store for him. They could see the train now as they ran down a ravine through sparse wiregrass. It was traveling just slowly enough for Andy to put his left hand on the latch of the open door of a freight car, just out of sight of the engineer and climb in. Andy pulled Lincoln inside and then Jacob, who was by then equally excited and terrified. If his parents knew, they would surely never speak to the Drake's again. Even Jefferson and Genevieve didn't know about Lincoln jumping the tracks.

The boys all yelled, "Whoohoo! Whoohoo!" They were impressed with themselves for miles, looking out the open door at all of the sights – pastures, farm houses, herds of livestock, lakes, distant communities – the three taking it all in. Jacob was in awe. They exited the train car when they saw something they thought irresistible to explore.

The trains that ran through Dothan were constantly arriving and departing, with Dothan being the peanut capital of the world. After the cotton crops were decimated by boll weevils in the early 1900s, the farmers of the wiregrass country started planting peanuts, as the sandy soil was perfect for growing them.

Dothan eventually came to produce over 65 percent of the United State's peanuts and the seasonal farm workers that planted and harvested the crops got to Dothan any way that they could. Dothan was equidistant from Atlanta, Jacksonville, Mobile and Birmingham, four hours south of Birmingham by car and near the Florida panhandle. The tracks ran in all directions.

All of Jefferson's family were farmers. Grandma Drake had picked cotton, peanuts, and velvet beans all her life. She grew her own food, made her own clothes and all her children's. She loved Dothan, and called it "God's Land." The name Dothan, found in the book of Genesis, meant "The Well." Jefferson called it "Wiregrass Country." Jefferson loved this part of Alabama. It was his home. He said that people from the Wiregrass were strong and survivors. He also loved Dothan because he was so proud of its rich heritage.

The black scientist, Dr. George Washington Carver, who was the honored guest at the First National Peanut Festival in 1938, developed over three hundred uses for the peanut. His inventions changed the region forever, making many very rich, and Dr. Carver a celebrated scientist among southerners, both blacks and whites. His success was the only proof the young Jefferson needed to realize that greed was a much more powerful emotion than racism. This fact Jefferson would take advantage of the rest of his life.

As the freight train glided over the plains, the boys were having a hard time deciding which intriguing site to explore. They finally agreed on a creek that was probably a finger of the Chattahoochee River.

"Jacob, are you ready?"

Jacob unaware of what was about to happen, answered, "Uh, yeah."

Andy threw Jacob from the train, then Lincoln, then he

jumped last. However, Jacob was unprepared and tumbled farther. He'd be ready next time. Andy had visited this spot often and Lincoln a couple of times. But, Jacob had never seen such a thing. They caught frogs and turtles, skipped rocks, and waded in the water up to their knees. An excited Jacob suggested swimming; and, although Andy and Lincoln wanted to, they resisted, as the water would turn their skin ashy white and possibly give them away to their parents. They had to keep their adventures a secret and the ashy skin would cause a lot of questions. Andy knew exactly how long they could stay before the returning trains became less frequent, although there had been times in the past when they had lost track of time and had missed the early trains. They had to get back before dark. That day they had pushed it, probably because they were with Jacob and having too much fun. But, like clockwork, a return train appeared in the dusk. The boys ran along side the train, and again Andy pulled himself up into an open freight car, then Lincoln, and lastly Jacob. This time, however, their giggles were interrupted by a cough, and, as the boys carefully turned around, the lighting of a cigarette.

The match illuminated a dark corner of the freight car, revealing two men. Andy whispered, "Hobos." Andy told Jacob and Lincoln firmly, "Turn around." He grabbed both by the shoulders, one in each hand, their shirts bunched up and held tightly in his hands. He said, "Don't look back."

The three boys looked out the door of the smoothly gliding, slow moving train. The only noise was an occasional cough, and the smell of the cigarette which reminded the boys that they were not alone. Jacob was trembling and Lincoln was ready to jump, but Andy in charge. The train rumbled along for twenty miles or so until the pastures behind Grandma Drake's croft came in sight. Andy jumped, holding onto Lincoln and Jacob. This time, they all tumbled hard, as Andy had not looked for a particular spot for their landing. Still holding them, he said, "Don't run." When the train was out of sight, he said, "Walk fast." Their hearts were still racing when Andy said, "If you ever see one of those hobos by yourself, run."

"But Grandma feeds them," Lincoln said.

Andy said, "Those are the nice ones. Some of them will kill you." Then firmly, he said, "Do you hear me, Linc? If you see them, you better run."

Jacob only had to be told once. He was convinced. He would run at first sight. As the boys approached the farmhouse, Andy said, "Never tell anybody about this. My daddy will kill me quicker than those hobos."

Lincoln's first experience with the homeless was one he would remember for the rest of his life. His experiences on the plains of the Wiregrass, with Grandma Drake feeding the homeless and the hobos on the train, were the events that more than any others, had directed Lincoln's journey and forged his attempts to bridge the polarized views of those who shared the values of Grandma Drake and those who were driven by fear, like his cousin Andy.

CHAPTER EIGHTEEN

The Good News

Piti and Lincoln had talked off and on as Piti prepared his case, but another two weeks had passed before Lincoln saw Piti again, as both were busy with their work and investigation. It was now the first week of February. According to the jail staff, Mack Oliver spent most of his time singing, but today had been an "outstanding day," Piti told Lincoln on the phone. He had called to arrange their meeting. Lincoln, too, was very excited about the news he was about to share with Piti. He thought it might save Mack Oliver's life.

The February day was icy and only twenty degrees at noon. The wind, though, was tame. There were no clouds in the sky, revealing a distant sun. The gray, dusty downtown even seemed calm, except for Piti, who was leaving the courthouse in his smoking and puttering, once yellow, but now faded to an indistinguishable color, 1974 Monte Carlo. Driving recklessly in and out of traffic, he thought, *I am going to be somebody.*

Although it had taken a full week longer than he told Piti it would to find Ezell, what Connolly and Franks found had Piti in an anxious fit. He couldn't wait to talk to Lincoln. Piti had demanded they meet at John's again. It was a place he thought brought him luck. Arriving early, Piti nestled into his favorite booth, happily speaking to everyone who walked by. He had been alcohol-free for over one and a half months; however, his weight was increasing as he ate even more, but attempted no exercise.

Becky, who had waited on him for years, could hold out no longer and had to ask, "Piti, what are you so happy about today?"

Piti, about to bust, released an uncontrollable giggle. He was bouncing his legs up and down rapidly on his tiptoes as he sat, wringing his hands.

"Just a beautiful day, Becky, that's all. Just a beautiful day," he replied, smiling from ear to ear.

"Uh huh." Becky raised an eyebrow and gave him a skeptical look, knowing there was more to it than that. "What you gonna have, Piti? Are you waiting on someone?"

"Yes, I'm waiting on someone. The doctor. You know – tall, black."

"Yes, I know him. I'll look out for him and bring him back when he arrives. You gonna wait on him before you order?"

"Well, is Mrs. Beulah cooking today?" asked Piti.

"What, do you have a special request, Piti?"

"You could say that."

Upon Lincoln's arrival, Piti was eating his favorite meal: a fried chicken liver sandwich with sautéed onions and a deep pink piquant sauce made of ketchup and mayonnaise. As Becky led Lincoln to the table, Piti licked his fingers. He had been kind enough to order one for Lincoln. Chicken liver sandwiches weren't Lincoln's favorite, but he didn't want to insult his new friend. He jumped right in and seemed to enjoy the meal, although he passed on the creamed corn and smothered scalloped potatoes. Both started to talk at once as soon as Lincoln was seated, but Lincoln yielded and Piti went first. It was clear that Piti just couldn't wait any longer.

"We're onto something big."

"What?"

Piti's fat hands squeezed his coveted chicken liver sandwich, carefully prepared by Mrs. Beulah. His sandwich was the only thing competing with his anxiousness to get his story out.

"Connolly and Franks. They found Roy Ezell. Roy Ezell!" Piti yelled, spitting small pieces of onions and chicken liver toward Lincoln. People sitting at tables nearby all looked towards Piti. Piti realized how loudly he had spoken and dropped to a whisper, looking both ways over his shoulders before he spoke again. "Roy Ezell – they found him."

"Where was he hiding?"

"He wasn't hiding. They thought he was at first. Hell, he's just stupid. He couldn't keep a job. He moved all over the place. Never had time to set up even a mailbox. They found him delivering pizzas in Nashville. He had a hell of a story." Holding up his left index finger, he gestured for Lincoln to wait a minute and took another massive bite of his sandwich, washing it down with a gulp of sweet tea. "Listen, he bought Mack Oliver's house for ten thousand dollars. He told Mack Oliver that he was from the city and that Mack Oliver had to sell. He told him his house was being eminent domained, and that Mack Oliver better sell right then or he'd get nothing."

"Ezell worked for the city?" asked Lincoln.

"No. He's no millionaire either. He's never had anything but delivery jobs, bus boy jobs, and service station attendant jobs. He showed up in Birmingham with half a million dollars and buys fifteen houses, then sold them to the city for one-point-five million dollars. He sold Mack Oliver's house alone for seventy-five thousand. But listen, that was the easy part. Connolly and Franks ordered a pizza from a hotel in Nashville and told the manager to send Roy Ezell because they were cousins and wanted to give him a big tip. Roy showed up, and when he saw Connolly and Franks, he wet his pants and told them everything. Get this," Piti concluded as he finished the last of the chicken liver sandwich, "Ezell, of course, wasn't the mastermind. He got twenty thousand for his effort and to keep his mouth shut. The old boy went to Biloxi and blew it in a week on quarter slots, blackjack and redneck hookers. If he wasn't so stupid, he would probably be dead, too."

"Too?" asked Lincoln bewildered.

"Well, hold on, I'll get to that. Listen, he told them that his cousin was the mastermind."

"His cousin?" Now Lincoln was even more interested, as he picked over the last remnants of his sandwich.

"His cousin's name is Ricky Luther, a petty thief and swindler with a record a mile long. He was in hiding up there. Connolly and Franks had the Nashville Police Department run his face on the local news as a person of interest in a crime. Some nosey neighbor ratted him out. When Connolly and Franks showed up, they said Luther seemed relieved."

"Relieved?" asked Lincoln.

"Yeah, that it was the police and not a hit squad."

"A hit squad? Piti, what the hell are you talking about?" asked Lincoln, whose nerves were now on edge. He wanted Piti to get to the point about Mack Oliver. But Piti was a lawyer who liked to develop a story.

"Hold on, doctor. This is two weeks worth of incredible lawyering and investigative work. Ricky Luther is the half brother of. . .you ready?"

"I'm ready, Piti."

"Jasper Thrash."

Lincoln leaned back into the worn vinyl of the old booth seat.

Piti, smiling, called, "Becky!"

"Yeah, Piti," she answered from across the room.

"Banana pudding. Want some, doctor?"

"Uh, no."

Moments went by as Lincoln absorbed the news. Piti helped to clean the table for Becky so she could deliver the pudding without interruption.

"Jasper hired him to buy the houses. Ricky Luther hired Ezell. This is enough to send them all to jail for fifty years, but that's not why Luther's hiding."

"Why is he hiding?"

"The bureaucrats at the city, the politicians, he knows everything. He knows where the money went - the million dollars a year Jasper got from the city. It only took three hundred thousand to run that shelter and that's at the high end. That's seven hundred thousand – minimum – every year. He knew who Jasper had to give the money to. Long-Hinkley Construction used him, too, to tote the money back to the crooks at the city that fixed the bids and got Long-Hinkley in. The bureaucrats trusted Jasper because he had played ball for so many years. He kept his mouth shut and delivered. Jasper brought in his brother, Ricky Luther, to add to the atmosphere of them all feeling like big-time players. Ricky, in those shit-kicker boots, biker glasses, Wranglers, a little fat belly that covered his oversized NASCAR belt, and his thug looks – he had the perfect redneck resume. From out of town, nobody knew him. Jasper played him up as 'The Enforcer.' Ricky was good. He helped Jasper deliver everybody's money. They all felt like spies and gangsters. Those articles in *The Birmingham News* about the corruption probably got Jasper killed. Somebody didn't want him to talk."

"The articles by Jacob Levin?" asked Lincoln.

"Yeah, him."

"He's a friend of mine."

"You know everybody, Lincoln, but that's good."

Piti's banana pudding had arrived. When he finished, he used his spoon to get every bit out of the corners, and eventually used his fat fingers to leave no traces of the pudding in the bowl.

"Luther also delivered the eminent domain scheme money the city paid to Ezell to Jasper and helped him deliver it to the crooks at City Hall. The whole one million dollars of it. Luther got fifty thousand and he's ready to name names."

"Why eminent domain?" asked Lincoln.

"The city crooks knew that the council was going to approve the city to buy property in Birmingham for the Wallace Corporation to develop. They were going to build condominiums. The mayor wanted middle-class folks to move back downtown. He wanted to increase the tax base and draw business back down there. The bureaucrats and a couple of crooked politicians wanted to buy up the property so they could make a little money for themselves. They couldn't use their own names and go and buy the property. That's illegal, of course, so they sent their old buddy Jasper Thrash. Jasper couldn't buy it because everybody would know that smelled funny. He's a homeless shelter operator with no money. So he got his convict half-brother, Ricky Luther, who nobody knew. But he was his brother and just as broke as Thrash, and a felon. A simple run of his Social would definitely alert the paper and your buddy Levin. Then, Luther had the bright idea to get Roy Ezell, a nobody. No one knew him. He's got no record, no history. No story. They dressed him up and no one paid attention. The property was bought from Ezell by the city at an inflated price. They all thought they had pulled off the crime of a lifetime. The mayor got his development property and gave it to the Wallace Corporation for a dollar. Wallace is building the condominiums and they thought all was well – until somebody killed Jodi Wallace and got Mack Oliver arrested. Mack Oliver in jail has made us overturn the stone about his house being eminent domained."

"Who knows about this?"

"Billy Penick knows, and us. Luther has a lawyer now, though, and like I said, he's willing to talk. But he wants immunity or some sort of reduced sentence. I think he'll get it. Billy and J. B. hate black corruption."

"Are all the bureaucrats and politicians at the city who are involved black?"

"No, some are, some aren't. And I know who."

"How does this help Mack Oliver?"

"Listen, if it wasn't for Mack Oliver, these guys might not have been found. We wouldn't have looked for them. They may not give Mack Oliver the chair if he's convicted. This may save Mack Oliver's life, man. But listen, there's still a better chance he's convicted than not, even if we think he's innocent."

"Well, that's good work, Piti. Good work. Congratulations."

"Well, shit, Lincoln. Don't be so excited," said Piti sarcastically. "Over one hundred homicides last year. Bodies are everywhere. Hundreds of assaults, robberies and burglaries – and now this. It's like the Wild West. Folks are coming unglued and we are in the middle of it," Piti said excitedly. "I remember now why I became a lawyer."

Lincoln couldn't help thinking, *Has the whole town gone mad, including Piti?*

He knew Piti was wrong, though, about the people coming unglued. Lincoln thought most of them had accepted the murders and assaults, the robberies, and the greed and ineffectiveness of the bureaucrats and the politicians. They had accepted it because it had happened gradually, in small doses over a period of time. As a psychologist, he had seen people live in and accept the most unimaginable conditions. Rape, incest, physical abuse, and torture. Most would reject this treatment if it just suddenly occurred, but in small doses over time, gradually they'd accept it. Piti looked at all this as an opportunity to prove himself, to exercise his great love for performing his profession. He had only known Mack Oliver for a little more than a month. Mack Oliver was only a client to Piti and Piti was right to keep his head and stay objective. Lincoln was close to Mack Oliver.

Lincoln could tell Piti wasn't drinking, although it was a subject they had only talked around, but Lincoln didn't want to push. Lincoln had watched as Piti was shedding the obvious signs of overindulgence in alcohol. He was proud of Piti and commented, "Piti, you look good. What are you doing?"

"Well, I haven't had a drink in forty days. I feel good."

"Great. That's great Piti. If you ever want to talk about it, I'm here."

A confident Piti responded, "Thanks. You've done more than you know. But what did you have to tell me?"

Lincoln hesitated to tell Piti of his discovery of Cassius Carey and Cynthia Bates, then remarked, "Nothing really. I just wanted to get together and get an update on Mack Oliver."

"Well, Mack Oliver tells me you haven't been to see him. Says he's called you several times. He really thinks a lot of you."

"Well, I've been really busy." Lincoln had been making excuses for not visiting Mack Oliver recently. In reality, he had felt powerless to assist Mack Oliver and was starting to think that optimism for the man was irrational and emotional. He also still felt great discomfort when at the jail, but he told Piti that he was planning to visit Mack Oliver that day. He needed to talk to him about Cassius Carey.

"Yes, I'm on my way to see Mack Oliver. I want to make sure he is still adjusting well to the medication. He did appear depressed during our last visit."

Becky interrupted the two. "Gentlemen, will there be anything else?"

Piti and Lincoln both replied no, and Piti added, "Please tell Mrs. Beulah that those livers were delicious." He turned back to Lincoln. "This news is going to hit the papers in a couple of days. The town will have more to talk about than Mack Oliver and Jodi Wallace. That'll help us. We start the jury selection soon. It'll be good to have Mack Oliver out of the papers. J. B. and Billy picked federal court to lessen the number of blacks in the jury pool. They think blacks are soft on crime. They wanted to send a message with this trial. They'll strike the few blacks that show. I'm going to try and keep as many revenge-minded rednecks off the jury as I can." Piti beat Lincoln to his pocket and bought lunch. Piti had a trial to prepare for, and Lincoln was on his way to the jail to see a depressed Mack Oliver.

As they parted ways outside the restaurant, Lincoln said, "Listen, Piti, I may be out of town for a couple of weeks. But if you need me, call."

"Where you going?" a startled Piti replied.

"Well, just personal business. I'll be in touch."

* * *

A few blocks away the district attorney's office was in the middle of a contentious lunch with the mayor's office. Billy Penick was accompanied by half a dozen of his assistants and the mayor had an entourage of lawyers. The two men had never gotten along, and it took that many associates to diffuse the situation and keep these meetings somewhat civil and productive. Billy had always distrusted the mayor. He honestly thought the mayor was corrupt, even though the mayor had never been convicted of a crime or even charged with one. Many at City Hall, some appointed by the mayor and many who were not, had been caught several times with their hands in the till. Billy, though, wanted the mayor.

Castelle, for his part, thought Billy unfairly persecuted him. He suspected that his motivation was racial, a bias against all black officials as corrupt and incompetent. He suspected Billy as one of the sources of the damaging *Birmingham News* articles, which Mayor Castelle also thought targeted him unfairly. Billy had denied it, but he was undoubtedly a source that leaked information about City Hall.

Billy had requested the meeting to discuss the Long-Hinkley Construction bribes. He had prolonged the investigation in hopes that he would be able to announce charges against the mayor when he brought indictments against the others involved. He had enough evidence to charge five city officials, like the news had reported. Billy had given up on trying to get the mayor in this round of indictments, but he still thought he could politically convict him and get him out of office.

Both men were politicians: a vicious, treacherous profession where the ends justify the means. The mayor had finally agreed to come over because he knew that if he didn't, it would be leaked to the news that he had refused to cooperate and was probably hiding something. Billy sat at the head of his thirty-foot-long conference table. Every one of his assistants white. Every assistant to the mayor, black.

Billy started with, "Do you mind if I tape the meeting?"

The mayor's lawyer and long-time friend, Lucius Jackson,

stated, "We do." That trap had snared the mayor before when out-of-context expletives were leaked to the press.

Billy asked, "You have nothing to hide, do you?"

Neither the mayor nor his lawyers retorted.

Billy got down to business. "We are going to bring charges against several of your employees and political associates tomorrow."

"Billy!" The thunderous Baptist voice of an angered Lucius interrupted. The loud preacher's voice from the large bow tie-clad advocate rattled Billy. "We came here of our own volition out of courtesy because we are high officials of the same city. You will use a more professional tone or we will go back across the street."

"Lucius, I just asked a question," a repentant Billy answered.

"You said employees of the mayor. These are city employees. They were there when he arrived. Secondly, the mayor is not the head of the city council. They are not members of his cabinet. They are an independent legislative body. Do you understand how the city's government works, Billy?" Lucius and Billy had had many confrontations in the courtroom. He was one of the few attorneys that could take on Billy and win, his style a mixture of lawyer, preacher and civil rights leader the perfect antidote for Billy. In a more paternal voice, Lucius directed, "Keep to the issue at hand."

"Would the mayor like to say anything in light of the developments?" asked Billy, more politely.

"By developments, I guess you mean the confessions of Roy Ezell and Ricky Luther, and the eminent domain issue we find ourselves with?" asked Lucius.

"And the murder of Jasper Thrash," added Billy with insinuation, purposefully goading the mayor to get him to make a comment.

"In any event, the mayor has no knowledge of any of that," replied Lucius.

But Castelle bit, interrupting his lawyer, not because he didn't know what Billy was doing, but he was a politician. He had to say something.

"I wanted a better City Hall and a more beautiful one. I recommended we renovate the building. It was falling apart. My knowledge of any bribes pertaining to the contractor is limited to what I've heard on television and read in the newspaper. I did not know the contractor, nor did I select the contractor."

"But it was a fiasco. People stole money and the construction is faulty," blurted out Billy. "What about the eminent domain scheme?"

"My knowledge of that is only this: I wanted to increase the city's tax base. I am building housing so the citizens can return to living in the city center."

"But again, people stole the money you paid to Ezell."

"The city paid," stressed Lucius.

Billy was starting to lose his temper. "You paid one and a half million dollars for property that Roy Ezell bought for four hundred thousand a few months earlier. Why didn't anyone check out Roy Ezell? It was incompetent not to do so. Did you care what happened to the citizens who were there in those properties?"

Again, Lucius fielded the question. "Billy, I'm sure he was more concerned than you. Do you have any questions, or is this just an attempt to embarrass the mayor?"

"You gave the property to the Wallace Corporation for a dollar to build the condominiums."

"The city gave the property to encourage the company to

move forward on a multi-million-dollar building project that will add millions more in tax revenue. It's called jobs and tax base, Billy. Who are you kidding? It's done all the time and should be done," explained Lucius.

"Mayor," asked Billy, "who are your largest campaign donors? Wallace Construction and Draper Wallace?"

"Billy, not even you are going to put that in the paper."

"Well, tomorrow one of your chief supporters, a campaigner of yours, and three city employees will be indicted on these steps for corruption, and we're starting an investigation into the murder of Jasper Thrash, which we believe is linked to this corruption. As mayor, do you have any comment?"

The mayor said, "Yes, I do," despite a disapproving look from the cautious Lucius. "I am the highest elected official in Birmingham. I love this city. The people entrusted it to my hands when I was elected, by a large margin I might add. The city has had many years to reach this poor condition. I accept full responsibility, that it is my job to lead the way in fixing it. We've done a lot, but it's not enough. We all must do more."

In context, the mayor's comments were benign, even encouraging, but out of context, they would be damning.

* * *

The next morning in *The Birmingham News*, coinciding with Billy's indictments, the mayor's comments were predictably printed out of context. The source, Billy Penick. "I accept full responsibility. . .the city is in poor condition. . .we have not done enough."

Billy Penick's press conference was at 7:30 a.m., February 15, on the steps of the district attorney's office. Billy wanted every household to hear his comments on the morning news while they were getting ready for work, eating breakfast, and driving the kids to school. The press corps had been camped out for an hour, fully aware he was grandstanding. But, he was the district attorney and had promised the broadest indictments in the city's history to end corruption. Billy approached the podium wearing only a suit – no coat, or hat or gloves. Just the suit to look athletic and invincible in the frigid weather. Those around him, including the press, seemed to be freezing. Billy, standing head and shoulders above the crowd, looked ominous. He appeared to be breathing fire as he exhaled into the cold air.

"Today is both a sad and happy day for Birmingham. Sad, in that the district attorney's office is indicting two of the city's councilpersons, Council President James Chambers and Council Member Brenda Lewis. We are also indicting three city employees - Bobby Dix, Charley Brill and Redd Phillips - on charges of bribery, conspiracy and money laundering. We have begun a murder investigation into the death of Jasper Thrash, which we have reason to believe is linked to this corruption.

"But it is a happy day for Birmingham in that we are sending a message. We will not stand for corruption and cronyism in this county. Our beloved city has deteriorated greatly over the past several years, as even the city's highest elected official will admit. The brutal murder of Jodi Wallace is just one horrible example. But as your district attorney, I pledge that we are going to make anyone involved in crime in Birmingham wish they had obeyed the law." Billy looked directly into the cameras, as if meeting the eye of every citizen in Birmingham. "I'll be happy to answer a few questions."

The press, as usual, jumped right in.

"Are you going to charge Peyton Castelle?"

"These are the only charges we are going to bring at this time."

"How is Jasper Thrash's murder linked to this corruption?"

"Sadly, we think he was involved in the money laundering and his connection may have gotten him murdered."

"Are you going to bring any more charges?"

"Let me just say this is an ongoing investigation. My office, as always, will keep the public informed. Thank you. Now we have work to do."

Billy was both campaigning and sending a message to potential jurors, both in the Mack Oliver Purifoy trial and trials of those he had just charged. His performance was masterfully orchestrated, although Jacob Levin's exposé on city corruption would not be kind to Billy Penick either, who had been the county's district attorney longer than Castelle had been mayor. Levin would write that the crime in Birmingham was unparalleled. He, however, made a distinction between hardened criminals and those who lived in poverty and were being run down by the police for burglary and theft, and even the one hundred murders that were mostly committed in crumbling neighborhoods, overwhelmingly against blacks. He called the crimes desperate, committed by people who felt hopeless and were locked out of society, and whose plight went unnoticed, except for the occasional white victim. In his opinion, the current indictments were overdue and just the tip of the iceberg of a system so corrupt that behavior like this had become commonplace. He accused the district attorney's office and most white officials of noticing the corruption now only because its leadership had been given a black face.

CHAPTER NINETEEN

The Birmingham Jail

Mack Oliver's appearance had changed significantly. The jovial Mack Oliver was now sedate; the laugh and demeanor that had once characterized him had been replaced with a solemnity Lincoln had seen overtake inmates before. Gone were his bangles and the rings on his hands and in his beard. He had gained weight, and now the bike-riding, very physical musician was reduced to depression and hopelessness. The guards described him as a noncompliant inmate who spent his days singing and withdrawn. Mack Oliver had never spent more than a day in jail and had not adjusted.

Lincoln could understand Mack Oliver's inability to adjust to the environment. He had always felt uneasy, even as a visitor, witnessing the lack of control prisoners had over their most basic choices. He knew his anxiety was common among black men when visiting a jail and being around cops. Most black men viewed the judicial system and cops as licensed lynch mobs. When visiting, you were told how long to stay and what time to arrive and leave, where you could sit, and you were searched. You were looked at with suspicion because you knew an inmate, who were all caged and treated like animals whether they had been tried and convicted or not. Only someone who was guilty deserved to be there, he felt. Lincoln couldn't bear to look at an innocent man like Mack Oliver endure this indignity. He had heard colleagues say that some people preferred jail, especially the homeless, because they were out of the hostile elements and well fed. The comment was among the most ignorant he had ever heard. He couldn't imagine that anyone preferred being caged to freedom. To have no control over ones own body and actions was akin to being subhuman.

Lincoln felt physically ill and depressed merely visiting the jail. After calming his feeling of panic, he noted that Mack Oliver was looking at him with understanding.

"Lincoln, I've missed you, but I understand why you don't want to come to the jail."

"No, Mack Oliver, everything is fine," Lincoln tried to put on a believable act. "I have just been so busy. I have been working so much lately, but I am still working with Piti on your case. That's why I'm here today. I need to talk to you about someone."

"Who?"

"Cassius Carey."

"Why do you want to talk about him?"

Lincoln did not want to tell Mack Oliver the truth. He only had a hunch, anyway – one he knew was a long shot and probably meant nothing. If it did, however, he needed to handle it carefully. What he could not tell Mack Oliver, and had decided not to tell Piti earlier at lunch, was that yesterday he had received a request for the release of information from the Atlanta Mental Health Center on a past patient – Cassius Carey. It was the same record Pam had retrieved for Lincoln two weeks ago. Lincoln was very familiar with these requests. He had himself requested previous treatment records on patients many times before. His signature was required before any psychological information on patients from the Catherine Fairchild Center could be released. The information was protected by the Privacy Act. A patient, though, could sign a release authorizing a treatment center to divulge confidential information. This is a customary practice for patients getting care at other facilities.

The signed release from Cassius Carey authorizing the release of information accompanied his current doctor's request. Cassius had entered Fairchild in April, ten months ago. So had Cynthia Bates, Cassius' girlfriend, the same month after the death of Tiffany Miller. Lincoln had contacted the family of Cynthia Bates who told him they were unaware of her whereabouts. She'd not been seen for nine months. Her family had reported her missing, but there had been no investigation.

The request did not say when Cassius had entered the center in Atlanta, but Lincoln was curious to find out if it coincided with the murder of Jodi Wallace. The record from Fairchild included Cassius' family's address in Atlanta, his mother's name and phone number as an emergency contact, and his employment history. It even had Cassius' Social Security number. Cassius had only stayed a few days, so the chart contained only an initial assessment of his problems by a junior staff member. Lincoln planned to hand deliver the medical record to the psychologist requesting it, a Dr. Samantha D. Williams.

"Mack Oliver, you mentioned to Mr. Pitman that Cassius Carey and Cynthia Bates were with you for a while at the abandoned house you and Tiffany found the night before she was murdered."

"Yeah, they were there."

"How long again were they there?"

"Just a couple of hours."

"Did they leave the house before Tiffany left?"

"No. Tiffany left first. She just left us all there. She had to go out. She wanted to use. We couldn't stop her. Cassius and Cynthia left after she did."

"Did you see Cassius or Cynthia again that night?"

"No."

"The next day?"

"I saw Cassius. He had used. He went into treatment for awhile afterwards."

"Did he act strange? Was anything different about him?"

"No."

"How do you know him, Cassius Carey?"

"He was friends with Cynthia, and Cynthia and Tiffany were best friends. He was also on the streets a lot."

"He was homeless?"

"Yeah. After Mom died, he and Cynthia stayed a while at the house."

"Do you remember how long?"

"Probably three or four weeks."

"Would you describe him for me?"

"He was a real nice guy, but nobody messed with him. He's not that big, but a real serious dude. He was real smart, clean cut, handsome, used to read all the time. He had a back pack full of Shakespeare novels. He didn't let anyone touch them."

"You said he was a nice guy?"

"Yeah, as long as you didn't make him mad."

"Did you ever see him mad?"

"Oh yeah."

"With who?"

"Many people."

"Tiffany?"

"Yeah. He said I deserved better. He didn't know what he was talking about."

"Mack Oliver, I have to leave town for a while. I have some business I need to take care of, but I will be checking on you. Piti is doing a good job preparing your case. Everything is going to be fine. Don't worry. It's going to be alright."

"When can I go home, Linc? I can't take it here. They've taken my bike, my horn, my brushes. They took all my jewelry. My momma left me that jewelry. I wore it all, every ring and necklace she gave me, to feel close to her. You aren't mad at me, are you? You know I didn't do it, don't you?"

"Yes, Mack Oliver, I know you didn't do it. I'm not mad at you. You're going to get out soon. Have you been able to draw with the sketch pad and charcoal I brought you?"

"Yeah, I got it, but I just can't draw in here."

"The guards said you're singing, though," Lincoln adds, trying to make Mack Oliver laugh.

"Yeah, some. Why are you leaving, Linc?"

"Mack Oliver, it's just something I have to do. It can't be avoided. I have to go. I'll be back soon. I brought you some more art books and a writing pad."

"Lincoln, I want to ask you a question," Mack Oliver said with a troubled gaze.

"What is it?"

"Why did you hesitate when I asked you what I should do when my lawyer wanted me to plead guilty? Why did you hesitate? You think I did it, don't you?"

"No, of course not."

"Then why would you hesitate?"

"I didn't want you to get the death penalty."

"So, you thought I should admit to a murder I didn't do? Would you ever admit to a murder you didn't do, Linc? You said you would fight, right?"

"Yes."

"You think that spending the rest of my life in jail would be acceptable to me for something I didn't do? I'd rather be dead, Linc. You thought life in jail wouldn't be so bad for me because I'm homeless? You've got it too, Linc."

"Got what, Mack Oliver?"

"You think you're better than me, too. I am a man, Linc. We're different, but you're not better."

"Mack Oliver, that's not what I meant."

"You did, Linc. You just didn't know it."

Lincoln knew that Mack Oliver was unfortunately right. He was guilty of the same thoughts he'd despised in others. Mack Oliver's insights had always shocked Lincoln. He decided to tell Mack Oliver his hunch about Cassius. Mack Oliver deserved to know everything.

The two men embraced as Lincoln left, the hug a little longer and tighter than usual. Lincoln reminded Mack Oliver, "I'll see you soon."

Mack Oliver replied, "You're my only friend, Linc."

Lincoln tied up the loose ends at his office and told Pam he would be on a personal leave for a couple of weeks. He called his parents and told them he would be away on business. He gathered his clothes, loaded the roadster and headed to Atlanta, hoping for anything that might save Mack Oliver from the electric chair or life in prison for murders he thought he didn't commit. He would tell no one else where he was going.

Lincoln wanted to leave for Atlanta that night. Cassius could leave treatment at any time, if he wasn't already gone, like he had left Fairchild after only a few days. He wanted to talk to him, but how? Lincoln wondered if Cassius would remember him. Should he drop a copy of the record in the mail, or should he just show up with it? If he just showed up, it might make the center's staff suspicious. He also didn't want Cassius to be scared off, if he had anything to do with the deaths of Tiffany Miller and Jodi Wallace.

After debating with himself, Lincoln decided to do the customary mailing of the treatment record and then drive over to the Atlanta Mental Health Center. But once he arrived, then what? No one was given free access to the center, just invited in. How would he gain entry? Lincoln would develop his plan on his 140-mile journey east from Birmingham to Atlanta, Georgia.

CHAPTER TWENTY

Progress

Dr. Sam had anxiously anticipated her session with Cassius. It had been three days since Family Night. Her trepidation was now replaced with understanding. Much had been revealed about the patient she was treating at the Family Night activities she had so masterfully incorporated into the treatment regimen. Mrs. Carey had opened a window into Cassius' mind for Dr. Sam. Mrs. Carey had also helped herself in the process. Dr. Sam saw the guilt and blame Mrs. Carey felt. She had blamed herself for the incestuous relationship with her father. She had found a way to excuse his behavior and that of her mother. Dr. Sam could only speculate for now, on the many variables that could characterize the abuse. When had it started? How long had Mrs. Carey endured the abuse? What was the reason for Mrs. Carey's mother's complicity in the abuse? What role, if any, had Cassius and Mark Antony's biological father had in their lives? What circumstances had led to their father being a pedophile?

Dr. Sam had had much experience with sexual abuse. The patients that entered the center had a disproportionate occurrence of sexual abuse within their past. The lives that many of her patients had lived had left nearly all with symptoms of post-traumatic stress and borderline personalities, and had blurred the boundaries of acceptable behavior. Abandonment issues, inability to establish meaningful, long-lasting relationships, sexual identity conflicts and chronic promiscuity, detachment from children, and compulsive and impulsive behavior that landed them in jail and addicted to drugs and alcohol. She knew she barely had enough time to address even one of the issues each patient had, but her patients did not have the luxury of in-depth, long-term treatment and most were not inclined to pursue it if it did exist. It could take months or years to explore any one of their many problems, and her patients did not have that much time. Dr. Sam worked with what she had.

For Cassius, that was sixty days, if he stayed, and hopefully Mrs. Carey would attend every Family Night. Dr. Sam wanted to get to the impetus of this treatment decision by Cassius. His pattern had been to enter treatment after life crises. His demeanor, his questions, and his history told Dr. Sam that there was much more to why Cassius had entered treatment on Christmas Eve. Why was he here this time?

Dr. Sam suspected Cassius' involvement in the suspicious death of his younger brother might have been an accident, although she knew that Cassius carried significant guilt about the incident. Betsy Carey had told the authorities it was an accident, and they had believed her story. But the death of Cassius' stepfather had also been under suspicious circumstances. Cassius had joked about watching him die and not being able to help him. Dr. Sam suspected his description was only bravado and animosity, but these incidents had preceded his first two treatment attempts. The third treatment attempt was ten months ago now. Cassius had told her about his brief stay at Fairchild, but did not say what event had caused him to seek treatment. She had requested the treatment record from the Fairchild Center in Birmingham over a month and a half ago and was still waiting for it to arrive. Nor had Cassius disclosed the events that led him to seek treatment on Christmas Eve, his current treatment attempt, number four.

She now knew he was the child of incest, the son of his mother and his mother's father. He had watched a probably innocent brother go to jail and subsequently die of AIDS. He had been mentally abused by a stepfather and reared by an overprotective, guilt-ridden mother who took him out of school at ten years old when he started showing the first signs of his antisocial personality. He was addicted to cocaine and alcohol and was homeless. Cassius had enough problems to justify a lifetime of psychotherapy, and Dr. Sam's experience was that they didn't have long. He was scheduled to leave in a few weeks. If they were lucky, he would stay and then come to aftercare meetings once a month for a year or so. She would treat Cassius for as long as he was convinced to stay. She was unsure if he would. Dr. Sam wanted to move more quickly to maximize the short time they had left.

Cassius, as usual, was on time for his session with Dr. Sam. He, too, was anxious to continue his treatment with her. The little he had done was having an effect on Cassius. In his mid-thirties, he had been lucky enough to reach an age where his chances of getting help and surviving were much better. For as long as he could remember he had been angry. He had felt bottled up and on edge. The turbulence in his body and mind was unimaginable to most. Dr. Sam had released some of the pressure Cassius felt, but what next? He was anxious to continue. His appearance was still improving. Cassius appeared to be a well-adjusted, healthy-looking thirty-five-year-old. His severe illness was neatly wrapped up for now.

Dr. Sam started where they had left off during their last session. "Cassius, you moved to Birmingham after your stepfather died. Why did you leave Atlanta so suddenly?"

"I just needed a new scene. I wanted to start over."

"How did his death make you feel?"

"I don't know. Like I told you, I was happy, relieved. He had been so evil to us – me and my brother, and my mother, too. I was relieved. I was glad he was dead."

"What about now? How does his death make you feel now?"

Cassius searched for an emotion for a moment and then replied, "Nothing. Strange to you maybe, but I feel nothing."

"You haven't thought about it?"

"No."

"It doesn't keep you up at night?"

"No."

"You told me a couple of sessions earlier that you were having trouble sleeping at night. Are you still having trouble?"

"Not as much, but yes."

"Tell me about Birmingham; when you left and went to Birmingham after your stepfather died."

"I was depressed for a while. I didn't have a job. I stayed on the streets and in shelters, but then I got a carpentry job. Everything changed. I was working and I got a little place. Everything was going well, but I started using again. I failed a drug test. They let me go, but said they would call me back sometime to fill in if someone was out sick or if they needed extra help on a big contract or something. They would pay me under the table. They couldn't have a drug user on the payroll. Insurance rates. I loved carpentry and the smell of wood, but I guess I liked the drugs more. I just couldn't quit. I lost everything – my place, my car. I went back to the streets. They have this fountain in Birmingham in the middle of an area they call Five Points South. I used to hang out at the fountain, the Storyteller Fountain, I think it's called. The people accepted me. I would do day labor at some of the construction sites, and in the evenings I would go there. I could get lost, nobody bothered me. It was the only part of Birmingham that stayed up at night. There are lots of clubs, restaurants, and street musicians. I met a guy there. His name was Mack Oliver. He played a horn. Best person I ever met. I could sit and listen to him play that horn all night. He should have been famous. I used to beg him to play. He had this one tune that he improvised, an old Lionel Richie song. He's from Alabama. He could make the horn sound like words. 'Father, help your children. Don't let them fall by the side of the road.' It was beautiful. We used to hang together. He didn't like the shelters. He was clean, though. And his mother died last year and we stayed together for a while at her house. She left him the house. She had saved a long time to get that house. She was a sweet lady. I had dinner with her and Mack Oliver a few times before she died. They were like my family."

"How did she die?"

"Heart attack or something. It was sad. Mack Oliver took it hard. It made him use, me too. He stopped, though, and went to treatment. Not me. I wasn't ready to stop yet. I stayed with Mack Oliver for awhile, but they took his house."

"Who took his house?"

"The City of Birmingham." Cassius' voice now grew firmer and deliberate, "They just took his house and tore it down. They gave him ten thousand dollars for a house worth four times that much and tore his damn house down to build some damn condos for rich people. Put him on the streets. And that stupid bitch girlfriend of his spent all his money on crack. She walked up and down the streets selling herself for two dollars to anyone who would walk by after she had spent all of Mack Oliver's money."

"Why are you so angry about that?"

"She was sleeping with the people that hurt Mack Oliver

– these men that took Mack Oliver's house. She spent his money. Mack Oliver just took it. Just played that horn on the corner and continued to take care of Tiffany, gave her all his money."

"That made you angry?"

"Yes, very angry." Cassius was obviously reliving the feelings. "She got what she deserved, though."

"What happened to Tiffany?"

"Someone killed her, threw her ass behind a dumpster. She was trash, so isn't that ironic."

"What was her last name?"

"Miller, Tiffany Miller."

"Do you know who killed Tiffany Miller?"

"No, but it was probably one of her white johns. Street hooker, crack-head, stealing people's money, could have been anybody. Mack Oliver was better off without her."

"When was she killed?"

"March, last year."

"Was anyone arrested for the crime?"

"Hell no. I doubt if it was ever investigated."

"You went to treatment in April last year?"

"Yeah, but there you go again."

"Why did you enter treatment at that time?"

"I was just tired and wanted to turn my life around."

"You stayed three days?"

"It wasn't what I thought." Cassius wanted to tell the whole story, but stopped short of incriminating himself.

Dr. Sam was quiet. She was not seeking confessions of past crimes. Cassius was now a patient, her patient, she had an oath.

"You stayed in Birmingham when you left treatment?"

"Yes. I liked Birmingham. My friend Mack Oliver was there. I stayed clean for a while. I was working more. Listening to Mack Oliver play every night. All that talent, playing on the streets for nickels and dimes. We had a lot in common."

"Like what?"

"The drugs, the streets. He should have been more, and me too. His father used to beat him. His mother just let it happen."

"Does she remind you of your mother?"

"I didn't say that and no, she doesn't."

"Your mother watched as the Reverend abused you."

"She thought she couldn't do any better."

"Like Mack Oliver's mother?" Dr. Sam asked.

Cassius ignored the question. "I got a job working on the condos they were building where they tore Mack Oliver's house down. They were building them to increase the city's tax base. They wanted more white people to move downtown, the papers said, but they called them middle-class people. That was code language," Cassius said meanly. "They wanted more people like you and less people like me and Mack Oliver. I used to go there everyday. Building the new condos for the rich white folks. They were on the news all the time at the site. The mayor and Draper Wallace, standing right on the spot where Mack Oliver's mother's house was. They didn't give a damn about the lives they wrecked to build those condos. Everyone thought it was a good thing. 'All the poor people are gone now, so please come back downtown.' Pathetic."

"Draper Wallace?"

"Wallace Construction. They were making a fortune. I worked for them. That's who fired me when I used. I hated them. The city gave them the land for one dollar, one damn dollar. People were moved on the streets, while the billionaire got the houses for one dollar. The city paid millions of dollars for the properties. They just gave it to him, but they don't want to give us anything. We should work. No handouts, they say, but give a billionaire millions. That's sick. I wanted to kill them."

"Who did you want to kill?"

"Draper Wallace and the mayor, but I didn't, so don't worry. That wouldn't have hurt them enough. I wanted to make them feel what I felt. I wanted them to ache with pain every night, as I did. They know pain and fear now. They needed to know what it felt like to lose everything, to have nothing, to be a failure, to lie at night and stare at the walls and wish you were dead."

"Is that why you are in Atlanta now? Are you hiding, Cassius?"

Cassius did not remember signing the release authorizing the Atlanta Mental Health Center to request past treatment records from the Fairchild Center in Birmingham. "You don't want to know the answer to those questions, doctor."

"Where's Mack Oliver now, Cassius?"

"He's in Birmingham. I'm sure he's playing that horn every night at the fountain, like usual."

"How do you feel now, Cassius?"

"I feel much better. I'm sleeping a little better, like I said."

"Is there anything you'd like to tell me, Cassius?"

"You said what we talk about is between us. I don't want anyone to know I'm here."

"They won't know unless you tell them, Cassius." Dr. Sam paused before asking her next question. "Is there anyone you want to hurt now, Cassius?"

"No."

"Yourself?"

"No. Now, have I admitted to anything that needs reporting, Dr. Sam? Just for the record, I didn't kill anyone at anytime."

"Cassius, let's talk about your progress on Step Five, Making Amends. You said you always had trouble with Step Five. Why?"

"I don't know."

"Are you ready to make amends? Are you sorry about hurting the people you've hurt in your life?"

"Sometimes I am. Sometimes I'm not. It's like a war inside my head. I go back and forth."

"What about today? Are you sorry today about any of your actions?"

Cassius thought intently about the question and seemed disappointed with his lack of remorse as he answered. "No. I'm not sorry today, but I feel sad for not being sorry."

"Is that a new feeling for you, Cassius?"

"Yes." Cassius hesitated for a moment. "Is that progress?"

"A little."

"But I'm tired, Dr. Sam. I just want peace. I want this war to be over."

Dr. Sam gave a reassuring look. "Then that's progress."

CHAPTER TWENTY-ONE

The Infiltration

The Atlanta Mental Health Center appeared much different from The Catherine Fairchild Center in Birmingham. Fairchild lived to be eighty years old and spent the last ten years of her life blind – a result of diabetes. She had dedicated fifty years to serving the poor and homeless. Her father and husband had both died from complications of alcoholism. Even with money, they had been no match for their addictions. Fairchild, who was from a political family, had once been appointed by the governor of Alabama to head his initiative on poverty. Catherine had left Charleston with her husband, a professional drinker and a bad politician. He mainly wanted to leave to get away from the watchful eye of Gayland Fairchild, Catherine's father, who was a long-serving state senator in South Carolina, and a controlling, chronic alcoholic. Unaware at twenty-three that she had wed a man worse than her father, sharing all of his bad traits and none of his good ones, Catherine sank herself into her charities as her husband's career and life were curtailed by bourbon. Her favorite charity became her center for the homeless, later named in her honor when she died.

Although located in Birmingham, Alabama, one of the poorest states in the union, with a well-earned bad reputation for giving very little to the poor, the Fairchild Center was an oasis. Catherine's reputation and connections and comfort among the rich had made the center a popular charity for many.

The well-financed center was well-equipped, too, compared to similar facilities and in many ways it rivaled private, for-profit treatment centers. Fairchild had insisted that it not look like the dreary and sad places the homeless men and women were coming from, but instead be a place of inspiration and high expectations. This philosophy had made the center competitive in attracting quality staff.

His father's illness brought Lincoln back home to Birmingham and the only place he had considered working was at the Fairchild Center. Catherine, who had no children of her own, had grown to love Lincoln as a son. His talents and Fairchild's love and connections had made the center the preeminent center for the homeless, not just in Alabama, but in the nation.

It appeared that the Atlanta Mental Health Center had no such benefactor as Catherine Fairchild. The center had not the resources or the benefits of Wallace Corporation donated construction and Fairchild fundraisers. Its chief asset was Samantha Williams.

Lincoln dropped the records of Cassius Carey, addressed to the Atlanta Mental Health Center, in a corner mailbox in Birmingham. He drove to Atlanta and got a room at the downtown Hyatt, where he had not been able to sleep a wink. He arrived at the mental health center promptly at 8:00 a.m., unable to wait a minute longer. He opened the unlocked door of the converted Garvey High School and walked in. No one asked him a question, as the dozens of patients rushed to classrooms in the center, and the staff monitored the halls and watched as the patients finished breakfast and started their treatment day. Lincoln was very familiar with the routine and felt at home, so he didn't look out of place to the employees who were preoccupied with their patients. His stomach was in knots. He looked down a corridor to his right and walked assuredly down the main hall toward a door marked Administration, hoping Cassius was still in treatment at the center. He wondered if he had already seen Cassius in the hallway and wondered if Cassius had seen him. He peeked around the heavy wooden door of the Administration office, meeting the flirtatious gaze of twenty-two-year-old Cicely Banks. Although he didn't know it, as soon as Cicely saw Lincoln, she decided she was going to give him whatever he wanted.

"Good morning," he said awkwardly, stepping through the door. "I'm uh…Ted."

"Good morning, Ted. I'm Cee. May I help you?"

"Yes, I'm from Georgia State. I'm a grad student and I, uh…am looking for a placement for my internship."

Cicely had begun playing with her hair and leaned back in her chair to get a better look at the full length of this Ted. She was quite happy with the idea that he might be around for awhile.

"So, Teddy, you need to show some ID."

"ID?" Lincoln responded nervously.

Slowly pronouncing each syllable, Cicely said sarcastically, "Identification."

Lincoln hesitantly took out his wallet and gave Cee his driver's license. She blew two full bubbles with gum she was chewing as Lincoln fumbled around to get her the license. She read it slowly, again, flirtatiously pronouncing each syllable, "Lincoln Theodore Drake from Alabama. Nice picture. I thought you said your name was Teddy?"

"Ted's short for Theodore." Lincoln's name was so unusual he didn't want Cassius to be alerted if he remembered him. "Listen, I really hate my name, so can you just call me Ted?"

"I like Lincoln. That's nice."

"I hate it. Ted, please. Can you just call me Ted, please?"

"Whatever you say, Teddy. I need to make a copy of your license and you need to sign in. We've had some problems with people coming in here with bad intentions." Slowly, she rose from her chair, swinging her hips as she walked languidly to the copier. As she made a copy of the ID, she added, "I used to go to college."

"Uh…who do I need to see?"

"You need to see Dr. Sam, sweetie, but you need an appointment to see her."

"Do you think it would be possible for me to see her today?"

"I don't think so. She has a very tight schedule."

"Well, it would be a big favor to me if I could see her today, Cee. Do you think there is anything you can do?"

"Here's your license, Teddy." Cicely held the license tightly as Lincoln tried to take it from her hand. Looking into his eyes, she blew another bubble and said, "You're gonna owe me." After releasing the license, she pressed the intercom button to Dr. Sam's office. "Dr. Sam, your eight-thirty is here."

"Cicely, I thought my first appointment was at nine?"

"I'm sorry, ma'am. Did I not tell you about the grad student that was scheduled to see you this morning? He called last week. I'm sorry. His name is Ted. Should I bring him down?"

"Give me five minutes, Cicely. I'm finishing some notes."

"Yes, ma'am." As she released the intercom button, she said, "You owe me big, Teddy."

"Thanks, Cee."

"You want anything else, Teddy?"

"Are there any other grad students here right now?"

"Not that I know of. They usually don't come here, or don't stay very long when they do. This is a tough neighborhood. I think you are the first one in a while."

"Good. Maybe she can use me."

Cicely responded, "I hope so."

As she walked Lincoln to his nonexistent 8:30 a.m. appointment, Lincoln thought, *What the hell am I doing?* He had broken at least six laws that he could think of. A good prosecutor could probably think of a half a dozen more.

He was careful not to make eye contact with anyone, but he observed that there were at least twenty file cabinets lining the walls of the office space behind Cicely's desk. He assumed they were patient records and they appeared, from the labels on the front of the cabinets, to be filed alphabetically. To look at one might be easy, but it was definitely a crime. Lincoln had shaved closely this morning trying to erase any signs of a Ph.D. and his thirty-five years, and he had put on his most collegiate-looking outfit. He was praying that Dr. Sam would not ask a lot of questions and would just be grateful to get some help. He was sure she was understaffed. He'd dated an actress for a while in L.A. and recalled reading lines with her. He hoped some of her acting skills had rubbed off. He hoped he was going to be able to be persuasive.

As they entered Dr. Sam's waiting area, Cee told him, "Have a seat, Teddy. I'll let the doctor know you're waiting. See you later."

Lincoln sat in the same chair as Cassius and many other patients who had experienced the effective treatment of Dr. Sam. Lincoln chose a sports magazine and thumbed through it as he anticipated Dr. Sam walking through the door. Cassius Carey, down the hall only seventy-five feet away.

Dr. Sam opened her office door and stepped inside the waiting area.

With her hand reached out, she said, "Good morning. I'm Dr. Samantha Williams. I'm so sorry about this mix up today. That happens sometimes."

Lincoln was stunned. Her presence. Her voice. Her beauty had taken him by surprise. He'd forgotten his rehearsed lines.

"I'm Lincoln."

"Lincoln?"

After a brief second passed as Lincoln composed himself, he stated, "Lincoln Ted Drake, but please call me Ted."

"Sure, sure. Come on in. I have just a few minutes, though. So, you're a student at Georgia State?"

Lincoln looked around the office. He sensed her competence. He saw her discreetly placed, but impressive credentials on the walls. She reminded him of a young, beautiful Catherine Fairchild and of his mother, Genevieve Drake.

"Yes, I'm at Georgia State, Psychology major, working on my master's. I need an intern placement."

"I have some friends there. Who's your intern instructor?"

Lincoln was dumbfounded and thought to himself, *I'm an idiot. Why didn't I look up some professor's names?*

Just when he thought his cover was blown and he needed to confess, Dr. Sam asked, "Is it Woo, Mincer or Haufman?"

"Mincer. It's Dr. Mincer."

"How is he?"

"Oh, he's great. You know, all business."

"Who, Mincer?"

"Oh, I'm just kidding."

"Listen, I'll help any way I can, but this is probably the hardest field placement you could have picked. Are you up for that?"

"Yes. This is exactly what I want. I want to work in a community mental health center when I graduate."

"Don't hear a lot of that anymore. Tell me why."

Damn, stumped again, Lincoln thought, but this time, Dr. Sam didn't save him. Lincoln just needed to go back in his memory and recall why he had became a psychologist so long ago.

He answered with a sincere and convincing, "The ruin of youth, crime, incarceration, homicide, disease, addiction, despair. What else should I be doing?"

Dr. Sam smiled, "Well, welcome to the solution, Ted. When would you like to start?"

"Today. Is that possible?"

"Eager, huh? Well, go back to Cicely's office. There's some confidentiality documents you need to sign. I'll send a staff person down to give you an orientation."

Lincoln's orientation lasted three hours. Cicely and the other two office staff persons, Donita and Jackie, had prolonged the encounter for the entertainment value. Men at the center were a rarity, as the pay was too low to attract many, and most males in the counseling profession worked at for-profit centers. Lincoln had gratefully played along. He did not want to cause any undue suspicion, but he was anxious to find Cassius.

Lunchtime arrived quickly. The patients were clamoring for the dining room. They eagerly awaited this midday break. They had prepared enough food to feed over sixty people, two helpings each, thirty males and thirty females, the parity a new phenomenon. In years past, the number of homeless and addicted males vastly outnumbered the number of females needing the services. The somewhat new chronic abuse of crack cocaine and loosening of social norms in the inner city had drastically changed the landscape. It had caused treatment professionals to rethink treatment approaches. The patients were no longer middle-aged and older men, but now young, urban men and women who were very immature, posing a myriad of new challenges. The scene resembled a school for emotionally afflicted, severely addicted adolescents who demanded maximum supervision and guidance, which was not present. Lincoln was saddened by the situation, but thankful and joyous as well that this group of people at the Atlanta Mental Health Center was trying so desperately to make a difference.

By noon, sixty ravenous patients were descending on the dining room from several directions of the large center, three staff people, walking with them. Dr. Sam was in her office, working, and would have lunch at her desk. Cicely Banks and two administrators also remained behind to have lunch later. Lincoln walked with the staff members. He looked at every males face and half of them looked familiar. His new colleagues had no clue as to the duplicity of their new intern. Lincoln felt both relieved and impressed with his four-hour infiltration. As they neared the dining facility, Ursula, a senior patient who had helped to prepare the meal, along with four other patients under the watchful eye of Mrs. Johnetta Watts, had been dispatched by her to alert the staff that an accident had occurred in the kitchen. Mrs. Johnetta, as the fifty-eight-year-old dietary aide was called, had called 911.

As they hurriedly entered the kitchen, the staff saw Damon Johnson lying on the floor, face up with a four-inch long laceration that extended from just above his left eye to his temple and was already swelling. There was a spilled boiler of peas beside him, and a broken pitcher of red juice or soft drink covering his shirt that first appeared to be blood. Jackie ushered the patients who were hovering over Damon out of the kitchen as Donita and Lincoln checked his vitals. He was unconscious, but breathing fine. Mrs. Johnetta held her chest as two patients fanned her.

Dr. Sam and the center's director, Floyd Bourgeois, arrived at the kitchen as someone asked, "What happened?"

The question elicited no immediate response. The truth, however, as usually was the case, would come out during group therapy as someone was making amends or coming clean. The paramedics arrived and calmly took Mr. Johnson to the county indigent care hospital, accompanied by Donita, where he waited for many hours to be sewn up and discharged. Then, Donita drove him back to the center. The incident, although not typical, was not enough to significantly interrupt lunch.

Dr. Sam and Mr. Bourgeois decided to join the staff for the noon meal after the excitement ended. Lincoln saw this as an opportunity. The other patients working in the kitchen that day – Demetrius, Clarence and Cassius – showed unusual politesse following the incident, making the staff duly suspicious of their culpability. The men all eventually made their way over to the table where the employees of the center were eating and, one by one, were introduced to the new intern, Ted. Teddy would be the preferred name for the females, the patients and the staff. Dr. Sam called him Ted.

The introductions gave Lincoln his first up-close look at Cassius. Cassius' stay at Fairchild had lasted only a few days. Lincoln didn't recall seeing his face, but Cassius thought Lincoln looked familiar.

"Do I know you from somewhere?" Cassius asked.

"I don't think so."

"Where you from?"

"Rhode Island."

"Long way from home."

"Where are you from?"

"Here and there."

Cassius gave him a suspicious look and returned to the other patients. Lincoln observed Cassius from across the dining room as he interacted with other patients. Although the one-hour lunch period had gotten off to a rocky start, the patients and staff had settled down. The heavy meal made the patients sleepy, something the staff appreciated after the lunchtime clamor. And

Lincoln, who had put on his best graduate student act for Dr. Sam, was fitting in. His ex-girlfriend's acting apparently had rubbed off on him, as he was totally believable and accepted.

CHAPTER TWENTY-TWO

A Boy Becomes a Man When His Father Dies

Cecil Pitman was not having as much luck in Birmingham. The assignment of Mack Oliver's case to federal court had had the predicted effect. There were very few black candidates in the jury pool. The few blacks that were called were successfully struck by Billy. Piti had eliminated as many whites as he could, that he thought obviously suffered from redneck neurosis, but the jury would still be a Billy Penick jury. All white, including the alternates. Piti was still sober, but not sleeping.

The newspapers and the television stations were showing particularly gargoylish images of Mack Oliver. His arrest photo and the pictures of him at his arraignment being restrained seemed to be on the front page and the lead story on television every day. The death of Jasper Thrash had given a modicum of relief for a few days. The story of Jasper being a crook and city bureaucrats and politicians being complicit were accepted by the community as common practice and to be expected. But the murder of Jodi Wallace was news. Mack Oliver was a pariah and the malevolence felt by the community about the murder was not going to subside. Piti found himself sinking into a depression.

Lincoln had gone to group therapy sessions and dumped trash, his past experience as an intern coming back to him. He had spent a lot of time in Cicely's office, unintentionally giving her the wrong impression, although it wouldn't have taken much. His goal was to get information about Cassius and Dr. Sam.

"Cicely, how long have you worked here?"

"Three years."

"Wow. That's a while. Do you like it?"

"Yeah, pretty much."

"What are your plans?"

"What do you mean?"

"I mean, do you plan on going back to college?"

"Maybe. I would make more money, but this is fine for now. I have a little boy. I need to work."

"It may be hard in the beginning, but it will pay off if you go back. What about Dr. Sam? How long has she been here?"

"Uh, longer than me."

"You like working for her?"

"Yes."

"What about Bourgeois?"

"He's okay."

"Just okay?"

"Well, he seems to care, but Dr. Sam is good. All the patients love her. I think I'd like to be a therapist."

"That's a great goal. Me, too. You say she works all the time?" Lincoln tried to be casual, talking while shredding old documents.

"Day and night. She doesn't have a life."

"No?"

"Well, no kids, no man. But she ain't gay."

"How do you know?"

"Well, she ain't never said nothing to me."

Lincoln tried a different approach. "What do you like to do when you're not working?"

"Well, I have Marlon, so I can't do much. But I like going out sometime when I can get my momma to keep him."

"Where do you like to go?"

"The Underground."

"You ever go out with Dr. Sam?"

"No," Cicely answered in a high pitched shriek. "We ain't that close. All she do is play racquetball anyway."

"Racquetball?"

"You know, racquetball, with that little racket, at the YMCA. Every evening, almost anyway. Sometimes she comes back here when she's done. What do you do, Teddy, when you are not in school?"

"That's all I do, go to school."

"You look like you're in good shape. Do you work out?"

"I play a little tennis."

"Look like you play a lot."

"Thanks."

Not wanting to look suspicious, Lincoln decided to leave early. He didn't want to hang around and seem unnatural. He had no reason to believe Cassius would leave the center that night, although he was concerned that the incident in the lunchroom would escalate overnight. Dr. Sam had started her evening sessions, and he didn't want to disturb her. He left a note thanking her and said he needed her to fill out some forms approving his internship that he would bring tomorrow. But he would forget, as he felt most students typically would.

Lincoln's phone call to Piti came at the perfect time, Piti thought. They were within two weeks to trial and he was feeling defeated and needing a drink.

"Piti, this is Lincoln. How are you?"

"I've been better, much better. How are you?"

"I'm fine, but I have a confession to make."

Piti was silent for a moment. He'd never known the serious, young doctor to ever joke with him. "Yeah? What is it?"

"I'm in Atlanta."

"Well," Piti said, "and that's the confession?"

"I'm at the Atlanta Mental Health Center."

Perfect, Piti thought, immediately assuming the worse. He asked sympathetically, "What's wrong?"

"I'm here on our case."

Piti thought to himself, *That's the first time he's said "our case."* "In what way?"

"Cassius Carey is here."

"Who's that?" Piti responded, not immediately remembering the name.

"Cassius is the homeless gentleman that Mack Oliver said stayed with him for awhile and was at the abandoned house with him early in the evening when Tiffany Miller was murdered."

"And?"

"He went into treatment immediately following Tiffany's murder."

"And?"

"He also went into treatment immediately following the murder of Jodi Wallace."

"And?"

"Well, I have a hunch. Just a hunch, though."

"What is it?"

"It's not uncommon for people to seek treatment after crises or crimes. Perhaps he felt guilty or he's scared and is hiding. I have treated many antisocials, like I think the person is that committed those crimes. We all think it's the same person because the murders were identical."

"So is this the guy who did it?"

"I don't know. I haven't talked to him or his therapist. It's kind of tricky."

"How did you get in the center?"

"That's complicated, too."

"How did you know he was there?"

"His therapist, a Samantha Williams, requested his treatment record from Fairchild. Something isn't right. Mack Oliver is no murderer."

"What about Mack Oliver? Does he know anything about Cassius' involvement?"

"No, no. He doesn't know anything. I asked him about Cassius. He just said he was real mean if you made him mad. Mack Oliver would not be a part of any murder."

"You seem more certain than you were before about Mack Oliver."

"Yeah, I am, but I never should have doubted him. I know him and even I was doubtful about his innocence. That's why I am here. No one is going to believe he didn't do it without the real perpetrator of these crimes being caught."

"What do we do now?" Piti asked. "I guess I should subpoena the records."

"I'd like to look at them first, Piti. I doubt if there is anything in them that would incriminate Cassius. A sociopath probably wouldn't confess to a therapist. And if she's not smart, he's already manipulated her. If she is smart, she doesn't want a confession, and treatment notes alone wouldn't be written in that sort of way. And therapists by law can't testify against patients, and, you're not supposed to know he's here. Treatment centers can't divulge that kind of information. We know he's here by illegal means. You can't call the judge and say, 'My friend, Dr.

Drake, just gave me confidential information.' Won't be admissible, and I might go to jail."

"Now what?"

"I'm going to get that record."

"Lincoln, don't get arrested."

"How'd it go with the jury?"

Piti sighed. "It's a Billy Penick jury, all white. Doesn't look good."

Lincoln took the MARTA the next morning to the Atlanta Mental Health Center. The morning was freezing in Atlanta, as winter had taken a full grip on the southern city. The rail train's route took him past many homeless, who appeared empty and dejected, squeezing their layers of sweaters and coats tightly to stay warm. The tin barrels lined the streets, filled with anything that would burn under bridges and corners surrounded by makeshift shelters, as many huddled around them. He thought how some had referred to the homeless as lazy, but he knew that no lazy person could brave ten-degree weather without food, or water or adequate shelter. Most people couldn't, but these people did. Everyday. Some with pocket change were riding the MARTA as well, a convenient refuge from the cold. They just rode as long as they could with no destination in mind, blank stares fixed straight ahead. This tactic would be tried on the buses and in public places, like the libraries and shopping areas. Some were more successful than others at not being told to move on.

Lincoln arrived at the center even before Dr. Sam. All the patients and staff were assembled in a large meeting space for a session referred to as Therapeutic Community, where the patients talked about hot issues, had devotion, read from the "Big Book" and offered measured support to each other. It was during yesterday's Therapeutic Community that Damon had openly doubted the sincerity of Cassius' motives in treatment, an affront that had caused Cassius to slam a large glass pitcher of Kool-Aid into Damon's face, knocking him unconscious and causing a gash that required twenty-five stitches, all while they were preparing lunch for the center. Cassius had committed the act between removing the chicken thighs from the oven and placing them on the buffet line. He gave no forewarning or apologies. Damon was back in treatment that morning and would not make such a mistake again; nor would anyone else.

Lincoln watched the interactions between the patients carefully, paying particular attention to Cassius, who sensed Lincoln's interest and still thought he knew Lincoln from somewhere.

Lincoln had been up most of the night, contemplating his situation. He had remembered writing a thesis many years ago during his graduate program and recalled that he'd interviewed a psychologist for insight. Maybe Dr. Sam would agree to an interview. He proposed that question to her at breakfast. It was 7:30 a.m. and Lincoln was not only thinking of Mack Oliver and Cassius, but had also thought about Dr. Sam as well, something he felt guilty about considering Mack Oliver's circumstances. He had wandered through Buckhead for hours without finding a spot that could hold his attention. He returned to the Hyatt at 2:00 a.m. and tossed and turned until 5:00 a.m., got up and shaved extra close, showered and made his way to the center. Dr. Sam's entrance into the dining room was a welcomed and anticipated sight.

"Good morning, Dr. Sam."

"Good morning, Ted. You're here early. That's a good sign. I wondered if you would return after yesterday. That sort of incident normally scares our intern candidates off."

"Dr. Sam, I'm contemplating doing my thesis on the treatment of antisocial personality disorders and I wondered if I could interview you sometime as a source. Do you think that would be possible? When you're not busy, of course."

"What about now? This is probably the least busy I'll be all day," she said. "Would you like to come to my office for privacy? Bring your breakfast."

Lincoln grabbed his plate and followed the very fit Dr. Sam, who walked briskly to her office holding a banana, an apple, and an orange. As they were seated, she asked, "What would you like to know, Ted?"

"First, thank you so much for this opportunity and thank you for agreeing to be interviewed," a very grateful Lincoln stammered.

"Sure, I understand, I've been there. Shoot. We have about thirty minutes."

"Yes, ma'am. Question one: how long have you been at the Atlanta Mental Health Center?"

"A little more than five years."

"Where did you go to college?"

"Brandeis."

"Why did you choose to be a psychologist?"

"I've never wanted to be anything else."

"Why the Atlanta Mental Health Center?"

"I see more here in a day than I would see in a month anywhere else. The people here need access to innovative treatment and have no choice of going somewhere else."

"It's a mission for you?"

"I guess so."

"Why?"

"Well, I'm sure you understand, millions of homeless people, the problem worse each year. It is probably our biggest disaster. America seems to have turned its head. Most Americans never look at a homeless person unless the homeless person makes the mistake of sitting too close to them or asking them for money."

"What's the solution that you mentioned?"

"Well, we need to change ourselves, not the homeless."

"That reminds me of something I heard Catherine Fairchild say," Lincoln said with dismay. "That the poor and the homeless will always be here. That they always have. That there is no cure for poverty. That it is those of us who are not homeless or poor that need healing. Only then will we make a difference in any individual's life who suffers the tragedy of being homeless."

"Ted, where did you hear Fairchild say that? She's been dead awhile."

"I meant, I read it." Lincoln kicked himself for not being more careful. "You've heard of Catherine Fairchild?" Lincoln added.

"Yes. She did incredible work and in Alabama of all places."

Lincoln quickly changed the subject. "Are you from Atlanta?"

"Athens, Georgia, about two hours east of Atlanta."

"Why did you come to Atlanta?"

"Atlanta is a progressive city, but has an awful problem with homelessness. The city also has the dubious distinction of giving homeless people one-way tickets out of the city when the Olympics were hosted here. The mindset, though, is probably typical. And my home, Athens, is close. Antisocials, though, you wanted to know about them?"

"Yeah, have you treated many?"

"Sure, we have a disproportionate amount in the population we treat."

"Why?"

"Who knows, but they are here."

"What do you do for them?"

"What can we do? Know they are here and that they might be violent. Confront the behavior. Give real consequences."

"What do you mean?"

"There is no treatment for sociopaths, Ted."

"Do they get better?"

"If they live long enough, some get better. After a while, they're just burned out, but often, they've left a lot of destruction before that happens."

"What would you do for a sociopath that was in your care at the Atlanta Mental Health Center?"

"Like I said, they're here all the time, so it's not a hypothetical. We treat their addictions and mental illnesses. We are aware of their manipulation and dangerous behavior."

"Why not just throw them out?"

"Society does that far too often for difficult problems, such as homelessness. Like the shepherd, the sheep you're most concerned about is the lost one. Should we discard a population of people? And maybe we do get through to some. Is saving even one worth it? We try to keep them alive and out of serious trouble long enough so that they might possibly change as they get older."

"How old before you start seeing any change?"

"Thirty or thirty-five."

"What if you knew or thought one was going to hurt someone?"

"Of course, we're obligated to report that to the authorities if we know any patient is going to hurt someone or themselves. Remember, there must be consequences. But therapists aren't supposed to be cops, no more than your doctor or lawyer."

"What if they had already hurt someone and were only in treatment out of fear, or hiding?"

"Everyone comes to treatment for a reason, and antisocials probably don't fear much, but they will hide."

"What if their whole treatment interest is just a manipulation?"

"That happens all the time, even among people who aren't antisocials. It's the nature of their addiction. Besides, any reason they have to get help, we have to take advantage of."

"Do you have any here now that I may be able to interview. Or, if that's not possible, review a medical record to get more insight?"

"Ted, why are you so interested in antisocials?"

"The prisons are filling up."

"There's more to that than just antisocial behavior. Let me think about it, Ted. These situations can get out of hand without some training."

"Like the situation in the lunchroom yesterday with Damon and Cassius?"

"Yes."

"You seem like you know what you are doing."

"Well, I'm glad you approve," Dr. Sam responded tongue in cheek.

"One more question. How old are you?" Lincoln blurted out.

"I think we're out of time, and none of your business," she said coyly.

Lincoln spent the week at the center having had many conversations with Dr. Sam. He'd become a welcomed addition to the staff. His knowledge, everyone thought, was way above average and unlike anything they'd seen before. He still awaited Dr.

Sam's answer about interviewing one of her antisocial patients. She had not forgotten, but still had not given Lincoln an answer. Lincoln's insight and intelligence had also made Dr. Sam fond of him. She trusted him now and had invited him to play racquetball with her several evenings. Lincoln learned quickly that racquetball and tennis had nothing in common. Dr. Sam beat him badly. The fact that it was just a sport, a game, provided her conscience the needed cover necessary for her not to feel she'd crossed the line. Ted was a student. She was his supervisor and teacher now. But there was something between them that Dr. Sam had not experienced before. Both were coming into the center earlier and staying later to spend more time together, the reality of which had Lincoln guilt-ridden and conflicted. He'd come close to telling her the truth several times, but he didn't know where to begin.

For as long as Lincoln had been back in Birmingham, he had lunch one day each month with Genevieve and Jefferson. He had not missed a day. His father's illness had made the time he spent with him even more precious. With his father's cancer much more advanced, Lincoln had to go back to Birmingham for the monthly lunch. He'd told the Atlanta Mental Health Center staff that he had to be in class and would see them next week.

Dr. Sam knew she would miss him. She remarked that she thought he was ready for the interviews he'd requested for the research for his thesis on antisocial personality disorder, and would get them lined up for him when he returned.

* * *

Jefferson Drake was enjoying the time he spent alone in the warmth of his comfortable study more and more. Genevieve found every excuse to interrupt him so she could sit beside him and reminisce with him. The cold days had robbed the abundant trees on the property they so loved of all their foliage. The oaks appeared white and lifeless, the ground brown and frozen. Winter had contained Genevieve to the indoors. Her precious garden was bare and anticipating her spring return. Only the hearty pansies remained. Her deepest fear was that Jefferson would not see spring with her. She sat with her feet curled up on the sofa beside him, both sharing a cup of tea and gazing into the blaze of a well-tended fire in the fireplace. The mantle was filled with memories. They anticipated the arrival of their son, but lunch today would be tomato soup, the only kind that Jefferson could keep down.

Lincoln let himself in quietly and took a seat near his parents by the warmth of the fire. Jefferson smiled with pride as Lincoln entered. Jefferson worried about Lincoln. He was thirty-five, unmarried, and with no family of his own. Jefferson had mixed feelings about the way he'd raised Lincoln. Lincoln had been raised with everything he needed, not because he was born to wealth, but because of Jefferson and Genevieve's sacrifice and sweat. Lincoln was shielded from the cruelty of Alabama, from racism, poverty and a second-class existence. Jefferson made sure Lincoln had never lost. He'd never had to sacrifice, but Jefferson and Genevieve's sacrifice had made him a doctor, prosperous and well adjusted. Jefferson's father many years ago had told his sons that a boy doesn't become a man until his father dies. Jefferson's father died when he was twelve. Jefferson worked on the hot plains of south Alabama until he was fourteen, when he ran away, lied about his age and joined the Army. He sent half of his pay home monthly to care for his brothers and sisters. He was a man at twelve and a war hero before he reached twenty.

"Lincoln," the still powerful voice broke the hypnotic allure of the fireplace, "How's your friend?"

Lincoln was distracted. He had been surprised at how rapidly his father's body was deteriorating. The once powerful and invincible-appearing Jefferson was now, at seventy five and his body overtaken by cancer, showing the first signs of vulnerability. "Who, Pop?"

"Mack Oliver Purifoy. His trial is next week. How's it going?"

"As well as can be expected."

"The paper says it doesn't look good for him," Jefferson gently tossed the newspaper toward Lincoln. "All white jury, not that it would matter."

Jefferson didn't mention the lead story in the morning paper, but Lincoln saw it as he flipped to the front page.

Rodney Thornton, boyfriend and campaign manager of Councilwoman Brenda Lewis charged with the murder of Jasper Thrash

> He was caught on videotape by a hidden security system entering Thrash's property the night of the murder and leaving hurriedly around the time the murder was committed. Previously fingered by Ricky Luther as the delivery man for bribes to city employees, Thornton now faces charges of first-degree murder, as well. Murder charges have been added to the bribery, conspiracy, and money laundering charges pending against Lewis. Council President James Chambers and city employees Redd Phillips, Charley Brill and Bobby Dix were also charged with second-degree murder. Thornton claimed self-defense and sources reported he was plea-bargaining for a lesser charge in return for his cooperation. Ironically, the surveillance equip-

ment that caught him was installed to catch thieves on Thrash's property after dozens of incidents of theft by petty thieves who found the donated property for the homeless irresistible.

The charges filed by the district attorney's office report that the five conspired to steal money from the City of Birmingham by using an elaborate labyrinth of bribes and money laundering to manage a criminal empire that has thrived for years. The charges allege that the group used an intricate scheme to purchase property from unsuspecting citizens using co-conspirators who posed as city employees, and then sold the property to the City of Birmingham at grossly inflated prices. The ill-gotten gains were then divided among the conspirators. The city bought the property under an eminent domain provision executed months ago. The affected houses were once located on the site where the Wallace Corporation is now building condominiums. These condominiums are nearing completion and providing jobs and needed residences for those migrating to the city center, bringing with them a much needed tax base. Sources in the district attorney's office say there is no connection between the Wallace Corporation and the conspirators. As yet, no charges have been brought against Mayor Castelle.

Jefferson interrupted Lincoln's reading. "You testifying?"

"Yes, if I am called. I mean, I'd like to." Lincoln's voice gained confidence. "He's innocent, Dad."

"Well, like I told you, I don't think he'll ever leave jail. Lincoln, prepare yourself for him being found guilty."

Lincoln knew his father was probably right. He'd been right about everything else.

"I met a girl," Lincoln said unexpectedly to his parents, changing the subject. Both looked surprised and Genevieve smiled broadly. Jefferson thought that Lincoln had had many girlfriends, but he was interested to hear more. But the statement Lincoln made had shocked him even more than his parents. It had just come out.

"Do we know her?" Genevieve asked.

"No, no. She's from Atlanta."

"So that's why you've been over there," Genevieve mused. "When do we get to meet her?"

"Well, I don't know. We are not actually dating or anything."

Jefferson stopped listening, assuming dalliance from Lincoln's statement.

Genevieve reassured Lincoln, "It started off slow with me and your father, too, you know. Camp Claiborne, Louisiana, where your father got his training." Lincoln had heard the story many times, but he learned something different every time she told it. "My mother worked on the fort," Genevieve continued. "I was only fourteen. She wouldn't let me see your father because he was a soldier. He told everyone that he was twenty-one, but he was only fifteen, you know."

"Did you know how old he really was, Mother?"

"No, not at first. He didn't want anyone to know. He thought he might get court-martialed."

"When did you find out how old he was?"

"When my mother threatened to go to his commanding officer and have him put in jail."

"So he had kinda lied to you. Did the fact that he had lied to you make you distrust him, or did it not matter?"

"Oh, it didn't matter? Not at that point. I was in love." She smiled over at Jefferson. "And that was a different kind of lie."

"What do you mean?"

"He had to lie. He couldn't have been in the Army otherwise." Genevieve knowing her son well asked, "Have you lied to that girl, Lincoln?"

He hesitated, "Kinda."

"Lincoln, if you lie to a woman, it's not a matter of if she'll find out, but when."

Jefferson was now interested again. He looked over the top of the book he'd picked up. He looked into Lincoln's eyes and saw his son's sincerity and obvious quandary. "Lincoln, your mother's family is Creole and your Grandma Drake didn't want any part of that. Plus, I'd run off and joined the Army. She thought I'd lost my mind, but I needed to find myself. I had three brothers to work the farm. They were happy doing it too. Those boys never left Alabama." Jefferson hated the wiregrass as a child, but had come to love it later in life. "You have to go after what you want, Lincoln. If you want her, tell her before it's too late. You have to create your own destiny. Nothing is guaranteed."

Lincoln rested in front of the fire with his parents. It was the first real sleep he'd had in weeks. Jefferson took the rest of the evening off. Genevieve was adjusting. The tomato soup had been filling.

CHAPTER TWENTY-THREE

A Different Kind of Lie

Lincoln was anxious to return to Atlanta. His excitement about being so close to Cassius, the person he felt had killed Jodi Wallace and Tiffany Miller, and his emerging feelings for Dr. Sam had him pushing the roadster to speeds that would rival Talladega Speedway. He needed to be honest with Sam about Cassius, and about how he felt about her. He was going to take his father's advice.

Cicely's broad smile greeted him as he arrived. She, too, had missed him. She, too, had emerging feelings. "Dr. Sam is looking for you. She's been in her office all morning, canceled her appointments. She said to let her know the minute you arrived."

Lincoln thought he too was anxious to see her. Cicely informed Dr. Sam by intercom that Ted had arrived.

"Yes, ma'am. I'll tell him to come right down." She turned to Lincoln, "She's waiting on you, Ted."

Lincoln's smile when he entered her office was greeted by an expression he'd not seen before on Dr. Sam's face. She appeared to have been crying, but she calmly asked Lincoln to sit down.

Avoiding his eyes, she uttered softly, "I called Tom Mincer to tell him what an exceptional job you were doing. He said he didn't know what I was talking about. Said he didn't know you. Of course, I thought, well, maybe I made a mistake. Perhaps you had said you had another instructor. So I called Jackie Woo. She'd never heard of you either. So I called Karl Haufman. Same answer. He'd never heard of you. But there are a lot of students at Georgia State. I thought, maybe they just didn't remember you. But the registrar confirmed that there was no Lincoln Theodore Drake at Georgia State."

Lincoln felt as though his heart had sunk into his stomach. "I can explain."

"I didn't call the police because I said to myself, there must be another explanation. I even called Georgia Tech and the University of Georgia. Perhaps there's another Mincer, but no such luck. But there must be a plausible explanation. You seemed so honest, genuine, special. I…I don't understand. Who the hell are you, Lincoln, Theodore, Ted Drake? Who are you?" Her soul crying, but she shed no tears.

Lincoln looked away, wondering now how to explain himself, how he could have handled this differently. He should have told her the truth. It just hadn't come out. He was going to. Now it was too late. The damage was done.

"My name is Lincoln Theodore Drake. I'm from Alabama. I'm a psychologist. I work in Birmingham at The Fairchild Center. One of my patients, a friend, has been charged with murder. His name is Mack Oliver Purifoy Jr. I don't think he did it. He couldn't have. He has been held in the Birmingham jail without bond for the past two months. His trial starts in a week and, if convicted, he'll be put to death. He *will* be convicted unless the person who committed these crimes is found, the true murderer of Jodi Wallace and Tiffany Miller. That's why I'm here…to find that person. You sent a release of information request to the Fairchild Center on a patient we treated last April. The patient entered treatment days after the death of Tiffany Miller. From the date on your request for information, it coincided with the date that Jodi Wallace was killed. I had a hunch that this person might be involved because his name was also mentioned by

Mack Oliver as someone who had stayed at his house. His name is Cassius Carey."

Dr. Sam looked angry now. "Your interest in antisocials, your *interview* with me, the request to interview an antisocial – all an attempt to get at Cassius?"

"Yes. I need that interview. His behavior is typical post-offense behavior. I'm convinced now that it was him."

"You're sick, as sick as you think he is. You lied. Who do you think you are? You're not a cop, a detective. So you decide to become a private investigator and break into a treatment center? A psychologist, a doctor, playing the sleuth? You know the rules. You know the law. The people here have rights, too. You know that. He's protected by confidentiality laws like everyone else that seeks medical treatment. Have you lost your damn mind?"

Lincoln leaned forward, speaking intently. "An innocent man is in jail. He will be put to death. Cassius was there at the time of both murders. He's a sociopath. He's hiding and he's dangerous. I need that interview."

"You won't get it, and if you don't leave, you're going to jail."

"Samantha, he's dangerous."

"Is being a fireman dangerous, or an airline pilot, or a cab driver? I know the risk, Ted, Lincoln, or whatever the hell your name is. How many of our patients have committed crimes, unthinkable crimes, and are also the victims of crimes? You've broken the law, too. Are you any better?"

"I know you're hurt. I know there was something between us, but you're not thinking," Lincoln said, his desperation clear.

All remnants of Sam's trusting and interested gaze were now gone, replaced by a look of distrust and disappointment. Her only response was, "Leave."

"Samantha..."

"Leave now, Ted. Don't come back." She'd keep his secret, but Lincoln knew he was now *persona non grata*.

Lincoln heeded her request and hesitantly left her office thinking to himself, *What now?* His options ran through his mind. *Don't leave and try to talk to her. Go to the administration office and snatch the record*. But that would be even more of a criminal act, which Sam would never forgive him for, and a line he wouldn't cross.

After processing these notions and wisely doing away with the thoughts, he hastily scribbled a note on his way out of the center. He gave the note to Cicely Banks.

"Cicely, give this to Cassius Carey. He's a patient here. Don't tell anyone, okay? Don't let anyone else see it. Oh, and get back in college."

"Are you leaving, Ted?"

"I'll be around."

She smiled. He knew she'd get the note to Cassius, and, at the lunch break, an aloof Cicely passed the note. "Cassius, Cassius," she called as the group of patients walked towards the dining room. "This is for you."

"What is it?" as Cassius took the folded note.

"I don't know," she snapped impatiently and walked away.

Cassius stopped and read the note: *I know you did it.* He looked around as if a light suddenly shone on him. His heart pounding, he walked hurriedly up to Cicely and grabbed her by the arm, his large hand immobilizing her.

"Who gave you this note?"

From his look and tone of voice, Cicely knew that she should answer. Without hesitation she said, "Teddy."

Cassius immediately thought to himself, *I thought he looked familiar. Lincoln. Fairchild.* He demanded, "Teddy? Where is he?"

"He left."

"Where did he go?"

"I don't know, but you better get your damn hands off me," she said frantically, as if trying to shoo a bear one comes upon unexpectedly in the forest.

Cassius composed himself, and said, "I'm sorry. I'm sorry, Cee."

"You better act like you got some damn sense," she said with indignation, although she was woefully unaware that her actions were like waving a red flag in the face of an enraged bull.

It was an intuitive gamble, but Lincoln, however, had accurately predicted Cassius' style and his actions that when he got the note. He would focus all his anger on Lincoln and he would run, and then he would machinate.

Cassius folded the note, placed it in his pocket, gathered his belongings, and headed to the railroad, where he would stow away on the first westbound train en route to Birmingham.

CHAPTER TWENTY-FOUR

Born Again

Sam had not returned any of Lincoln's phone calls. Piti would have offered his friend a drink – who appeared to need one – but Piti had thrown out every bottle at the house and was still sober. The Homewood house was starting to look like it was part of the community. The shrubs were cut away from the windows. The windows were cleaned and sparkled, allowing sunlight in that highlighted the shiny hardwood floors and a new, soft yellow sofa that didn't look like Piti had selected it, in a neat, tastefully decorated living room. The old newspapers had been discarded and the pizza boxes gone, revealing a dated but quaint kitchen filled with old appliances. It gave the appearance of being frequently used. There were small baskets of tomatoes, potatoes, and squash, and assorted spices on the counter. The kitchen showed a woman's touch. Piti was neater, sober, and even more robust. Lincoln knew instinctively what Piti didn't say. There was a woman, but it reminded Lincoln of Sam, of what might have been.

The neat kitchen was starting to steam up from the boiling oil on the small, white stovetop. Piti was battering whole catfish, with nothing missing but the head – the fins and tails still intact. The fish seemed larger than usual, but Piti compensated with an oversized skillet. As he laid the fish in the scalding grease, the oil roared and popped pieces of hot batter onto Piti's hands and the stovetop. Piti never flinched, his skin accustomed to the hot oil. Lincoln shielded himself with his palms up toward the direction of the hot oil. Piti was adroit and nimble in the kitchen. He had prepared coleslaw, fried chips and fried, hot water bread as complements to the fried catfish. He served Lincoln the meal on a plate the size of a turkey platter.

As Piti started to drown his fish in hot sauce, he told Lincoln that his trip to Atlanta had been a success - although if anyone at the Atlanta Mental Health Center wanted to press it, he could lose his license. Luckily, though, no one had. The involvement of another homeless man in the murder of Jodi Wallace had enabled Piti to quickly get a subpoena for Cassius' medical record, but, just as Lincoln had predicted, the record had not implicated Cassius. Cassius had wisely talked around his involvement in any crime. The notes that Sam had written could mean anything, although they did illustrate the life and thoughts of a severe sociopath. But without her testimony, they would not point to Cassius as the perpetrator. It was unclear if she thought he was guilty anyway. Regardless of the thoughts she might have, she couldn't testify against him. Their conversations were protected. Piti knew the courts were clear on that issue. Verdicts had been overturned on appeal when a therapist testified against a patient and that testimony resulted in a guilty verdict. The reason for the meeting at Piti's Homewood residence was to discuss Cassius' return to Birmingham, something else that Lincoln had correctly predicted. There were two days before the trial of Mack Oliver and last night, Connolly had been called by his informant, Charles Tolbert.

"Cassius was at that fountain on the Southside. He'd been asking about Mack Oliver and you. He didn't know what had happened he said. Said he'd been away and that he and Mack Oliver were friends, wondered if anyone knew where you lived. Tolbert was suspicious. Connolly had asked him to call if someone or something seemed suspicious, relating to the Wallace girl's murder. Tolbert called him at midnight. Connolly and Franks picked Cassius up on the usual charge used to pick up the homeless when they needed to be questioned, drunkenness and public nuisance. They went out and got Cassius at two a.m. Imagine that – only Draper Wallace could get two cops out of bed at two a.m. to arrest a homeless man."

"Where is he now?"

"Downtown. They took him without incident, but they can only hold him for twenty-four hours without charging him with something. But he's not talking. Said he wasn't going to say a word without an attorney present. I want to get him on the stand, break him down."

"I don't think anyone can. Look, there's less on him than what they have on Mack Oliver, Piti." Lincoln was agitated and desperate thinking how close he had come to getting his parents or Samantha killed.

"This is all we have. There is no other option. If we don't put him on the stand, they convict. If we do, something might shake loose."

"Piti, he's a sociopath. We've talked about this. He's as smart as anyone in the courtroom, if not smarter, and he is crazy. You're not going to break him down. He's not weak. He's not scared. He's not stupid."

"What do you want me to do, doctor? We go to trial in two days. That's all I've got. It's a miracle we have anything. Have some faith. You did it – found him, got him back to Birmingham. If you hadn't found this man, there would be no hope for Mack Oliver, trust me. That's genius, doctor."

"Thanks," Lincoln said, dryly.

"Are you worried, Lincoln?"

"Of course. This is Mack Oliver's life."

"No, I mean about you. You think he came back to Birmingham for you? Are you worried?"

"Not about me."

"Who then?"

"Sam. He may think she set him up. My mother and father. He won't let this go if he gets out."

Piti put his fork down in the middle of a bite. Lincoln had never seen him look so serious. "Then we better keep him in jail."

CHAPTER TWENTY-FIVE

Judgment Day

Mack Oliver never knew his grandparents. Neither his paternal or maternal grandmothers were married and both were dead before he was three. He had grown up in poverty, and had been physically and emotionally abused by his father and ridiculed by playmates and classmates. His mother was too depressed to offer him much protection or guidance. He was small, maladjusted, and would become addicted to drugs in his teens and show the first signs of schizophrenia while in his twenties. He had not had any substantial job during his life, no children, no sisters or brothers. He had one girlfriend his whole life, Tiffany Miller, who was severely addicted to drugs, a prostitute and now dead, with Mack Oliver charged with her murder. He had one friend – his therapist, Lincoln Drake – and a lawyer, Cecil Pitman.

February 25 had arrived. Mack Oliver was sedate the morning of his trial. To him, it seemed a likely end to the life he'd led. He wasn't outraged or asking, "Why me?" Long ago, he had gotten over asking that question. Lincoln brought Mack Oliver a new suit and shoes. Against Piti's wishes, however, Mack Oliver had refused to shave or cut his hair. He looked very much out of place in the suit Lincoln had selected. The shirt and tie seemed to have him sewn up, pulled as tight as a corset, making his body uncomfortably erect. Mack Oliver appeared gaunt. He had not been able to eat or sleep and his lips were badly chapped.

The disruption of his medication, the murder charges, the confinement, the confiscation of his belongings, his bike, his art, the regimented days had all taken their toll on Mack Oliver. His eyes appeared hollow and lifeless.

He sat with Piti at the defense table in front of a packed spectator gallery awaiting J. B. and a jury of his peers. The only eyes he looked into were Lincoln's, who sat behind him on the first row. Piti had been awake all night, rehearsing his defense of Mack Oliver. He was sweating profusely. The top of his collar was wet, and the perspiration was visible on the back and underarms of the light-weight khaki suit, but now he wore a new tie and a white shirt that had been ironed, thanks to the new girlfriend. The defense table seemed bare, with only a couple of legal pads and three or four pens lined in a row.

Piti's mind cataloged each piece of evidence against Mack Oliver, his position, and what would surely be the prosecutions position going through his mind. He rehearsed the issues and trouble spots and his plausible explanations. *He was there the night of the Wallace girl's murder; so were many others. She hugged him. It sounded plausible, but a white jury would not comprehend that a beautiful, rich white girl would hug a homeless black man. The hair had to get on her from his forcible contact. His bangle in her hand. He gave it to her for giving him the five dollars. He wanted to feel like he wasn't just accepting a handout. She pulled it off his arm during a struggle. He was seen by the store owner "harassing" her will be his testimony. The Winters and Drover girls saw him trailing her towards her car where she was killed. He admits he trailed her, hugged her, said goodnight and rode his bike to an abandoned house, where there was no alibi to speak to his demeanor when he arrived. Tiffany Miller was his girlfriend. His DNA was present in her body. She was killed in the same manner as Jodi Wallace and only one hundred feet apart. He was black and he was homeless.*

Billy Penick radiated confidence, as did his two assistants at the prosecutors table. He was still standing, greeting the Miller family, who starred in the direction of Piti and Mack Oliver. He'd place his large left hand on the back of all those he talked to as he stood over them, and squeezed their hands with his right hand. The Miller and Wallace families were sad images to observe. Draper and Millicent Wallace looked out of place as a victim's family. This was the first time Millie had ever been in a courtroom. It was Draper's second time, with Mack Oliver's arraignment being the first, and neither had ever visited anyone at a jail. This was the territory of lawyers, the poor and minorities. But the courtroom today was mostly white and voters, and Billy took full advantage of this opportunity. There had only been two months since the tragic murder and emotions were still raw. The mood was somber and angry. Billy sat down only moments before the bailiff cried out and brought order to the awkward whispers.

"All rise. The Honorable J. B. McPeake presiding."

The words cracked the air and startled the spectators. The large chamber echoed as the words came forth, causing stomachs to churn, light-headedness and panicked nerves. Piti's hands shook. The bailiff's announcement was all too familiar to the Millers. The Wallaces squeezed each other's hands tightly. Billy relaxed in the thought of having a friendly referee.

J. B.'s walk seemed extremely slow as he made his way to his towering bench. He knew Jodi Wallace, he knew her family. He'd visited their home, golfed with her father at the club, and so had every other judge or notable citizen. This was a victim he could relate to. He was a judge, a professional, but this time he felt the grief, the loss.

"Ya'll be seated. Mr. Pitman, good morning."

"Good morning, ya honah."

"Is the defense ready this morning, Mr. Pitman?"

Piti's mind responded, *No*, but his mouth uttered a timid, "Yes suh, ya honah."

"Mr. Penick, are the People prepared to begin this morning?"

Penick responded with an intrepid, "Absolutely, ya honah."

"Bailiff, bring in the jury."

Nine a.m. The moment had arrived, more ominous than any imagined; there was no turning back. J. B.'s steely gray eyes, his pale skin, white hair and black robe on the bench focused the attention of the courtroom. There would be no talking except when directed, no outbursts. This was J. B.'s domain and there was no second in command. Even Wallace was frozen to his seat.

After welcoming his jury and giving instructions, J. B. directed for the trial to begin. "Mr. Penick."

"Thank you, ya honah. Good morning, ladies and gentlemen. I'm Billy Penick, your district attorney. Thank you so much for your service. I don't think there is any higher civic duty than your honorable sacrifice to serve as jurors. We are a nation of laws, not men. No one is above the law. I beg you to keep that in mind as you witness the testimonies and evidence here today.

"Today, you will decide the fate of the murderer of Miss Tiffany Miller and Miss Jodi Wallace. On March thirty-first of last year, this defendant killed his girlfriend, Tiffany Miller, in a drunken rage. His motive - a lethal mix of jealousy and crack cocaine. The defendant will offer you no plausible alternative scenario.

"Late at night on December twenty-third, the defendant again committed this ultimate act of hatred. Again, he murdered, sexually assaulted and robbed eighteen-year-old Jodi Wallace, a freshman student at the University of Alabama, home for the holidays, shopping and enjoying an evening with her friends on the Southside. But that night, the unsuspecting young victim was being stalked by a cold-blooded murderer, emboldened possibly because he thought he had gotten away once before. Eyewitnesses will place him at the scene, harassing the young girl, asking for money. When she told him she had none, he waited for her menacingly outside on the corner, intimidating her while she talked to two of her long-time friends and tried to have a cup of coffee in peace. She felt compelled to ask her friends for money to give him, hoped he'd leave her alone. One of her friends gave her a five-dollar bill, which she then gave to that defendant. Perhaps that night he just needed more money and found the young girl too easy a target to pass up, three shopping bags and her purse with credit cards. But, whatever the reason, he followed Miss Wallace to her car. Two eyewitnesses saw him pursue her into a dark alley, the last time anyone saw her alive. Miss Wallace was strangled and sexually assaulted with a wine bottle in that alley, her hand broken as she tried to defend herself. She was shoved in the trunk of her car and left for dead just minutes before Christmas Eve. She was a student, well liked, from a good family and a virgin."

Billy paused for effect. "But let me warn you about this up front: the defense undoubtedly will try and smear Miss Miller. They may bring up she had an addiction. Perhaps she had to resort to prostitution because of that addiction. They'll say anyone could have killed her, anyone except Mack Oliver Purifoy, Jr., whose semen was present inside Miss Miller at the time of her death. She'd been out all night, hadn't come home, and the semen of at least two other men was found in her body. The defendant was jealous and angry. He had motive and opportunity, but he has no alibi. Even so, he covered his tracks pretty good. The murder went unsolved for nine months. But mercifully, Mr.

Mack Oliver Purifoy left a trail, though that led back to him with Miss Wallace. His hair was on her mitten. A bangle that he made was clenched in the young victim's hand, appearing desperately to point to her assailant, Mr. Purifoy. He had motive, money, and opportunity. He was the last one seen with her before her murder. He won't be able to hide behind young Jodi's lifestyle as a defense like he will do so cowardly with Miss Miller. And, ladies and gentlemen, there is an eyewitness to this crime. Yes, someone saw this murder, but was so terrified that he is just now coming forward." Billy's revelation of an eyewitness jolted the spectators, the jury and J. B., and a murmur went through the courtroom. Piti sprang to his feet.

"Ya honah, I object."

"Approach the bench," J. B. commanded. "Billy, what's this about?"

Billy looked smug. "Ya honah, this evidence was just discovered yesterday."

Piti sweating harder than before, said, "This is outrageous, ya honah. The defense has no knowledge of this so-called eyewitness."

Billy said laconically, "Ya honah, Mr. Pitman has known about this witness for some time. His name is Mr. Cassius Carey, a friend of the defendant. Perhaps he thought he'd hurt his case."

"Mr. Pitman, is this true? Did you know of the existence of this witness?"

Piti hesitated, thinking he'd lost before he stood up. Billy was better, much better. He was outclassed. Duped. Who was he kidding?

"Mr. Pitman, go to your seat. Overruled. Mr. Penick, continue."

Piti's shrunken confidence as he walked back to his seat communicated defeat to the courtroom and grave concern to Lincoln. Lincoln's eyes asked Piti, *What is this about?*" Piti shrugged his shoulders and shook his head.

After the sidebar with J. B., Billy approached the jury and announced calmly and slowly, pointing back at Mack Oliver, "There sits the murderer of Tiffany Miller and Jodi Wallace. If it wasn't true, I wouldn't be standing here saying so." He looked into the eyes of each juror and then took a deliberate walk back to the prosecutor's table, stacked the papers on it neatly, as if to communicate that all things significant had been said and to stop listening. The trial was over, he seemed to be saying.

Piti had a lot to overcome. Mack Oliver sat emotionless.

"Mr. Pitman." A few moments went by. "Mr. Pitman," J. B. repeated, sounding impatient.

Piti stood, his status, presence and delivery the antithesis of Billy's. He adjusted himself. The courtroom was silent. Piti's steps seemed to squish on the marble floor. The first words shook around in his mouth before he got them out.

"Mr. Purifoy is no more a murderer than you or I." Piti's statement again focusing minds. "I don't have an alibi either for the night Tiffany Miller was murdered. I was home in bed, just like Mr. Purifoy. But Tiffany's death is tragic. Like her family, Mr. Purifoy mourned her death. He loved her. He went looking for her the next morning when she didn't return home. He went to the Storyteller Fountain on the Southside. He found out she had been murdered at that very moment when friends there told him. He talked to a dozen people at the rehabilitation center where he was receiving aftercare addiction treatment about the loss of this young lady he loved. Sure, his DNA was present in her body. She was his girlfriend, a fact you heard the prosecution concede. He wasn't arrested for this crime nearly a year ago now.

He wasn't even a suspect. And why not? One large hand killed Miss Miller, the hand of a very powerful man. Mr. Purifoy is five-feet, seven-inches tall and weighs under a hundred and fifty pounds. He is an artist and a musician."

Piti's voice grew stronger. He seemed to be getting into his stride. "Now let's move to the night of December twenty-third. There were over fifty homeless men on the Southside and dozens of other people. At Christmastime, people are more generous, I understand, prone to giving when at other times they may not be. The prosecution would have you believe that because Mack Oliver asked for money, he's guilty. Because he was in the vicinity, he must have killed her. He is homeless, isn't he? Yes, my client is homeless. He has a drug addiction, which he has overcome, and he suffers from an illness, schizophrenia. But, regardless of your feelings about his affliction and his lifestyle, as Mr. Penick pointed out earlier, we are a nation of laws, not men. Mr. Penick also told us that no one is above the law, and he's right. But no one is below the law either. Mr. Purifoy's status in life makes him no less a citizen than you are. He is equal under the law, as equal as any of you. He must be presumed innocent. No guilt can be assigned to him because of who he is, only for what he's done. The question is, can the prosecution prove beyond a reasonable doubt that he is a cold-blooded double murderer?

"I submit to you this morning that their rationale is flawed and their evidence doesn't even come close. What happened to Miss Jodi Wallace on the Southside two months ago is a tragedy that no one will soon forget, and we should not. And the person who killed her should be brought to justice and punished to the full extent of the law, but it is important to punish the right person. Both Miss Miller and Miss Wallace deserve that. Their families deserve that. Mr. Purifoy was on the Southside on December twenty-third. He asked Miss Wallace for change to buy food, get a hot cup of coffee. She told him she didn't have any money. Mr. Purifoy has heard that answer many, many times. It didn't anger him. As a matter of fact, Miss Wallace returned later and gave Mr. Purifoy a five-dollar bill, which you'll hear testimony of, because her heart was moved to help a man in need. Contrary to making Mr. Purifoy angry, that would make any homeless person very happy. In return, Mr. Purifoy then gave her a bangle that he had made because he likes to give something to people who give to him. The bangle wasn't lost during any struggle between Mr. Purifoy and Miss Wallace. It was a gift. Yes, he did ride his bike behind her as she walked to her car, an attempt to make sure she got there safely. As they approached the car, she hugged him and said, 'Merry Christmas.' She felt she knew him and she liked him because she would sit and listen as he played his horn at the Storyteller Fountain. He rode away as she was placing items in her trunk. The hair from Mr. Purifoy found on the victims mitten was transferred during that innocent embrace.

"When Mr. Purifoy left Miss Wallace, she was alive. The prosecution tells us that there is an eyewitness, a Mr. Cassius Carey, who has decided – after two months – to come forward. Where has he been for the past two months? What the prosecution didn't say was that this man was picked up on the Southside for public drunkenness and nuisance. What are his motives for coming forward now? How reliable is his testimony? Where was *he* that night? The investigation into this murder that led to the arrest of my client only lasted two and a half days. The haste to arrest someone because of the victim's family's status and prejudice toward the accused has us here trying the wrong man. I only ask this, that you be open minded. This is a murder trial. Two people have lost their lives and this man, Mr. Purifoy, is on trial for his." Piti took his seat.

Even J. B. was impressed with Piti's opening statement. Billy had not seen this defense attorney standing before the court in Piti's skin. He was no longer the drunken ambulance chaser today that Billy had come to know and beat easily. Today, he looked competent and like the friendly, fat uncle that every juror surely had and probably liked.

The prosecution called Marion and James Miller, humble people who described the loss of their daughter, Tiffany. They were followed by Draper and Millicent Wallace to establish the circumstances under which their daughter came to be on the Southside on December 23. The presence of the four parents describing the ultimate loss was dispiriting. Piti did not cross examine.

The prosecution called the Jefferson County coroner, Reuben Knox, to establish cause and time of death.

"Dr. Knox, how long have you been a coroner?"

"Over twenty-two years."

"I would imagine you've determined cause of death for hundreds of people."

"Thousands."

"You ever testified in court before?"

"Dozens of times."

"You graduated from the University of Alabama?"

"Yes."

"Fine school."

Dr. Knox was sixty years old. His expertise was not in question. Billy wanted to leave no possibility that his word could be disputed. Knox was prone to speaking mechanically, giving a clipped response with no change of expression, regardless of the question. He showed no emotion and talked about the victims as one would discuss inanimate objects.

"How'd Miss Miller die?"

"Asphyxia."

"Asphyxia?"

"A lack of oxygen, in this case caused by strangulation."

"What time did she die, Dr. Knox?"

"Approximately one a.m., March thirty-first."

"Any DNA present in or on Miss Miller's body matching the defendant?"

"Yes."

"What type?"

"Semen."

"Dr. Knox, how was Miss Wallace murdered?"

"Asphyxia caused by strangulation."

"Any other damage to the young victim's body?"

"Yes."

"What, doctor?"

"A broken hand in the carpus region and two broken phalanges on the same hand."

"In other words, a broken wrist and two broken fingers?"

"Yes."

"Which hand?"

"The right hand."

Billy turned to the judge, "Let me introduce into evidence, ya honah, that the victim was right-handed." Again, he addressed Dr. Knox, "Could the broken hand have happened by trying to defend herself?"

"Objection," Piti interjected. "He's a coroner."

"Who has given his opinion about causes of death in thousands of cases," Billy retorted.

"Overruled."

"Doctor?"

"Yes. In my opinion, she was trying to defend herself."

"Doctor, you also found a single strand of hair on the victim's right-handed mitten?"

"Yes."

"Doctor, has there been a positive match of that hair?"

"Yes."

"Whose is it?"

"The defendant's."

"Which part of the body did the hair come from?"

"The head."

"Doctor, Miss Wallace was also raped?"

"Sexually assaulted."

"What do you mean?"

"The perpetrator used what appeared to be a wine bottle with a chipped edge. There were lacerations and bruises to her vagina and the vulva and anal regions."

"A wine bottle?"

"Traces of wine were found in the vagina and on the victim's body." Billy introduced the coroner's pictures of the victim's body. Her family, some spectators and a few of the jurors began to cry. Billy then held up a bangle made of twisted aluminum wire.

"Doctor, what is this?"

"It appears to be a crude bracelet of some sort."

"This was retrieved from the victim's left hand?"

"Yes."

"Do you know where it came from?"

"No."

Billy brought out a large poster board with Mack Oliver's ominous-looking arrest photo, dozens of silver chains around his neck visible. Then he presented photos of his hands, a ring on each finger, and dozens of silver bracelets to the elbow, most homemade and many identical to the bracelet in evidence. The picture communicated exactly what Billy knew it would.

"Doctor, could the victim have pulled this bracelet off the defendant during a struggle?"

"Ya, honah, I object." Piti stood up this time.

"Sustained."

"What time was Miss Wallace killed?" Billy wrapped up.

"Between eleven and eleven-thirty p.m."

"No further questions, ya honah."

"Mr. Pitman."

Piti approached the coroner with a contemplative air, "Dr. Knox, was there other semen present in Miss Miller, beside that of the defendant?"

"Yes."

"How many other donors?"

"Two others."

"Do we know who they are?"

"No."

"Doctor, Mr. Purifoy was Miss Miller's boyfriend. Is that consistent with his semen being present in her body?"

"I would imagine."

"Doctor, to your knowledge, do you know of a wine bottle being recovered at the scene of either crime?"

"No."

"So there are no fingerprints of Mr. Purifoy on a wine bottle?"

"No."

"Mr. Purifoy also doesn't drink alcohol. He wouldn't have a wine bottle with him. You say that the victims died of asphyxia?"

"Yes."

"It's your belief that it was one gloved hand?"

"Yes."

"A big hand?"

"Impossible to know."

"There were two cracked vertebrae?"

"Yes."

"Then a powerful person?"

"Yes."

"Can hair be transferred to clothing or gloves by mutual casual contact like hugging?"

"Yes, of course."

"The prosecution offers that the bangle came off during a struggle. Could he have just given it to her?"

"Ya honah," Billy cried.

"Withdrawn, ya honah. No further questions."

Billy redirected. "Doctor, I've read that men in rage, especially those mentally ill, can show incredible strength, regardless of size. Have you read that?"

"Yes."

"Dr. Knox, one last question. Was Mr. Cassius Carey tested as a donor of the semen you found in Miss Miller?"

"Yes."

"And what was the result?"

"The preliminary results are negative."

"Negative? He wasn't a donor?"

"Doesn't appear to be."

"No further questions, ya honah."

Billy next called Alan Alman to the stand, who testified that he'd suffered from harassment by Mack Oliver and other homeless people on the Southside for years. He said that he'd seen Mack Oliver harassing Miss Wallace the night of the murder. Allison Drover and Stephanie Winters described a menacing defendant who followed their friend into a dark alley. They said that they felt nervous about her walking alone and regretted not walking with her. Piti established that none of them saw Mack Oliver commit murder, but their testimonies confirmed that the person last seen with her between 11:00 p.m. and 11:30 p.m. was Mack Oliver, in conjunction with the coroner's timeline for when she was killed, which no one disputed.

Finally, J. B. asked, "Mr. Penick, how many more witnesses do you plan to call?"

"Just one, ya, honah."

"Well, let's take a lunch break and resume at two o'clock p.m." He looked over to Piti, "Mr. Pitman?"

"That's fine, ya honah."

The gavel adjourned the court.

"Bailiff, see the jurors out."

Piti asked the guard to give him a few minutes with Mack Oliver. Lincoln offered a supportive hand on his shoulder.

"Mack Oliver, Cassius Carey will say he saw you murder Jodi Wallace."

Mack Oliver shook his head. "He's lying. I didn't do it."

"Was there anyone else in the alley when you left Miss Wallace?"

"Not that I saw."

"Did you see Cassius?"

"No, no."

"Alright, that's alright. Guard." Lincoln did not say a word until Mack Oliver was taken back.

"Piti, you did an excellent job this morning."

"It won't be enough."

"Let me buy you a cup of coffee." They walked silently to the cafeteria. They'd both take it black. Neither had an appetite. Lincoln finally broke the silence.

"It's my fault."

"What's your fault?"

"Cassius being here. It's my fault."

"It wouldn't have mattered, Lincoln. If anything, he hurts their case a lot. He's a wild card Billy didn't count on. Billy wishes he'd never shown up. If he hadn't, the jury would be able to follow along simply. Cut and dried. But these antisocials, doctor, what can I expect? Cassius is the only other witness he'll call."

"He's going to lie and he's going to be believable."

"You said I wouldn't be able to trip him up."

"I don't think so. What about me, Piti? Are you going to call me?"

"No. I'm sure Cassius has told Billy about your exploits in Atlanta. You'll be badly impeached, but I wasn't going to call you anyway during Mack Oliver's defense," Piti said, trying to make Lincoln feel better. "If he's convicted, we can use you during the sentencing phase. You'd make a great character witness."

"What about Mack Oliver? Will you call him?"

"No, absolutely not. It would be disastrous. Billy would eat him alive."

Two o'clock p.m. arrived much sooner than Piti would have liked. He found himself exactly where he'd started two months ago. Lincoln, offering no advice, and had a look of dread on his face. Mack Oliver's eyes were affixed straight ahead.

"Ya honah, the People call Mr. Cassius Carey. Mr. Carey, please state your full name and address for the record."

Cassius was clean-shaven with an erect bearing, unlike the person Piti had imagined in his mind. He appeared well adjusted and stated his name articulately.

"Cassius Carey, Seven-sixteen, Fifth Avenue West, Atlanta, Georgia."

Billy began his questioning. "Mr. Carey, what's your relationship to the defendant?"

"We're friends."

"How did you come to know him?"

"I met him on the Southside where he used to play his horn. His deceased girlfriend, Tiffany, and my girlfriend were also friends."

"Miss Miller?"

"Yes, Tiffany Miller."

"How long have you known the defendant?"

"More than two years."

"Mr. Carey, where have you been for the past two months?"

"Drug treatment. I'm a recovering alcoholic and addict."

"How long have you been clean?"

"Over two months."

"I'm glad to hear that. You said you and Mr. Purifoy are friends?"

"Yes."

"How close?"

"I love him. He's my best friend."

"Mr. Carey, did you know Tiffany Miller well?"

"Yes, like I said, she was best friends with my girlfriend, Cynthia. We used to hang out together with her and Mack Oliver. He had a house on the Southside that his mother left him."

"Do you have any knowledge of who murdered Tiffany Miller?"

"Somewhat."

"What do you mean somewhat?"

"I knew Mack Oliver was angry with her."

"Why was he angry?"

"When he sold his house, she stole the money and used it to buy drugs. He said his mother bought that house with insurance money she received when his father died. She loved that house and died there."

"Why did Mr. Purifoy sell the house?"

"He was told he had to."

"By whom?"

"By the city. They eminent domained the house. He had no choice."

"Do you know how much he sold the house for?"

"Only ten thousand dollars. He thought he should have gotten much more."

"Let's go back to Miss Miller for a minute. Did he ever tell you he was going to hurt her?"

"Yes."

"What did he say?"

"I'm going to kill that..."

"I'm sorry, Mr. Carey. Could you repeat that, please?"

"He said, 'I'm going to kill that bitch.'"

"'I'm going to kill that bitch,' and of course, he did."

"Objection."

"Sustained."

There was satisfaction in Billy's voice. "Mr. Carey, you said the house that Mr. Purifoy owned was *eminent domained* by the city?"

"Yes."

"Mr. Purifoy sold his house for ten thousand dollars?"

"That's what he told me."

"The court record of the transaction bears that out. The house, according to comps in the area is worth forty thousand to sixty thousand dollars."

"Mack Oliver was very angry when he found out."

"Do you know how he found out?"

"Well, after the money was all gone, he started asking around. People told him he got cheated. Then he was even angrier. I think he just snapped. His mother used to be able to talk to him, but she's gone."

"Who did he blame for losing the house?"

"Tiffany and the billionaire, Draper Wallace. The city gave Draper Wallace the house, all the houses, and the land where he's building those condos for one dollar. They were on the news all the time talking about how good it was for the city for the old houses to be gone and others to move in. Middle-class people, white people, is what they meant. He said he wanted to kill Draper Wallace, but that wouldn't hurt badly enough. He wanted him to die everyday for the rest of his life."

"How was he going to do that?"

"He was going to take what he loved the most and destroy his life the way he had destroyed Mack Oliver's life. His daughter. He was going to kill the girl."

"Mr. Carey, why didn't you tell someone?"

"I don't know. I'll have to live with that for the rest of my life. It has made me sick inside. I relapsed because of it. My mind has been so messed up, I couldn't think straight. But I tried to stop him that night. He had been looking for an opportunity for six months, but she was away at school. He just knew he'd run into her that night. I asked him why he wasn't playing his horn that night. I thought if he played he wouldn't get into trouble. He didn't answer me. He was just sitting and waiting on her and drinking heavily. I saw him asking her for money. I took my eyes off him for just a little while. By the time I got to the alley, he was just standing there. The girl was in the trunk. I'll never forget his eyes. He was out of his mind."

"What did you do next?"

"I ran. I didn't stop until I got to Atlanta, but I couldn't take it anymore. I came back."

"Why did you come back, Mr. Carey?"

"I was working the Steps. There are Twelve Steps to recovery from addiction. I was working Step Five. It's called Making Amends. 'Admit to God and to another human being the exact nature of our wrongs.' I needed to come back and come clean so these families could have peace, so I could have peace. That's why I came back."

"Mr. Purifoy's lawyer may say you killed Tiffany Miller and Jodi Wallace, and that you're blaming Mack Oliver to save your own hide. How do you answer that?"

"I can understand that a lawyer should do whatever he can to protect his client. I was willing to run away so I didn't have to betray a friend, but after getting treatment and working the Steps, I knew I must tell the truth. Besides, what motive did I have? This killing just has to stop. Mack Oliver has to be stopped."

"That's all, ya honah," Billy took his seat.

Cassius' story had sucked the air out of the room. The jurors could not take anymore. The Wallaces were leaving the courtroom.

"Mr. Pitman, in light of the hour and to afford you an uninterrupted cross, I think we'll end for today. Mr. Carey, you will be remanded to the custody of the court until the conclusion of this trial. Do you understand the charge of this court?"

"Yes, your honor."

"Court will resume tomorrow morning at nine a.m."

Mack Oliver did not object. He didn't protest. He just sang as the guards returned him to his cell. The gavel sounding did little to bring the court to recess. The jurors were ushered out by the bailiff, but most spectators just stood there after J. B. walked out, unsure of what to do next.

Cassius wanted to know how Lincoln knew he was in Atlanta. What had Mack Oliver told Lincoln about him? Was Dr. Sam in on it? Cassius' rage was nicely wrapped up, however. He looked sincere, believable. He was calm and seemed to have remorse for Mack Oliver. He would have testified all evening. He loved this stage. Having control of a courtroom, an audience, and someone's life were reinforcing to Cassius, that he was smarter than anyone in the courtroom. The more time he spent on the witness stand, the more believable his story would get. Piti and Mack Oliver were no match. Was anyone?

Lincoln Drake's experience with sociopaths made him the only one not shocked at the story that had unfolded in this late afternoon. Cassius would stop at nothing to keep his freedom, even if it meant sending a friend to jail. Cassius had reached an age where most sociopaths were tired, burned out and wanted to rest, but these urges were suppressed now and his only motive was his own life. Lincoln anticipated that it would be impossible to make Cassius stumble on the witness stand. Lincoln knew Cassius probably had believed parts of his own story and felt himself a victim.

Mack Oliver was expendable, weak, and Cassius wasn't going to jail for what he perceived as trying to help Mack Oliver. Mack Oliver had been stupid to sell his house for $10,000. He had been even more stupid for letting Tiffany Miller steal the money. He had been weak to do nothing about it. He should have taken care of Tiffany and Draper Wallace himself. Cassius was only trying to help him.

Lincoln had to talk to Sam. He knew the answer had to be in Atlanta. They needed her help.

CHAPTER TWENTY-SIX

Forgiveness

The two-and-a-half hour drive had Lincoln standing on the corner outside of the Atlanta YMCA at 8:00 p.m. Sam's anger had subsided to some degree. She even seemed to be expecting his arrival. She had hoped he would come anyway.

"Sam, I'm sorry," was the first thing out of his mouth.

"Would you like a cup of coffee, Lincoln?"

"God, yes."

"There's a great place around the corner." Their walk was silent and slow, both secretly relishing every step. Sam ordered apple cobbler with her coffee. Lincoln took his coffee black.

"I don't know your patient, Lincoln," Sam said after Lincoln had filled her in on the details of the day. "I can only imagine someone that you think innocent being on trial for murder. I have had a patient be put on death row. I have some spending the rest of their lives in prison, dozens with sentences of more than twenty years. I know you've had many, too. What would you have me to do? Your lawyer has the medical record. He has my thoughts about Cassius. He is a drug and alcohol addicted sociopath. I have others like him in the center on any given day. Testifying against him is unethical and not permitted by law. I'm his therapist. He's supposed to be able to confide in me. What would I say? He has never confessed a past crime or any intent to commit a crime. What would I say, Lincoln? Would I say he seems like a likely candidate to have committed a crime?

A murder? Don't you think the D.A. could match that with their own expert who would say that Mack Oliver is a likely candidate as well? This is a job for the lawyers and the courts, not doctors."

"I can't give up, Sam."

"Why? You've had many people you've treated that have committed crimes, Lincoln. What is it about Mack Oliver that is making you so desperate?"

"Have you ever witnessed someone die? By lethal injection? Or in Alabama, the electric chair? Have you ever seen that?"

"No."

"It changes you." Lincoln was silent for a moment. "Mack Oliver never had a chance. I can't watch an innocent man die. Mack Oliver has no one else."

"Pretend I'm your therapist, Lincoln. What else is there?"

Lincoln had broken the law and not been able to sleep for two months. The truth was he had treated many sociopaths and schizophrenics. He had had fugitives use his treatment center as a safe harbor. He had heard confessions of all sorts that he chose not to hear. Sam knew it. On some level, Lincoln knew it. Why Mack Oliver? Dr. Sam knew he was struggling with more than Mack Oliver's fate, as if his own was tied to it.

"What is it, Lincoln?"

Lincoln exhaled, losing his controlled, rigid bearing that had been trained into him and expected of him his whole life. Sam was looking at him the way she had a week earlier.

"I was raised in a carriage house," Lincoln stated. "The servant's quarters of an estate in one of the richest suburbs in America. My father dropped out of school in the eighth grade. My mother was a house servant. For whatever reason, they were born with incredible strength. I have known many very successful men and very powerful men, but I have never known anyone as strong or as smart as Jefferson Drake. I'm sitting here with you drinking a five-dollar cup of coffee with a Ph.D. and an inheritance of over sixteen million dollars because I just happened to be born one mile down the road from Mack Oliver. My father just happened to be Jefferson Drake instead of Big Mack Purifoy."

"Lincoln, do you feel unworthy?"

"I am unworthy."

"Many people have had the great fortune you've been blessed with."

"Not many people from where I'm from. Maybe where you're from, Sam. Jefferson Drake fought for me. He fought for me so hard that I lived, that I succeeded. I triumphed, but he did it. I didn't do it. He did it for me. No one ever loved Mack Oliver more than they loved themselves. He was born to lose, to be homeless. He was dealt a bad hand from the start, in the womb. I feel like I have to do this for Mack Oliver."

"You pity Mack Oliver. I don't know him, but I'm sure he doesn't want your pity."

Lincoln was silent for a moment, perplexed at the idea. "He said the same thing. But there is no truth to that. I don't pity him."

"What did he say?"

"He said I was no different from others who thought they were better than him, but that's not true."

"It's not, Lincoln? You wouldn't want to be Mack Oliver, would you?"

"No, of course not."

"But you think he would want to be you? Tell me about him, Lincoln."

"He's an artist, extremely talented. He's very intelligent, uncanny at times."

"But he's poor and he's schizophrenic, so you think these talents are lost. You quoted Fairchild when you interviewed me. You said she said that it was us who needed help, not the poor. She meant our hearts needed more compassion and understanding, that there would always be an ample supply of poverty."

Samantha covered Lincoln's hands with both of hers. She looked at him and said, "I don't think Mack Oliver wants a five-dollar cup of coffee. I don't think he wants your sixteen million. It hasn't made you happy. And what about me, Lincoln? How do you feel about me?"

"I love you, Sam. I love you."

"And you feel guilty about that, too. And even guiltier that you think I may love you."

"So you've diagnosed me."

"Yes, unfortunately."

They'd both smile. Lincoln felt somewhat relieved.

"Perhaps Mack Oliver has had someone he loved very much, Lincoln, and doesn't envy you with me. When I first met you, I asked you why you wanted to be a therapist and work with this population. You remarked 'What else would I be doing?' as if you had no other choice. It struck me that you had a heavy dose of guilt motivating you. There are many other things you could be doing, Lincoln. What if Mack Oliver also pitied you? Wouldn't that be a twist? You have to do this for you, Lincoln. Know who you are doing it for."

"So, doctor, what's my diagnosis?"

"Survivor's guilt, but your prognosis is good."

Lincoln knew she was right. "So, you love me," he added.

"Let's talk about that later. What are you going to do about Mack Oliver?"

"Is there anything you can do to help, Sam?"

"Cassius is my patient. Our communications are privileged. My talking to you about him is against the law. He has made intimation about crimes, but nothing though that we haven't heard before. Without the information you've given me, Lincoln, the things he suggested wouldn't have meant anything. I have to act like I didn't hear them. With more treatment and at his age, he is really at a point of breaking through. I can't talk to you about Cassius." Sam wanted to help Lincoln. She hesitantly offered, "But I can talk to you about his mother."

"His mother?"

"Yes. She's not a patient. She's his chief enabler. She's very sick, but on some level, she knows. She knows who Cassius really is. I would be careful, though. She's protected him his whole life. Cassius won't discuss his mother. He protects her as well."

"In Cassius' testimony today, he blamed Mack Oliver for murder. If he's not impeached, Mack Oliver dies. I have to talk to the mother."

"Her name is Betsy Carey."

"Yeah, she's listed as the next of kin on the admission forms at Fairchild."

"That should give you an address and phone number."

"What do I say? She doesn't know me. Maybe you should call for me," Lincoln suggested, but Sam shook her head.

"No. That's all I can do. You're the man that broke into a treatment center and impersonated a grad student looking to do an internship. I'm sure you'll figure something out. After you do, ask her about the death of her son, Isaac, and her husband, the Reverend. She's protective of Cassius, remember that."

"And he's protective of her?"

Sam answered hesitantly, not wanting Lincoln to go any further with questions about Cassius. "Yes, he is."

Lincoln added, "She knows. Is there incest?"

Sam didn't answer.

"She's the key. Their relationship is the key. She has to come to Birmingham. She has to be put on that witness stand." Lincoln was thinking out loud. Sam sipped the warm coffee, fully understanding Lincoln's obsession.

Their meeting ended abruptly, as Lincoln stood and said, "I have to go. I have to call someone." He wrapped his arms around her and she returned the embrace, "Thank you, Sam."

"Lincoln, be careful. I know I don't have to tell you this, but Cassius is sick. Don't push...well, you know what I mean."

CHAPTER TWENTY-SEVEN

Hope

When Lincoln called, Piti was in the last round of a staring match he was having with a half gallon bottle of Jack Daniels Black Label he'd picked up from Toddies Package Store on his way home after leaving the courthouse when J. B. adjourned the court. Losing to Billy had always been a trigger for Piti. He had never beaten him, or even come close. He knew of no way he could overcome Billy's skill and Cassius' eyewitness testimony.

"Piti, you need to subpoena the mother."

"Who's mother, Lincoln? Where are you?"

"I'm in Atlanta. I'm on my way back to Birmingham."

"Atlanta?"

"Yes, but you need to subpoena Cassius' mother. She's here in Atlanta."

"Why?"

"She's the key."

"What do you mean, Lincoln?"

"She knows the truth about Cassius."

"What makes you think she'll talk?"

"She's the only chance you have."

"But a subpoena will take two days, minimum, even with J. B.'s influence. She's in another state."

"Listen, I grew up in J. B.'s backyard. I know him and I knew his father. If they want something done, it happens. If you say there's a two-day minimum that means he can have her there tomorrow. And don't forget, this is Draper Wallace's daughter. You just have to convince J. B. that he needs to do it."

Piti hesitated a moment and with a defeated voice, asked, "Lincoln, why wasn't Mack Oliver playing his horn the night of the murder of Jodi Wallace? And why didn't he play it on Christmas Eve? It just doesn't add up."

"Do you still not trust him, Piti? I warned you Cassius would be believable. He's lying. He's a sociopath. Mack Oliver's mother introduced him to music. She loved music, but Big Mack wouldn't let her play the piano or sing in the choir. Mack Oliver used to play for her. She died last Christmas. Playing at Christmastime would have reminded him too much of his mother. He thought he might relapse, use drugs again. That's what happened last year. That's what made him relapse. We talked about it. I told him not to play at Christmas."

"Triggers, right? You told me about those. I have some, too," Piti sighed. "J. B.'s not going to listen to me, Lincoln, especially not after today. He gave me that disgusted look after I objected to Billy calling Cassius and Billy told J. B. I knew of his existence. He'll hang up on me."

"But he'll listen to Wallace. You have to figure out how you're going to get Wallace to call J. B.," Lincoln insisted.

Then Piti thought of Connolly. "Connolly knows something isn't right. Connolly can get Wallace to call J. B."

"I called the center and got Mrs. Carey's address. You give it to Connolly, Piti. I have another call to make."

After he hung up the phone, Piti tossed the bottle from his back door into the alley, where it sounded like a small hand grenade hitting the street. The noise woke the neighbors and caused a chain reaction of barking dogs. It was the first time Piti had ever awakened the neighbors when he had chosen *not* to drink.

As Piti predicted, Connolly's call to Wallace incited him to arouse J. B., and an Atlanta judge issued a subpoena to Betsy Carey to appear in court the next morning at 9:00 a.m. Connolly and Franks picked her up at the Alabama state line the morning of February 26. The order had taken only two hours.

Lincoln made his call to Jacob Levin at *The Birmingham News*. He wanted to get a story out about Mack Oliver and a second suspect, Cassius Carey.

"Jacob, this is Lincoln."

A shocked, but happy voice responded, "Lincoln?"

"Yes. How are you?"

"Great. It's wonderful to hear from you. I saw you in the courtroom today. It doesn't look good for Mr. Purifoy. I'm sorry. I hear he's a patient of yours."

"Yes, that's why I'm calling. He's innocent, Jacob."

"It doesn't look like it."

"You've known me all of my life, Jacob. He didn't do it."

"Who did?"

"The man who was the eyewitness, Cassius Carey. He's a cold-blooded, sociopathic murderer. If he is turned loose, there will be more deaths. I'd like to give the jurors something to think about at least. They are not sequestered." Lincoln described the events that had led to his phone call.

"What do you need?" Jacob asked.

"I was hoping we could get a friendly article out about Mack Oliver in the morning paper."

"Lincoln, I'd like to help, but the morning edition has already gone to press. It's not like it used to be. I think I could get a *Rushed to Judgment* segment on the morning television news, though. Everybody watches the news on television now." Jokingly, Jacob said, "The only two loyal readers I have left are my mother and your father. How is he, Lincoln?"

"He's not so well these days."

"He's a great man, Lincoln."

Lincoln was silent for a moment. "I saw your mother at the…uh, holiday party at the club. We sat together. It was good to see her. My mother really enjoyed talking to her."

"It's okay, Linc, you can say it. It was the Christmas Gala. She's never missed that party. It's the biggest event of the year, and she's got to know what's going on. Listen, I can get you a headline in the evening edition. The consensus is the trial will go into jury deliberation tomorrow. Lincoln, I hope he prevails."

"Thanks. It's good to talk to you, Jacob."

"We should stay in touch."

"I'll see you in the morning at the trial."

"Yeah."

CHAPTER TWENTY-EIGHT

The Verdict

On February 25 and 26, there was no more important an event in Birmingham, Alabama than the murder trial of Mack Oliver Purifoy. The attention that had been given to the murder of Jodi Wallace had climaxed even more dramatically than anyone had imagined. The day and night news coverage for the past two months now seemed appropriate. The Millers were thankful that they would have closure, but the Wallaces would never be the same family again. With Jodi gone, their faces portrayed doused hope, purpose and expectation. The large courtroom seemed to be even more crowded, but much more still.

It was five minutes before 9:00 a.m., and even the normally profligate Billy was in his seat. Mack Oliver appeared bedraggled, even in the fresh shirt and tie he was wearing. The thoughts of Cassius' accusations had caused him to suspect himself. Lincoln had accurately assessed a mild temporary psychotic break. Piti was right; that he could hurt himself if he took the witness stand. Piti and Lincoln had conferred most of the morning over breakfast. Neither had an appetite. A taciturn Betsy Carey waited in a witness room. The bailiff would announce the arrival of J. B., his entrance having no less of an impact than the day before. Piti had asked J. B. if he could begin his cross of Cassius after the testimony of Cassius' mother.

"Mr. Pitman, Mr. Penick, approach the bench. Mr. Pitman, I've read your motion. Mr. Penick, any objection?"

"Ya, honah, the Court has made great accommodation to have Mrs. Carey brought here to testify. I hope this is not just a Hail Mary on Mr. Pitman's behalf that will needlessly cause these families additional and avoidable distress, but it's his client, ya, honah. The People will yield."

"Mr. Penick, you have no other witnesses?"

"No suh, ya honah."

As Piti had requested, Connolly and Franks had arranged for Cassius to be outside the courtroom when his mother was brought in, affording him the full impression of an ambush, which Lincoln thought might unnerve him. He then would be taken back to a secluded witness room to await the continuance of his testimony.

Mrs. Carey entered the courtroom unsure of the level of her son's involvement, but she had had a lot of experience with being put in the situation of being asked about Cassius. First, when he was a child in school. In the community when there would be trouble. Church. The job. All of his life, one occurrence after another. She protectively referred to it as the persecution of her son.

Mrs. Carey walked gently up to the stand and smiled at the jurors and the judge. She initiated a "Good morning," and J. B. and each juror were compelled to answer back in unison, "Good morning."

She gave the impression of being an honest, concerned elderly mother who had probably raised an honest son, who had just fallen on bad luck. Piti had to be careful. A harsh direct could alienate the jury, but he trusted Lincoln who'd told Piti he had to break her.

"Mr. Pitman, you may proceed."

"Good morning, Mrs. Carey."

"Good morning, sir," she replied in a soft, polite voice.

"Mrs. Carey, do you know why you are here this morning?"

"I was summoned by the court to be here. I am here as the judge ordered." Her voice was articulate and soothing.

"Mrs. Carey, there have been two murders here in Birmingham last year of a Miss Tiffany Miller and a Miss Jodi Wallace. Do you have any knowledge of those murders?"

"Yes, of course. The whole nation has either read about that in the papers or watched it unfold on the television."

"My client," Piti said, looking toward Mack Oliver, "has been charged with those murders."

"Yes, I am aware of that. But, sir, what does any of this have to do with me?"

"Mrs. Carey, your son has said he saw my client commit these murders. Mrs. Carey, I believe your son is not telling the truth. I believe that he is the true murderer of these two women." Piti was taking a gamble that shocked the spectators, causing J. B. to use his gavel.

"Ordah! Ordah!"

"For heavens sake, how could you say such a thing?" Mrs. Carey sounded shocked.

"Mrs. Carey, have you ever had a conversation with your son about these murders?"

"Yes, I have. Last night. He expressed deep sorrow."

"Did you know that he knew the defendant?"

"No, I did not."

"Is that something that you think he would leave out accidentally?"

"He might."

"Did he tell you that the woman he calls his girlfriend, Cynthia Bates, has been missing for nine months?"

Mrs. Carey hesitated.

"Mrs. Carey?"

"No, he did not."

"Mrs. Carey, according to records obtained by the court, it appears that you home-schooled your son. Is that accurate, ma'am?"

"Yes, it is. I home-schooled both of my boys."

"How many children did you have, Mrs. Carey?"

"Three."

"Mrs. Carey, what were the circumstances that led to the decision to home-school Cassius?"

"They said he was unruly, but..."

"Mrs. Carey, would you be surprised to know that there is a teacher who still remembers your son, who said he was the most unruly and troubled child she's ever taught in her twenty-five-year history?"

"Objection," Billy said, almost lazily.

"Sustained."

Piti continued. "The medical records of Mr. Carey indicate that there were antisocial features in his personality and a conduct disorder by the age of nine, and two diagnosis of antisocial personality disorder from two different doctors that I will introduce into evidence now. The most recent diagnosis of antisocial personality disorder was just two months ago, by a Dr. Samantha Williams at the Atlanta Mental Health Center.

"Do you know what a sociopath is, Mrs. Carey? It's a person who has no regard or empathy for others. One who can lie and kill and have no remorse for his actions. Did you know your son was a sociopath, Mrs. Carey?"

"Ya, honah, she's not a psychologist," Billy interjected impatiently.

"Mr. Pitman," J. B. cautioned.

"Just bear with me, ya honah. I'm not asking her to testify to his mental status."

"No, he's just needlessly badgering his own witness and grabbing at straws," Billy countered.

Piti could see that he was starting to lose some of the jurors, who saw Mrs. Carey as a harmless elderly woman and Piti as a bully.

"Proceed, carefully, Mr. Pitman," J. B. advised.

"Mrs. Carey, you said you had three children?"

"Yes."

"Where are the other two?"

Mrs. Carey began to cry. This part of Lincoln's instructions given had been accomplished. But Piti feared the impression it was making on the jury, who was beginning to like him. But Cassius needed to see his mother in distress.

"Where are the other two, Mrs. Carey?"

"They are both deceased."

With his next question, Piti was breaking a cardinal rule of lawyers: Never ask questions to which you don't already know the answer. But Lincoln urged Piti at breakfast to concentrate on the deaths of Mrs. Carey's other children and Cassius' involvement. This felt like a time to make an exception to the cardinal rule.

"Mrs. Carey, how did your children die?"

Mrs. Carey dabbed her eyes with a tissue, "My oldest son died of a prolonged illness. His name was Mark Antony. My youngest son, Isaac, died of injuries sustained in an accidental fall."

Piti looked at Lincoln, who at breakfast had urged him to

concentrate on Isaac's death and Cassius' involvement in it. Piti glanced at Lincoln, then continued.

"How old was he when he died, Mrs. Carey?"

"He was five."

"Where was Cassius when your son fell and died?"

"What do you mean?"

"Was Cassius there when he fell?"

"Yes, but he had nothing to do with his fall."

"Did anyone ever say he did?"

"Only his stepfather."

"His stepfather?" Piti held his breath. He was venturing into dangerous territory, appearing to know more than he did.

"The Reverend blamed him for everything. It was an accident. He just persecuted Cassius and Mark Antony. He called Mark Antony gay and sinful. He even liked Cassius more than Mark Antony, but he said Cassius was lazy because he was a carpenter and was wasting his mind. But after Isaac died, he hated Cassius."

"Where's your husband now, ma'am?"

"He's deceased."

"How did he die?"

"He choked while eating. He'd had a stroke."

"Was he feeding himself?"

"No."

"Who was feeding him, Mrs. Carey?"

"Ya honah, this is ridiculous," Billy complained.

"Overruled." J. B. was cautiously allowing broad latitude. This trial was about murder, and he'd called a Georgia circuit court judge at 11:00 p.m. and a deputy had aroused Mrs. Carey at midnight with a subpoena to get her in the courtroom this morning. She'd been driven to the state line by two troopers with flashing lights and speeding the whole way. Wallace wanted to hear her testimony. Billy and Piti were both shocked by the power and haste of the court when a citizen like Wallace was involved, and Piti was taking full advantage of the latitude.

"Mrs. Carey, you may answer the question," the judge directed.

"Cassius was feeding him."

"Cassius?"

"Yes."

Piti's mind had shifted to the coroner's report. The statement Mrs. Carey made about her son being a carpenter brought him to something that had troubled the coroner: a wood splinter in Jodi Wallace's neck.

Thumbing through his report, "Is your son right-handed, Mrs. Carey?" he asked.

"Yes."

"No further questions, ya honah." Piti ended abruptly.

As Billy stood, he pulled together his coat and looked at the jury with a bewildered gaze, wanting them to feel the same way. He shrugged his shoulders, saying sympathetically, "Mrs. Carey, ya honah, I have no questions for this witness."

The bailiff assisted Mrs. Carey from the stand. As she was guided to a seat that Piti had strategically selected, to afford Cassius a plain view of her when he took the stand, Mrs. Carey recognized a familiar face that elicited a smile. It was Samantha Williams, who had inconspicuously taken a seat on a rear pew. Lincoln, noticing the expression, turned to see Samantha as well. She left her seat to join Mrs. Carey.

A recalcitrant Cassius entered the courtroom. His sociopathic cool-headedness had been interrupted. Incensed that his mother had been dragged to Alabama for Draper Wallace, his eyes affixed on Lincoln, the person behind this plot, the reason he had been arrested and was in court. Then he turned his ominous gaze on Piti, and then on Mack Oliver.

As he was seated, he saw that the eyes of his mother had obviously been crying, and that Sam had taken a seat next to her. The presence of Sam and his mother made it more difficult for Cassius to be dishonest. He had to appear in control, uncompromised. He gathered his composure, but the damage was done. The jurors had seen the other side of him that quickly, and he knew it: the dark side of his personality that was so different from a day earlier. He awaited Piti's questions.

"Mr. Carey, what is your vocation? I mean, what do you do for a living?"

"Mr. Pitman, I know the meaning of the word vocation."

"The clarification was for the jury, Mr. Carey."

"They probably need it, don't they, and I think you know the answer to that question."

"Yes, I think I do. Ya honah, could the court reporter read for clarification, when I asked Mrs. Carey where Cassius was when her son, Isaac, fell and subsequently died of suspicious injuries?"

J. B. nodded in the affirmative.

The reporter took a minute, the suspense tormenting for the spectators. She cleared her throat and read the transcript, "Where was Cassius when your son fell and died? *What do you mean?* Was Cassius there when he fell? *Yes, but he had nothing to do with his fall.* Did anyone ever say he did? *Only his stepfather.* His stepfather? *The Reverend blamed him for everything. It was an accident. He just persecuted Cassius and Mark Antony. He called Mark Antony gay and sinful. He even liked Cassius more than Mark Antony, but he said Cassius was lazy because he was a carpenter and was wasting his mind. But after Isaac died, he hated Cassius.*"

"Ya honah, she can stop there. Because he was a carpenter and was wasting his mind. A carpenter. This piece of evidence, until now, was puzzling. It was always the missing piece of evidence that has given me trouble for two months. But ya honah, I'd like to bring to the attention of the court the coroner's findings of a small splinter of wood in the neck of Jodi Wallace and splinters of wood and sawdust on the neck and body of Tiffany Miller. That is consistent with the sawdust and wood fragments that would be on a carpenter's gloves. Someone who had on the same clothes and gloves they'd worked in on a construction site as a carpenter. Mr. Carey, isn't it a fact that you worked for the Wallace Corporation as a carpenter?"

Cassius didn't immediately answer, prompting J. B. to direct him, "Mr. Carey, you must answer the question."

"Yeah."

"As a carpenter on the very site where the condominiums are being built?"

"Yeah," Cassius answered with satisfaction.

"Also, ya honah, I will point out that the coroner's report said the murder was committed by the one-gloved right hand of the assailant. Mr. Carey is right-handed and a carpenter. My client is not a carpenter and is left-handed."

Cassius' court-appointed lawyer stood and motioned to Cassius to stop answering questions.

Cassius looked directly at Piti, "I'm done here."

"Mr. Carey, isn't it true that you killed Miss Tiffany Miller because you despised her for spending Mack Oliver's money, which he received for the sale of his house and that she used to buy drugs? That you felt the only fitting judgment for her was death? That you lay in wait in that alley and killed her with those large hands that were gloved with the same gloves you used at the construction site, where you worked for the Wallace Corporation? Isn't it true that you killed Jodi Wallace to punish the man you felt was ultimately responsible for putting you and Mack Oliver on the streets? The man building the condominiums? The man that received the properties for one dollar, Mr. Draper Wallace? You were in that alley drinking and hiding in the shadows to kill Tiffany Miller and Jodi Wallace. Isn't it also true that you, a parricide, a sociopath, killed these people in a drunken fit of revenge and hate? Isn't it true that you checked yourself into the Fairchild Center after murdering Tiffany Miller, and then checked yourself into the Atlanta Mental Health Center after murdering Jodi Wallace? That both times you were running and attempting to hide and avoid the authorities? Isn't it true that you were willing to let an innocent man be put to death to hide your crimes? One last question, Mr. Carey. Where is Cynthia Bates, your admitted girlfriend who has been missing for ten months?"

Cassius repeated, "I'm done here."

The relationship with his mother, the lies, the protection had been unspoken between them – an understanding they both tucked away in the darkest recesses of their minds. It would stay tucked away. Neither was able to allow the other to see any acknowledgment of their awareness of their deeds. Cassius would not answer.

Piti looked to the jurors, suggestive of Billy's style, and then to Mack Oliver, and then to Lincoln, and lastly to J. B.

"Ya honah, there sits the killah of Tiffany Miller and Jodi Wallace. I have no further questions of this man, ya honah."

After what seemed to be several minutes with spectators, jurors and the prosecution unsure of what they had witnessed, J. B.'s voice brought the surreal moment to reality.

"Mr. Penick," J. B. summoned.

"Yes, ya honah." Billy got to his feet slowly after a brief pause, "The People have no further questions of Mr. Carey."

"Mr. Penick, how do you wish to continue?" J. B. asked with a sapience that tacitly told Billy not to go on.

A shocked and uncharacteristically uncertain response came out. "Ya honah, the People will drop all charges against Mr. Purifoy, and, ya honah, we will file charges immediately against Mr. Cassius Carey for the murders of Miss Tiffany Miller and Miss Jodi Wallace."

As dramatically as the trial had begun, it had ended. But the pain of no closure would still be with the families of Tiffany and Jodi for months to come.

"Mr. Purifoy." J. B.'s voice brought order to the courtroom, "You are free to go."

He released the jurors, and the sound of his gavel adjourning the court had a delayed effect in ending the dramatic conclusion in the courtroom and the sanguineous tale that had unfolded.

CHAPTER TWENTY-NINE

The Passing of an Era

The walk down the drive felt different that night when Lincoln arrived at the Titusville house his father had built. He'd offered Mack Oliver refuge at his loft or a hotel, but Mack Oliver had declined. He wanted his bike, his horn, his rings, and bangles and he desperately wanted out of the suit Lincoln had purchased for him. He planned to spend the evening at the Storyteller Fountain. He played through the night to approving admirers. His cigar box was full of dollar bills and coins. Piti wanted to celebrate. He had many alternatives, however, when Lincoln told him he just wanted to spend the evening with Jefferson and Genevieve.

Sam made the journey back to Atlanta alone.

Betsy Carey kept a vigil for as long as she could at the jail where Cassius was being held.

Jefferson was having good and bad days. Today had been one of the good days. He and Genevieve were in the dining room when Lincoln arrived. Jefferson startled Lincoln, who didn't see him standing in the bay window, anticipating his son's arrival. Lincoln saw the approving smile gazing through the window as he stepped onto the porch. Jefferson had not touched his soup that evening. A hug first, and then a proud mother offered Lincoln a bowl of soup. He had no appetite yet, though. Jefferson took Lincoln into the study. He wanted him all to himself. Genevieve would understand. She would have much longer to spend with Lincoln than Jefferson. Jefferson's decline was not interrupted by good days. He carefully took his seat on the worn end of the sofa, where he'd sat for many years. Lincoln appeared to fade into the large recliner next to the fireplace facing his father.

"This article in the evening paper by Jacob is good." The voice not as strong, but was still reassuring to Lincoln. "'Mack Oliver Purifoy, the homeless man that changed Birmingham.' He plans to do a series on the homeless. Lincoln, you saved the man's life. I was wrong, you were right."

"Wrong about what, Pop?"

"I said he'd never leave jail. I was wrong, you were right." Lincoln thought to himself that he'd not recalled Jefferson being wrong before. Jefferson then said, "You made the right decision."

"The right decision, Pop?"

"Yes, the right decision. Life is nothing if not choice. You made the most difficult choice, the one that no one else would've made, and it was right. Lincoln, everyone has an opportunity during their life to make a difference. We all have a chance to do something great. I used to think that my chance happened on the battlefield in Europe. Now I know that my chance at greatness was when I had you. The decision you made to help this man was an opportunity at greatness. I'm proud of you son."

"Thanks, Dad. Thank you for being a father. I love you."

"Lincoln, two things. First, you need to find that girl in Atlanta and make up to her. I don't know what you did, but your mother thinks it was bad."

"You're the matchmaker now, Pop?"

"Your mother says that you love her. If you do you better. . .well, I think you'll know what to do. Second, I want you to tell me about your friend. Who's Mack Oliver?"

Jefferson and Lincoln talked and laughed through most of the night. Jefferson had poured the good scotch and Genevieve joined them when the fun seemed too irresistible to pass up.

It was the passing of an era for the Drakes and Birmingham.

Peyton Castelle and Draper Wallace's condominium project was a success. The middle class returned to downtown Birmingham in droves. The success of the project would cost Peyton the election – the new voters, mostly white, choosing not to go with him. William Penick III became governor. He was sworn in by Alabama Supreme Court Chief Justice J. B. McPeake.

Mack Oliver continued to play at the Storyteller Fountain almost nightly to even larger crowds, now that most people felt the City was safe.

Piti was no longer on the rotation of lawyers for the indigent and homeless. And with memories fading, he was now regarded as one of the top defense attorneys in the state.

Jefferson would succumb to cancer two weeks after the trial just shy of spring. The day of Jefferson's funeral would be the warmest on record for that date. The minister would remark that it was God's way of saying he was pleased with the life Jefferson had lived and was welcoming him home.

Lincoln Drake had become a man.

CHAPTER THIRTY

Letter from Home

The Pacific showed great agitation, as winter was losing its grip and giving way to spring. This Saturday morning, the Drakes were taking advantage of a much needed morning of doing nothing. The doctor had ordered rest for Samantha. The house they'd purchased only six months earlier felt as though they'd lived there for years. Samantha decorated the cottage using light, airy colors, appropriately complementing its ocean views. Genevieve helped select the fabrics and furnishings, a needed diversion to help her cope with the loss of Jefferson. She'd stayed in California with Lincoln and Samantha for two months after their marriage, but wanted to return to the house she and Jefferson had shared for two decades.

Samantha reclined in an overstuffed, wicker rocker on the large, rear porch of the beach house, while Lincoln finished a mid-morning run. As Lincoln made his way up the steps of the porch, he greeted Samantha with, "Good morning," and gave her an extra-long kiss.

Samantha responded, "Good morning."

"What are you doing up? Did I wake you? It's just eleven a.m.," Lincoln said jokingly.

"No, your daughter did. I think she was hungry."

They both rubbed Samantha's stomach. She was in her second trimester.

"Have you seen the dog?" Lincoln asked.

"No, I haven't."

"Unlike her."

"Well, you got her from the pound. They said she was a roamer."

Lincoln called for the dog. "Murphy…here, girl!" Lincoln then walked through the house to the front porch and retrieved the mail from the mail box. Some windows were open, the soft drapes moving in the gentle breeze that flowed through the house. He whistled for Murphy again, "Here, girl!" even louder, before he returned to the rear porch.

"I'm sure she will be right back, Lincoln. Your mother called twice yesterday and so did Piti. We must have been asleep."

"Piti? He probably needs more marriage tips. He thinks I'm an expert."

"I called your mother back while you were running. She said she wanted to talk to you. She seemed a little upset."

"I'm sure she's just missing Dad. It's been a year. They always looked forward to spring. I'll give her a call. You want something to drink?" he asked. He pulled back the screen door and handed Sam the mail, while delivering another kiss on her cheek.

Lincoln retrieved the phone and dialed his mother. "Mom, it's Lincoln. Are you okay?"

"God, yes. I'm fine. Just worried that I couldn't get you last night."

"Were you having trouble sleeping, Mom?"

"Listen, I'm fine. It's not me."

"What's wrong?"

"It's Cassius Carey."

The name sent chills down his spine. "Yes?"

"He escaped."

"Escaped?" Lincoln repeated in a low voice, as he walked back to the porch to look in on Sam, who was going through the mail. He walked back into the house. "Mom, when did this happen?"

"Thursday night."

"Thursday?"

"It's all over the television."

Lincoln absorbed the news. "Well, it's nothing to worry about, Mom. I'm sure they'll have him back in custody soon. This happens. They always get caught within a few days. Don't tell Sam, okay? The baby and all." Then he added calmly, "Mom, I want you to stay at the McPeakes for a few days. Can you do that? Spend some time with Mrs. McPeake. It'll help you sleep, take your mind off Dad."

"Well, okay, but nothing will take my mind off of your father."

"Just for a couple of days, okay? Can you go now?"

Lincoln ended the phone call with his mother and began to dial Piti. He had nervously dialed a few numbers when he heard Samantha's shrill voice call him. "Lincoln!"

He dropped the phone and rushed back to the porch. Samantha was clutching a letter, her eyes wide with shock and fear.

"What is it?" he asked.

"This. . .this letter," with a trembling hand, she handed the letter to Lincoln. "It's from Cassius. What's going on?"

Lincoln sat down and began to read the letter:

Dear Dr. Sam,

I hope my letter finds you in good health and good spirits. I hope all is fine with the new marriage, although I don't think he deserves you. I read that the doctor proposed to you at a restaurant.

Seems a little tacky. The pictures of you in the paper didn't capture the joy I hope you felt that day. You looked quite sad.

I wanted to thank you for your commitment and loyalty. I know you genuinely cared about me and did not betray me. You obviously took your oath to your profession seriously. That's a whole lot more than I can say for your husband. I read about his father. I'm shocked his father could sire such a lying sap. I know you weren't a part of his deception. He manipulated you the way he has manipulated people his whole life. He's dragged you into something you should have never had to be a part of. I'm very sorry. He'll have to pay for what he has done.

I have discovered who my real father was. I understand that you knew. It seems that my mother wasn't what she professed to be, acting like the old schoolmarm. The Reverend knew all along. They deserved each other after all.

I felt that there was a connection between us. I could sense how you felt about me. I hope that by the time you receive this letter that I will be a free man again.

Keep your fingers crossed.

Cassius

Lincoln gave Sam a reassuring embrace. "Honey, come inside. I am going to call Piti. I'm sure it's nothing to worry about."

An anxious-sounding Piti answered Lincoln's call. "Lincoln, I was just about to call you again. Have you heard?"

"Yes. Is he back in custody?"

"No, not a trace of him."

"He sent Sam a letter."

"What did it say?"

"You can imagine – veiled threats against me, but not her, thank God. It was mailed from Alabama days ago. It didn't go through the jail's mail system."

"What do you think, someone mailed it for him?"

"Had to if he was in jail. My mother said he escaped Thursday. The letter was mailed Tuesday. How the hell did he get out?"

"He manipulated the psychiatrist, Dr. Farah. He conned her to put him in a minimum security area of the jail for psych testing. They were about to begin his trial. They took their time this time. They didn't want to be embarrassed again. Wallace wouldn't forgive another screw up." Piti continued, "But listen to this – the girl, Cynthia Bates, that we thought was dead..."

"Yeah?" Lincoln was now anxious for Piti to continue.

"She's not. Cassius' defense attorney met with her. She said she wanted to talk to him about Cassius' defense. She said she had been in Atlanta waiting for Cassius to get out of treatment. The attorney thinks she put a gun in his briefcase. He entered the jail later that evening for an appointment with Cassius. The attorneys don't have to get searched or go through the metal detectors, they waved him through. He unknowingly brought Cassius an automatic weapon. When he got there, Cassius grabbed the briefcase and knocked him unconscious. He put the gun to Dr. Farah's head and jumped out her window, then drove her car off the premises. She reported it two hours later. She said she was distraught and afraid. It's the damnedest thing I ever heard. They found the car abandoned and no one has seen him. Everybody is in a panic. It's a manhunt."

"Any leads?"

"No, but Connolly is on it. Says if Cassius is on earth, he'll find him. How's that baby?"

"Fine, fine."

"You enjoying teaching?"

"Yes."

"Back at your old alma mater, huh, California boy? How's

Samantha? Does she like that treatment center out there? Homeless folks out there any different from those here?"

"Probably not, Piti. I hear you're a big-time lawyer, now."

"Memories fade fast, don't they?"

"How's Mack Oliver?"

"Just fine, still at the fountain on the weekends and still in the apartment you got him."

"Good," Lincoln responded. "Ah, there she is. The dog," he told Piti. "Come here, girl. Where you been? You had me worried. You're gonna make me get the leash." Murphy ran down the beach to the porch and rested at Lincoln's feet.

"You think he'll disappear, or do you think he's coming out there?"

Lincoln was silent for a moment, staring at the turbulent waves of the ocean. Then he answered, "What do you think, Piti?"

THE END